WITHDRAWN

CHIMES

THE MACMILLAN COMPANY
NEW YORK · BOSTON · CHICAGO · DALLAS
ATLANTA · SAN FRANCISCO

MACMILLAN & CO., LIMITED
LONDON · BOMBAY · CALCUTTA
MELBOURNE

THE MACMILLAN CO. OF CANADA, LTD.
TORONTO

CHIMES

BY
ROBERT HERRICK
Author of "Together", "One Woman's Life", etc.

*"For life is, after all, nothing but the
capacity to assert a condition of inner
equilibrium within the transition of
external circumstances."*

44692

New York
THE MACMILLAN COMPANY
1926

All rights reserved

PS
1922
C4
1926

Published in the United States of America by
THE FERRIS PRINTING COMPANY, NEW YORK.

PART ONE

CHIMES

CHAPTER ONE

The new university! . . . A river of yellow prairie mud lay between the young man and the flat campus dotted with a half-dozen stone buildings, some still unfinished. Clavercin edged his way across the muddy ditch on his heels, trying not to destroy the polish that the Pullman porter had given his shoes that morning, for he wished to make a good impression on this his first personal interview with the President of Eureka, whose curt telegram of invitation had drawn him agitatedly a thousand miles. He landed, not too damaged, before a long low yellow brick structure, its gravel roof supported by wooden girders.

"The university gymnasium and temporary library," a lanky youth informed him, with a slight grin.

"Temporary!" Clavercin judged that was the present note of this institution for higher learning which the prodigious energies of Dr. Alonzo Harris, combined with the fabulous wealth of an old lumberman, were calling into being here on the flat sandy soil of the Middle West.

He had ample time that first visit to meditate on the contrasts between his own old college and this new one, while he sat in the outer office waiting to see President Harris. The great man was busy, and the harassed middle-aged woman who acted as stenographer and secretary gave the young man a bored, hostile glance while she took down his name, as if he had already been forgotten.

Outside there was much passing in the corridor, students going and coming from classes, professors hastily donning the academic costume of cap and gown for

1

chapel service, which apparently was held in a big room at the other end of the building. There were many women's faces among the students; not pretty faces, rather drab, uninteresting ones. Out here in the great West they did not divide the sexes. He would have to teach women in his classes,—that would be a novelty! He believed in sex equality and all that, but something romantic in him was offended by the evidence of co-education. He liked to think of women as apart from the commonplace of life—as decorative, provocative, mysterious,—and how could one when they stuck pencils through their hair and stood on one leg gossiping with fellow students or bent nearsightedly over a grimy class-room bench?

The bare office where he waited was adorned with an ambitious water-color sketch of the campus as it might be one day,—a crowded, pinnacled jumble of Gothic buildings. A vision to cheer the spirits of the faculty, to whet the imagination of possible donors. Opposite this hung an engraving of "Our Founder",—the old lumberman and "wood-pulp millionaire", James S. Larson, whose initial gift of two million dollars was converting this piece of raw prairie into the architectural dream displayed on the opposite wall. Clavercin examined the features of "Our Founder" with keener interest than the "Plan of Eureka University", trying to discover in the bony structure of the face, the bushy overhanging eyebrows, the close-set little eyes, and the loose mouth the impulse that had led this pioneer to turn his devastated miles of virgin timber land into "libraries, laboratories, and museums", with their human adjuncts, "for the enlargement of the domain of knowledge", as one of President Harris's flamboyant announcements had phrased it. He gave it up. That must remain part of his general bewilderment for the present.

Within the cubicle, divided from the outer office by a ground-glass partition, the President of Eureka was functioning busily, judging from the number of persons who entered and emerged through the glass door. Occasionally high notes escaped through the thin wall, subdued by a deeper voice murmuring huskily. This he attributed to the President. Once through the open door he had a glimpse of a short, thick-set, smooth-faced man seated in a swivel office chair.

He was meditating on some of the fantastic rumors about this new meteor in the University world, when the middle-aged woman addressed him.

"Dr. Harris will see you now."

Before the young man had made up his mind whether he ought to take his coat and hat with him or leave them to chance in the mob of the outer office, he found himself grasped in a fleshy white hand and drawn irresistibly into the cubby-hole, coat and all. Dr. Harris held his visitor's hand, squeezing it momentarily while he smiled warmly through his gold spectacles into the young man's face. Clavercin, remembering the awesome greeting of the great man in his own college, tried to extract his hand from this too familiar welcome, aware of what was befitting an underling like himself from a college president.

"Glad to see you, Dr. Clavercin—"

"Mr. Clavercin," the young man corrected with a sudden stiffening of his mental muscles. This new American habit of making every teacher into a "doctor" was extremely offensive to him.

"Ah, not yet taken your doctorate? We'll make that right soon. You can take the degree with us while you are teaching." Immediately the president made an entry in one of the fat red morocco-covered books that lay on his desk. Then he looked up brightly with a full smile which was completely disarming, free from all guile. "Glad you are to be with us!" Clavercin felt that he meant it, although he had skipped bewilderingly all formality of acceptance and appointment. "Just a

moment!" as the worried secretary whispered something
in the president's ear.

This gave Clavercin an opportunity to examine the
celebrated head of the new university more closely. His
first impression was that he need not have worried over
his own personal appearance: President Harris's shoes
had not been shined for days and showed traces of
campus mud. They were of soft leather with elastic
sides, a kind of shoe one should not wear outside his
bedroom. Also, his trousers were too short, with curling
frayed bottoms, and they bagged at the chubby knees.
His new black frock coat was plentifully sprinkled with
dust and dandruff, and down the black ministerial waist-
coat there was a visible stain, possibly from coffee-drip,—
Clavercin observed a thick china cup on the desk among
the papers and note-books. These trivial personal details
filled the young man with confidence. Compared with
the president of the new university he himself was
dressed like a gentleman, as it was understood in the
East.

But his attention quickly moved on to more important
matters. That round smooth face, framed in gold spectacles, beneath a tousled mop of black hair, was both
youthful and grave,—and just now evidently contrite,
as if the confidential stenographer was lecturing him
about something forgotten! The soft lips covered a firm
chin which had the grip of pure will. A short thick
neck joined this head to a stout loose trunk. It was not
a delicate body, spare and lean as the scholar's should
be, but powerful, with the fleshiness of the "corn-fed"
American. Two shrewd little brown eyes turned once
more on his visitor, not unfriendly eyes,—they were
trying to see the other as he saw himself. Dr. Harris
had tipped back in his swivel chair, exposing a soiled
white sock, garterless; his fat short legs stretched his
trousers out of shape, while his hands were clasped behind his head; altogether a most relaxed attitude, so

unlike the Jovian majesty Clavercin was accustomed to find in this office. The fingers, he noted, were short and thick, not the hand of an artist; the square nails were grimy,—in fact the president proceeded to clean them with his penknife as he talked.

"You find us," he was saying, "in all the confusion of moving day so to speak: we are just moving into the university as distinguished from the college. . . . It is this new spirit of the university which will be the distinguishing feature of American education . . . ", not notable generalities, which Clavercin promptly forgot.

They were interrupted again by the secretary, who remarked impatiently as a nurse might to a child with whom one must be firm, "Dr. Harris, there is the board meeting at four, and the Trustees' dinner to-night, and Mrs. Cordell Clumpton's. . . ."

"Yes, yes," the round head nodded indomitably; meanwhile extracting another note-book from the pile before him, the president concluded his interview with the young man briskly: "May I repeat, Mr. Clavercin, that the doctorate is the teacher's certificate of competence. May I not suggest that while carrying on your work with us you prepare yourself to take the appropriate higher degree? This is a university, not a college!"

"But, but . . . " the young man stammered, for the university president had risen finally to his feet and was holding out the fat white hand in dismissal, with another broad cherubic grin.

"I am glad you are to be with us, Dr. Clavercin," President Harris concluded genially.

And the young man found himself in the outer office, bewildered, created a doctor of philosophy by main force, all those delicate matters of salary, title, courses, departmental relations, and so forth, which had been the subject of so much eager meditation since he had first received that inciting telegram, not even mentioned. "But, but . . . " he was still stammering as at the door into the outer office (which was more jammed than ever with persons waiting to see the president) he almost bumped into a dark-eyed, resolute looking woman and a gray-haired short man with a bushy black moustache.

"Ah, Mrs. Crandall," the irrepressible president exclaimed heartily, "I want you to meet our new acquisition, Dr. Beaman Clavercin from Harvard, who is to be with us in the department of general literature." (Thus the young man realized that one more of those important points which had not been referred to was already settled, and the decision communicated to him in this aside, as well as the objectionable doctorate fastened upon him for life!) "Just a moment, Mrs. Crandall . . . Dean Dolittle!" and Dr. Harris waved adieu to the young man, while the gray-haired dean inserted himself swiftly into the cubby-hole with a bundle of official looking papers, together with another worried secretary, a yellow telegram in hand.

"It's our busy day," Mrs. Crandall remarked merrily, "but every day is busy with us!"

"It's . . . it's too wonderful," Clavercin stuttered, trying to find the precise figure that would convey his bewildered state of mind. "Like a big department store or a factory,—yes, a factory geared up for overtime."

"But you mustn't say that!" the agreeable Dean of Women of Eureka University corrected good-naturedly.

And he recalled with dismay that this eager, kindly woman must be *the* Mrs. Edith Crandall, so well known for her efforts in the higher education of women, formerly professor in a state university, later married to a distinguished English physicist, whose tragic death in his laboratory had sent her back to her former field. Beckwith had talked about her last summer. She was one of the most influential persons in the new university. Clavercin liked her at once, as did all the world, and he felt that his untactful remark had not caused offense.

"Of course, Mr. Clavercin," Mrs. Crandall remarked

with a broad motherly humor, laying a gloved hand on his arm, "we may be the Barnum of education, but we don't like to have it said too frankly. As I tell my young friend Miss Stowe" (which served as an introduction to a pretty young woman, who stood demurely by during this conversation), "we must put our prejudices in our pockets and see things out here in the large, the very large,—in the future!" And she laughed again sympathetically.

At this point the door to the cubicle opened, and the dean shot out, a scowl on his clay-like face in response to Mrs. Crandall's introduction of the newcomer. Clavercin read dislike to new "acquisitions" in the yellow eyes of the dean, especially of those from the critical East, though the tone of his voice was silky, diplomatic. Indicating by a wave of the hand that he had prepared the way for her with the Power within, Dean Dolittle hurried off.

Mrs. Crandall paused long enough to say, "Jessica is my *alter* ego,—she will explain everything to you!" and disappeared behind the glass door.

The two young people thus left together in the outer office looked examiningly at each other. Clavercin with his instinctive prejudice against the higher educated female recognized that Miss Jessica Stowe was dainty, dressed like the young women he knew who led purely social lives, in contrast even with the attractive Mrs. Crandall. She was tall, delicately molded, quite blonde, with a fuzz of reddish hair under the large "picture hat", which in obedience to the prevailing fashion she then wore. Her features were small, firm, a very definite little chin (which might sharpen and harden with age), a slightly ironical droop to the upper lip that might turn sullen, and tiny, exquisite hands. Altogether she was an agreeable contrast to the drabby, homely young women who had been pushing through the hall outside.

"So you are in it too?" Clavercin inquired curiously.

"Experimentally, for the present," Miss Stowe replied with a priggish precision of speech, yet being agreeably modulated in tone as the speech of the East, he found it a relief. "I am assisting Mrs. Crandall in organizing the woman's side of the university and working in my subject, social science, at the same time."

She did not say that she was a doctor of philosophy, having passed a very brilliant examination for the degree at Johns Hopkins, and that her thesis, about to be published by Eureka's new Press Department, upon *Primitive Marriage Forms* was likely to attract considerable attention.

"This growing industrial centre is a rich field for social research," she explained condescendingly. "We are about to open a university settlement in connection with my department out in the steel works."

"Ah!"

There was an ironic tone to the young man's exclamation: they did not consider the new science of "sociology" highly where he came from. . . . By this time they had abandoned the stuffy anteroom and were standing on the entrance steps to "Founder's Hall", a little to one side from the throng of incoming students.

"It's all so queer!" the young man confessed, with a puzzled expression on his rather delicate, fair face.

"Why so?" Miss Stowe demanded roundly. "It's new of course,—what did you expect? I find the newness stimulating."

(Along with "temporary" and "contact" Clavercin placed "stimulus" on his private index of words that must never be used.)

Miss Stowe's asperity indicated a suspicion that the young man, fresh from the old puritan tradition, was tainted with dilettanteism, popularly supposed to be the secret vice of Harvard. She herself being more robustly nurtured did not find the bustle of the raw campus displeasing.

"Our faculty has already some quite distinguished names," she continued, "and Dr. Harris is gathering new ones all the time to round out the departments."

"I know, I know," the young man mumbled, wondering if ability to write verse and a yearning to make plays could be reckoned as suitable credentials for membership among these important names. Some of the more renowned "acquisitions" Miss Stowe pointed out to him as they loitered near the entrance.

"There's Professor Emanuel Harden." She indicated a wizened, stooping old man with a shawl wound loosely around his chin, a cloth sack of books under his arm, the "typical" figure of the college professor, already almost extinct. Clavercin knew Harden by reputation, of course, a fiery historian of revolutions whose acceptance of Dr. Harris's invitation had influenced lesser men to listen to the song of the "New Barnum". . . . "The tall man with him is Professor Hanks, formerly President of an Iowa college, now head of the department of zoology, and the short dark man behind them is Dr. Stern, the great chemist, and there's Bock, head of mathematics. We are strong in the sciences," Miss Stowe commented complacently. "The idea is first to build up postgraduate work in science. The humanities don't count as they once did."

Coming from an institution that had long been famous as the home of the "humanities" Clavercin felt that he ought to resent this slur, but it was too obviously true; all American universities were madly developing their science departments. That was what "the new education", so much talked about, meant,—science.

Just here a young man with an erect, brisk carriage came up to Miss Stowe, who promptly introduced him to Clavercin as "Dr. Edgar Mallory, my head!"

At first glance Dr. Mallory looked as if he might have been transferred from the accounting department of the wood pulp business to a more responsible post. His

clothes were new, neat, and fitted him. He spoke briskly
with a touch of jocular irony and a little smile. Clavercin immediately pigeon-holed the man as "efficient Yale
Y. M. C. A." which, while not exhaustive, was not far
wrong. . . .

"Looking us over?" Mallory inquired pleasantly.
"We are used to it. Don't say that our campus lacks
walks and that our buildings are mostly on paper. I've
been trying to see his Majesty all day on some very
important matters." (This Clavercin recognized, was a
professorial formula, which he himself would often
employ,—meaning anything that one had very much on
one's mind.) "But what with the Trustees' dinner
to-night, and stray grandees from Persia and South
Africa, and Mrs. Cordell Clumpton's ball, there's no time
for such minor matters as our new social laboratory in
the steel district. . . . Ah, Mrs. Crandall," he interrupted himself as that lady emerged from the vortex
about the door, "you managed to see him, of course!"

"Just a wee moment," that gracious lady beamed back,
thus removing the sting of her preference, "about the
dinner to-night, and the plans for my new girls' dormitory, and a few other things . . . I didn't forget the
settlement. . . . Just listen! He wants to cut out the
reception rooms in the dormitory as so much 'waste
space'! 'Earnest students,' he said, 'don't have time for
visitors or take them to their rooms!' Imagine! It took
me at least five minutes to convince him that some
earnest students," she paused to squeeze Miss Stowe's
arm, "do have time to receive guests whom they do not
care to take to their rooms." She laughed merrily,
adding, "Do come over to my place, all of you, and
talk."

The longer Clavercin was with her the more he was
drawn to this vivid woman. She, too, was of the blood
of the pioneers, like Harris and the ex-lumberman
Founder. She had the same energy, enthusiasm, force:

she came from the same strong prairie soil, but instead of going to loose flesh as it had with Harris, her inheritance had gone into bone and muscle. Something Scotch in her Minnesota ancestry had given her that hard, clear grit, and her wide experience as teacher and executive, her European residence, had refined not only her speech but her outlook on life. While President Harris still had the soil of the prairie clinging about his untidy person, Edith Crandall had it well packed and trodden under her competent feet.

Clavercin had of course heard much about this famous woman,—who in the university world had not?

As Dean of Women in the State University, then commissioner of education, she had received more publicity of the newspaper, lecture platform sort. Interspersed somewhere with this was the romance of her marriage to a famous English physicist, melodramatically cut off by the fatal accident which had killed him. Clavercin recalled this as she chatted to him, and he could believe all of it and more,—how indomitably, her personal life thus cut short, she could pick herself up and plunge back vehemently into the lives of others. There was romance in the woman, imagination, and, as he divined, more than romance, more than ready sympathy,—a diplomatic shrewdness, a man's grasp of the actual, and the urge to mold life.

Abruptly turning from her humorous account of her own job she asked him, "Did you get from the president what you wanted?"

'I can't say I got anything" the young man answered ironically, "except a doctor's degree,—which I don't want!"

They had reached the bare apartment, fitted in the prevailing Grand Rapids style, which Mrs. Crandall shared with Miss Stowe. She apologized with a comical wave of her hand for the confusion of hats, coats, books, and papers that cluttered the small living room, for the

weak tea and the tasteless bread and butter which after
some trouble finally was extracted from the hotel management. After serving the tea Mrs. Crandall returned
once more to the young man's personal situation. That
was one of her engaging peculiarities,—although as easily
distracted from her theme as any quick-witted woman,
she never quite lost sight of her objective and sooner or
later closed with it.

"Beckwith told me all about you," she began.

"Norman Beckwith!"

"Isn't he splendid? I made up my mind we needed
you here, just your kind, but it had to be managed
tactfully, you understand. Dr. Harris had already filled
up the English department with a lot of university extension material, you know, and Dean Dolittle was not
favorable. But Mr. Gorridge, the president of our
Board is a very intelligent man, anxious to secure the
best for the university. And it is just your type, the
cultivated Harvard sort, that we need in this place."

The young man, who after his flurried reception by the
president was unaware that his appointment was of any
concern to anybody but himself, was agreeably gratified,
and warmed still more to this eager woman. It was
thanks to her and to that casual meeting last summer
in Switzerland with Beckwith,—they had made a couple
of ascents together,—that he had received the Harris
telegram.

"You know," Mrs. Crandall continued, confidentially
lowering her voice as if she were about to confide in him
an important secret, "Dr. Harris with all his great
gifts,—and he is a wonderful man,—hasn't much dis-
crimination. He likes to think of all men as well as
they think of themselves. He is too—optimistic!"

There was evidently plenty of politics in the new
institution. At Harvard it was the fashion to look
down on college politics, to pretend they did not exist.
Whatever wire-pulling went on was discreetly kept out

of sight, at least of the younger men. At Eureka the game was played boldly in the open, and Clavercin felt duly excited at being inducted into the best clique. Before his watery tea had quite cooled Mrs. Crandall had extracted from him not only all these conditions of departmental position, of courses and pay and rank that he had thought to settle with the president, but also many of his inmost, shyest ambitions,—*The Masque of May*, performed by a group of young people at Mt. Desert, his poem in "The Atlantic" so widely quoted the past winter ("The Pleasant Walks of Academe"), the edition of Keats which he had been asked to prepare for a publishing house,—all the little structure of his literary dreams. It seemed perfectly easy and natural to display them before this older woman, with her warm, eager smile of comprehension, her glowing brown eyes.

"You must come and see me often," she urged as he rose to leave. "And we haven't talked of Beckwith!"

Both paused, lips parted in a smile, half humorous, half tender, as if the picture of the absent Norman Beckwith was too complex for hasty exploration.

"He'll be so glad to find you here!" she said. "It's—it's lonely sometimes!"

Clavercin agreed: for all the bustle and excitement of the new Eureka there must be many lonely moments when one felt banished from the amenities, the suavities of an ancient university.

"Oh, stay and see these men," Mrs. Crandall urged, "they are our sort!"

One of the newcomers to whom she immediately introduced Clavercin was Augustus Langdon, professor of international law, a thin, sandy-haired man with a precise, not to say mincing, habit of speech. Clavercin thought him tiresome and patronizing, but Mrs. Crandall handled him with a silky deference. With him was a stout, rosy-cheeked little man, Alfred Cox, professor of Latin, who was of the college politician type; also a slender, sickly looking older man, whose wide mouth trembled humorously when he spoke. Thomas Bayberry, he gathered, had recently returned from Athens to teach Greek in the new university,—"If I can find anybody who will take it!" as he explained to Clavercin.

He left the Veronica in a comfortable glow: Eureka would not be quite the desert island he had feared. Mrs. Crandall came into the hall to repeat, "Now, Edgar, see he gets a good seat at the dinner to-night and meets the right people,—you know!"

In spite of this last touch of maternal friendliness and the picture of Mrs. Crandall picking up the afternoon paper from the floor and waving it to him in farewell with another of those instantaneous and irresistible smiles, oddly enough the dominant image that Clavercin carried away with him was that of the still, self-contained girl, wholly impassive, who had watched Mrs. Crandall as one might watch a noted actress, not critically, but neutrally. There was not much of importance that escaped those gray-green,—or blue-gray—eyes set rather far back within the well shaped brow of Jessica Stowe. He could not refrain from asking Mallory, as they emerged from the Veronica together, "Who is that Miss Stowe,—what is her connection?"

Mallory with his air of secretarially efficient young America, whose business it is to know everything about everybody and who has no objection to imparting discreetly what he knows, replied readily, "She's a daughter of Senator Stowe, the Cotton Thread Stowes of Connecticut,—you know, the largest manufacturers of cotton thread in the world, just being made into a trust. She met Mrs. Crandall in Europe and became greatly attached to her,—or Mrs. Crandall to her, which is the same thing. Mrs. C. induced her to go into graduate work in social science instead of doing New York society, as her people expected, and brought her out here for assistant. She is to give a course next year. She is

very intelligent,—an unusual young woman," he repeated
as if that, too, did not wholly explain a smile of private
appreciation.

"He hopes to marry her," Clavercin thought. They
were proceeding in the direction of the suburban station
which was engulfed in a mound of sand to be used in
elevating the tracks.

"You'll find it different out here," Mallory threw out,
gropingly, as if he were taking measure of the slim figure
beside him. "Doing everything at once in a hurry,
education also. But that makes it more exciting, so
much opportunity to make yourself felt."

He talked on jerkily, easily, in assorted phrases. He
was a graduate of Yale addressing the "Harvard man"
in that queer tone of condescension and antagonism
which in popular conception must always mark the
difference between these two old institutions. "As a
Yale man," he seemed to be saying, "I am not supposed to be as refined, as finished a product as they
make about Boston, but I am more virile and American
than your kind, less of the dilettante, better adapted to
understanding the great public and making my place in
a thoroughly American environment like this one. I am
not as intolerant and unsympathetic as you are likely
to be. I can understand different sorts of superiority,
while you admit only your own kind." And the other
was thinking,—"He's a good sort, one can see that,—
but nothing fine. Just like him to be going in for a
pseudo-science like sociology which we don't recognize.
They never did know what scholarship means at Yale,
nor what the American university should do for its
students,—try to rub off some of their barbarism."

Meanwhile Mallory informed him that the majority
of the Eureka faculty belonged to the Yale camp: a few
came from Princeton and Cornell, a number from small
Western colleges, only a handful from Harvard. The
Harvard representatives were not popular, he gathered,

because they expected all to bow down when they announced with an air of finality, "We do thus and so at *Har-vard*."

"You'll see the whole show at the dinner to-night; we all perform!" Mallory said in parting.

The young man decided to defer his departure until a later train so that he might "take in the show". The Trustees' dinner was one of those get-together affairs of which the West is so fond. "We must get acquainted," everybody kept saying.

The dinner was held in a big new hotel which the smoky atmosphere of the city had already tarnished, making it shabby before its time. The public dining-room had been preëmpted for the occasion, which was the first grand demonstration of the might and majesty of the new university,—"the Harris School", as the press familiarly dubbed it. The faculty assembled in cap and gown according to the university regulation, while Trustees and Distinguished Guests were conspicuous in evening clothes.

The food did not occupy much time. It was showy but frugal: one felt that it had been ordered in a mental conflict between a desire to be lavish and a restraining realization that the academic purse could not stand the strain. "We can't be wasteful," as Dr. Harris said, cutting out an entrée from the menu submitted to him by one of his secretaries. So they got more quickly to the talk which pleased Clavercin, who hoped to have some of his perplexities answered.

The president first rose and stood while the student's band, playing brassily in the gallery, was being quieted. Short, thick, with the round face of a gnome beneath the gold tasseled flat cap, his mussed silk gown swelling comically about his bulky body, the President of Eureka University was in total contrast with the stately figure that in Clavercin's experience embodied academic dig-

nity. Yet, when the tight-pressed lips parted and the
first words came, everyone must understand why the
man was there.

First he recounted in figures the miracle that he had
accomplished in three short years,—the buildings built
or to be built, the numbers of students enrolled, the
size of the faculty. "And this is but the start! From
this we must go on until our university equals the great
city of its birth, the great country in which we live."
So far, just a forthright business address to business
men,—an architect's speech. Was this to be all? Not
a word about the function of a university. He was
saying, "We must carry the higher education into office
and factory and home,—that is the mission of the new
education!"

"University extension," some one near Clavercin commented sneeringly, "popular lectures!" As if the speaker
had caught the slur, he described his own struggle for
an education, the illumination brought to him by his
first college lectures. "We must give to all who will
take it the precious revelation of truth," he ended
emotionally.

Clavercin, applauding mechanically with the others,
caught a glimmering perception of the idea within
Eureka: the university should be not for the few, the
select, the endowed, but for all, so that they might
gain each within his capacity the larger life of the mind.

"A new religion," he whispered across the table to
Miss Stowe, who returned a stony glance, as if her
"science" did not admit any such emotional extrava-
gance. . . .

Clavercin thought her charming in her black gown,
her reddish hair rippling beneath the mortar board, and
wished that he were sitting beside her. . . .

After Dr. Harris's speech, Samuel Gorridge, president
of the Inland Steel Company, spoke for the Board of
Trustees, describing in dry humor the compulsive power

of the university president's enthusiasm which had enlisted him in his effort to make a university. "This is a great country, a great city, and we must have a first-class university," he said,—and beneath his commonplace words it was difficult to detect any comprehension of what a university should be,—"the best men, the best plant," he repeated and sat down. Mallory spoke for the faculty, "in the lighter vein" for which he was noted. He recounted some of the comic aspects of the new campus, and switched finally into the theme of university usefulness, stressing the importance of a university to a city, what it did for "the larger life of the community".

Only one of the speakers, the old German, Harden, really attacked the idea of what universities existed for, and he spoke with such a strong accent and so vehemently that it was difficult to follow him. It was clear that he did not like faculty meetings, committee meetings, public dinners: he demanded libraries, seminars, capable students, and again and again came the phrase, "We are to find the tru-uth!" which sounded almost pathetic. At the end he turned his back on the room and, clenching his fists, adjured the president and the trustees as they wished to die peaceably to enable him to get the documents and the assistants he needed to complete his great work. Then he whipped around and clenched his fists at the faculty, as he had the habit of doing in faculty meeting, and told his colleagues that they did not know what scholarship was. Everybody laughed more or less. Old Harden was a "character", and every university must have a few "characters", like ivy and parchment. The trustees looked amused for the first time.

The last speaker was a gentleman from Oxford who made a pleasant little talk about old and new colleges, contrasting his own Corpus Christi with Eureka. "Another thousand years," he said consolingly in conclusion, "and you may have some grass on your campus like our English turf,—and that is what makes a university!" They laughed at his little joke.

"All the same he is nearer the mark than the others," Clavercin confided to Miss Stowe, as the diners rose with relief from their seats. "But not one of them seems to know what a university should be!"

"Perhaps they think that is obvious enough," the young woman retorted priggishly.

"But it isn't so obvious!"

"It isn't just a museum or a plant. It isn't just a place for Harden to write history in or to train other historians to write history. It isn't, as Mallory seems to think, a school for educating helpful young men like himself to be good citizens!"

"What do you think it should be?"

"I don't know exactly,—after to-day," he laughed back. "I must come out here to find out. . . . As the Englishman said, it's a place where you grow turf,— but as Harris feels not for just a few to walk on!"

"So that's the Harvard idea?" she demanded suspiciously.

"It's my own idea—what's yours?"

"I don't know that I have any worth stating," she replied snubbily and turned back to wait for Mrs. Crandall, who was talking vivaciously with Gorridge.

Clavercin sauntered down the boulevard to his train, utterly wearied from the jumbled impressions of the day, confused in mind, and troubled over his own decision, which loomed momentously before him. The moon emerging from a bank of black cloud illumined fitfully the still lake, and revealed the classical outlines of the new art building in face of a giant unfinished skyscraper. Beyond was a grimy jumble of shacks beside the "temporary" railroad station. That was the city of Eureka, a jumble of efforts and makeshifts, to which a university was now being added.

"The university will change all this," he muttered sleepily, "no, I mean change the lives of people so that they can't endure all this. Oh, hell, do I know what a university is for,—except to pay salaries!" But he woke in the middle of the night as his car bumped over a crossing saying, "I have it,—a university is to discover and teach the Art of Life." Having settled this he went back to sleep quite soundly, knowing that he should accept the invitation to "join the circus," and find out more clearly what he meant. It was in fact the only way in which he could marry Louise, and that seemed to him then of paramount importance.

CHAPTER TWO

"It seems to me, Mr. President,"—that was the formula used by most of the speakers in faculty meetings. Why could they not say simply, "I think so and so,"— or blurt out whatever they had on their minds, as old Bayberry, the archeologist, did on the rare occasions when he opened his twisted, trembling lips to emit some pithy irony? And why were they possessed to speak, voicing their commonplaces, heating themselves to feeble passion over trivial differences? After the first few times, when the novelty and dignity of being a full fledged member of a university faculty had led him to hurry into his alpaca gown after his late class, Clavercin, like most of the younger men, had become slack in his attendance at faculty meeting. At first it gave him an uneasy feeling to ignore the typed summons, also a sense of recklessness: it was generally believed that the president's confidential secretary listed absent members. Well, Clavercin was not yet sure that the university was to be his life forever, and in any case he did not intend to be the slave of an empty form. Little Stover of the Political Science Department never missed a meeting and rarely failed to speak, after clearing a catarrhal throat. (Usually he remarked somewhere, "We used to do that at Ri-pon," as if anybody cared a damn what they did in the little Minnesota college where Stover had been hatched!)

President Harris, surrounded by his officials, sat dumpily in the chair, either listening to the tiresome discussion in an abstracted muse, or reading some document which a Dean handed over to him ostentatiously, or glancing

through one of the innumerable fat morocco leather
notebooks that contained his mountainous memoranda.
It was obvious that he was bored or resting, that he
attended faculty meeting like chapel, as a necessary part
of the ritual of the university. It was rumored that he
found these general faculty meetings wasteful of time
and had in mind a scheme of abolishing them altogether,
substituting a series of little Boards to be dominated by
officials, where business could be put through expedi-
tiously as in a meeting of directors.

But before that happened there was one meeting of
the faculty over an issue that aroused general interest.
It was when the president's committee, appointed to
inquire into the system of entrance requirements, reported in favor of substituting certificates for examinations. The certificate system of accepting students from
schools was in vogue everywhere in the country
except in a few of the older universities. The new
university had begun bravely by examining candidates
for admission, "just like Harvard or Yale." But within
a few years it was painfully apparent that the community did not take to the examination system: students
preferred colleges that accepted them graciously by
certificate. Eureka might have a large endowment, a
distinguished faculty, better equipped buildings, and
facilities than its rivals, but it did not attract students.
The trustees, expected to meet the mounting deficits,
scrutinized the attendance as directors would the cost
sheets and sales of a corporation and asked difficult
questions. Finally it came to a head in this report: the
certificate system and athletics, they made the successful
college, not the faculty, or the libraries and laboratories.
It was futile to point to the growth of the graduate
school: postgraduate courses did not pay their cost.
To run a large university it was necessary to have a
strong college. From the start two currents of opinion
had developed in the new faculty,—those who believed

in numbers and those who heroically stood out for
quality. The "Eastern men",—and most of the younger
men,—were for maintaining high standards: the Middle
Westerners" (including the Deans and office force)
favored the letting down of the barriers, "popularizing
the school". It came to an issue in the presentation of
this report which verbosely favored the certificate system
"modified and adapted", "safe-guarded", and so forth. . . .
It was a full meeting. All the older men spoke. Clavercin glowed under the furious eloquence of old Harden,
who denounced this "American get-learning-quick idea,"
and recalled tenderly his own German university. "What
business have we teaching riff-raff from the streets?" he
hurled at the president, shaking his fist. "Gift me that
library you promised me when I came here and those
advanced students!" The faculty tittered, recalling the
miserable shack at the other end of the campus which
housed the famous library bought at auction from a
second-hand dealer, and the President actually blushed
through his sallow skin. The elegant, foppish Sidney
Lamb, of the department of philosophy, spoke at length,
harping on the terms "form", "culture", "crudity". He
did the cause little good because so many of the faculty
disliked him personally, considered him a snob. Then
Mrs. Crandall poured oil on the harassed state of mind.
She spoke graciously, suggesting that it was too soon to
condemn the new university because it had failed to
attract large numbers,—they really had more as it was
than they could properly care for. "Yes, women!" some
one sourly remarked. "But what we want is men."
And Mallory spoke, entertainingly, vigorously, with
frequent sarcasm, ridiculing the "Harvard attitude of
heaven-born superiority". Everybody knew that he had
written the report at the instigation of the President.
While he spoke, Dr. Jessica Stowe, who was present
because she was teaching in Mallory's department,
looked demurely into her lap. It was the gossip that

she was to marry the popular Dean in the early summer.
Clavercin thought her prettier than ever and wondered
if she approved the glib argument of the man about
to become her husband. Nothing of course was resolved by all the talk,—it never was. Two hours of
oratory left the question just where it started, with
those who wanted numbers obviously in the majority,
and the others bitter; some of those near the door slipped
out in the growing obscurity. Then the electric light
was turned on, and the bare factory-like room gleamed
in hard brilliance, while outside a pitiless winter rain
beat across the unfinished campus in wild gusts.

Just as the president was bestirring himself to finish
the futility, Norman Beckwith rose in the rear of the
room and, in a voice so hoarse with a strange emotion
that Clavercin scarcely recognized it, began to speak.
The Dean, he said, had treated the question as a joke;
the Dean was fond of his little joke. Perhaps education,
the university itself, was a joke: it remained to be proved
whether they could make of Eureka anything better than
a joke,—a stupid joke perpetrated by a rich man. The
faculty leaned forward, moving uncomfortably in their
seats, as if on the edge of a scandal. One did not say
that sort of thing openly like that,—one hardly said it
privately among friends unless one happened to be a
frivolous scoffer from the East. Clavercin listened
amazed at the words coming from the man he was living
with, his most intimate friend in the faculty. Of course
he knew Beckwith's general views about "Barnum's
Show". But with the reticence of his breed, Beckwith
had never opened the serious depths of himself like
this. And the faculty listening, as they had not listened
to the other speakers, however much they might dislike
his doctrine: they were listening to this young man
who, turning scornfully upon the official bench of pop-
ularizers about the president, asked them in the words
of old Harden,—"what is a university for? To attract

students by athletics and fraternity houses, who hope
to mount from one social stratum to a little higher one,
thanks to their college associations? Or is it for those
who desired to follow the long hard road of science
and scholarship, to keep alight the sacred fires of learning?" Jessica Stowe, Clavercin noted, was watching
Beckwith narrowly, but her still face made no sign
that he had convinced her. Beckwith went on to paint
the scholar's life, lean, lonely, unlovely, wholly absorbed
in its devotion to immaterial things, its reward an inner
reward. "And to them you talk about numbers!"

"He speaks like a priest," some one near Clavercin
remarked. It was apt. Yes, Beckwith was an ascetic
at heart,—though last night he had been quite drunk,
Clavercin recalled. This was the creed of his spirit, the
monastic creed with its denials and exaltations..."If
you want to play the business game, why don't you get
out into the city and play it with men, for profit and
power? The university is no place for money changers!"
Stocky, with a bony high forehead, graying hair, a
rugged mountainous face, Beckwith stood exceedingly
straight, his hands clasped behind him.

"That is all so!" Harden commented loudly when
Beckwith suddenly stopped, as if pierced by a sense of
the futility of his passionate words. Mrs. Crandall
leaned forward and smiled at Beckwith across the president's fixed, glowering gaze. Others mumbled feebly
their "it seems to me." The crowd had been irritated,
not persuaded, and Mallory scored cheaply by remarking that possibly Mr. Beckwith had missed his vocation:
he should seek a seminary. Beckwith flushed, half
rose, but the president interfered bulkily and raised
his pudgy hand to quell the antagonisms. "Mr Beckwith has mistaken the purpose of the report," he said.
"It is not designed to lower the standards of the university, but to make the opportunities we have to offer
the youth of this community more easily accessible.

Shall we set ourselves above the community—or meet it?" One could see that he was endeavoring to reconcile his own passionate desire to "make the university count" with this move to lower the banner of "high standards" so proudly raised. In the end some sort of vote was taken, the report adopted, and before the president could pronounce, "The ayes have it," the members of the faculty were hastily donning rain coats and overshoes and hurrying into the hall.

It seemed to Clavercin as he listened to the president's hurried, "The ayes have it," as if the doom of the new venture had been pronounced; that there was nothing now to be done except to write Louise they could not be married this June; he must resign and hunt for an honest job elsewhere, in competition with those other vulgarians who sweated frankly for the right to live in the grimy offices of the city. Beckwith's laughter greeted him at the entrance. "Well, old man, they had us on the run!"

Miss Stowe, who was waiting in the vestibule with Mrs. Crandall while Mallory hunted for a cab, remarked, "Does it make so much difference,—I mean the university will get just about the same sort of student either way!"

"Perhaps," Beckwith admitted; "all the same it makes a difference, all the difference there is between pretending and being."

The young woman challenged this statement with a little smile that said,—"Is there any such distinction?"

The arrival of the cab cut off the retort to this mute question. Mrs. Crandall remarked, by way of consolation, as she stepped into the cab, "This vote isn't the last word. We must keep up the fight! Sorry to leave you, but we are due at a party at the other end of the city."

She waved the young men farewell as the horse cab set forth into the downpour. The faculty in bunches of twos and threes were streaming across the open campus with coats close-buttoned, bending under umbrellas, bound for home and supper. Their thin legs and fluttering coat-tails presented a ridiculous exterior.

"Well, shall we go over to Fleshie's for a drink to get the taste out of our mouths?" Beckwith suggested. Instead they ate the frugal meal offered at the faculty club and returned to the rooms they shared in one of the new dormitories. These were bare little cubicles designed for the occupancy of divinity students, a few of whom glimmered about the corridors wanly. Across the way lived two other instructors, Walter Snow in Sanskrit, round-faced and jovial, and Sugden in church history, cadaverous, with glittering restless eyes, who played the races and cheered the athletes. Before attacking the night's task the four occasionally read aloud a canto of the *Purgatorio*. Clavercin, who had once studied Dante under a famous professor of *belles lettres*, felt that the practise restored the amenities so woefully slaughtered at Eureka. He had a sense of defiance in reading out the passionate phrases of the fierce Italian, whose symbolism seemed so alien to the flat world around him. To-night the rain beat gustfully against the windows, the boisterous wind swept papers and rubbish across empty lots. Bent over the littered table beneath the unshaded drop light the four repeated the sonorous words of the text and forgot the dribble of the day, the class routine, the futile discussion in faculty, examinations, standards, and all. Clavercin had the impression, so often repeated in this university world, that no crisis was real. Its significance looming importantly beforehand already began to retreat into the dull commonplace, to be repeated in a slightly different form another time. And so on. Men talked and heated themselves about ideas, principles, theories, policies. Some sort of action was taken, and the world remained as flat, as unmoved as before. The hills of momentous decision always receded into the distance.

The canto finished, they turned to the night's tasks, correcting papers, preparing for the morrow's classes. Sugden was writing a text-book from which (and from the ponies) he expected to make enough money to retire to Europe. Snow was editing a text that might bring him the desired promotion. Beckwith lighted his pipe and gathered up a fistful of history test-papers, over which he dropped sardonic comments,—"My God, Lizzie Goldering thinks Martin Luther was the author of the Decretals. Try again, Lizzie!" . . . "What these people lack is a sense of reticence: they keep nothing back!" Clavercin, having written a long letter to Louise in a gloomy mood, where the shortcomings of Eureka were inextricably mingled with doubts about their future, went off to bed, leaving Beckwith sitting in the fumes of his pipe. Beckwith might sit there all night: Clavercin had never seen him go to bed. Apparently he never felt fatigue.

Before putting out the light in his own cubicle Clavercin looked down on the bare campus, lighted sparsely by solitary arc lamps, which revealed black pools of water, not yet absorbed by the sandy soil. A few stunted oak trees, relics of the original prairie, raised gnarled branches to the dark heavens. The skeleton of the new commons building at the further corner could be seen, also the new biological laboratories already roofed in. A lonely figure moved across the deserted quadrangle below,—some belated student coming home from the library. There had been holdups on the campus,—a divinity student had been robbed of his silver watch and one dollar and sixty-two cents the week before. . . . President Harris must have a stout heart; Beckwith too had something within to sustain him, at least an indomitable humor. Clavercin, contrasting the desolate space of the empty campus with

the lovely intimate quads of the English Cambridge
that he had visited one vacation, shivered. "A thousand years to grow turf like that!" yes, easily. Eureka
was so ugly, so raw, so flat! One must live here for
the future. He wanted to live in the present. Had he
the courage to quit, now that he knew what it was
like! Louise expected they would be married in the
spring. She couldn't understand. No, he hadn't the
courage. He pulled his clothes over his head and tried
to forget it all, murmuring inappositely the sonorous
words, *"Sua voluntad è nostra pace,"* which somehow
comforted him.

CHAPTER THREE

There was the alleviation of Flesheimer's. Beckwith had discovered this beer-garden saloon, one among many on a disreputable avenue not far from the university. The old Bavarian and his fat, fresh-faced *frau* had kept the place since those prehistoric days when farmers with their produce on their way into the growing city had stopped there to bait their horses and have a drink of bitter Milwaukee beer. Flesheimer kept his place with German neatness and decorum, serving Rhine wines and excellent Kentucky whiskey as well as the bitter domestic beer. Behind the saloon was the "garden," a tiny graveled spot containing a few old poplar trees, some benches and tables, an "arbor" of course. Here Beckwith with his following would come on pleasant afternoons to drink beer and talk. College teachers were not supposed to frequent such places any more than the clergy,—and that made it pleasantly exciting to go to Fleshie's, as they called it. When, some case of student discipline being up in general faculty, Dean Dolittle had remarked dryly, "Inasmuch as certain members of this faculty are known to enter saloons," accusing eyes immediately sought out "the Harvard gang", as they were called.

"Yes, I go to Flesheimer's," Beckwith admitted promptly, flushing slightly. "Why shouldn't I?"

Mallory, who was presiding, turned the matter off with a joke, but the student's case was dropped. After this to go to Fleshie's became all the more a symbol of freedom, a way of shaking one's fist at the hypocrisies of Eureka, like cutting faculty or abstaining from chapel. Dolittle, Mallory, Mrs. Crandall, the twin snobs, Sidney Lamb and Aleck Harding, and a few others like "heads of departments," might frequent the houses of the philistines in the city, eat of the fleshpots to be had there, being asked patronizingly to dine, to go to the opera. But for impecunious young instructors such social expansiveness was impossible. A few glasses of beer at Flesheimer's, a steak in onions when they wanted to escape the monotony of faculty club meals, was their single compensation. They wiled thither as many of their colleagues as they could, making their simple conviviality a test of superiority. Mallory came a few times to demonstrate his broadmindedness and ostentatiously drank ginger ale. Also Bert Sanderson, an energetic young westerner recently appointed to the chair of Geography, and the statistician, Will Ampthill, who had wild, goggly eyes and a slobbery uncertain mouth. Sanderson smiled at the free talk, the flourish of revolt: he was an "arrivist," as they dubbed all those who followed the rules and voted with the administration. He was just married and determined to make of his new chair of Geography a stepping stone into office.

They talked wildly, condemning the university's "advertising methods," its thin program of expansion, its pretentious announcements, university extension, co-education, all the novelties, then occasionally got off into wider topics of the day. Beckwith and Snow talked as if they were socialists,—it was the period of Shavian Fabianism, and the proper pose was to question the foundations of society. Cast up in the midst of a rich city whose only standard of rank was wealth, they affected a social dispassionateness. Beckwith was the most outspoken of the crowd, the best informed and the least personal. He did not seem to care for good clothes, for fashionableness and social pleasures. Mallory was using him in his new settlement where his

classes in economic history were attended by young
Jews, Italian and Russian, who he said were keener
than any of the university students. Snow knew a
circle of people that sympathized with the so-called
"Chicago anarchists", and Ampthill had his differences
with the timid head of his department on the question
of "trusts", which were then very much on the public
mind.

"Just because some fat-head millionaire took a fancy
to start a university instead of a racing stable, and a
lot of bank presidents and trust magnates meet Prexy's
deficits, there is no reason we shouldn't say what we
think about these things," Ampthill blustered.

They were all much agitated when Ampthill was summoned to the President's office and solemnly warned that
he must take "strictly impersonal and scientific" views
in his teaching about public utilities. There was agitation just then over the street car lines in Eureka, which
a skilful gambler had amalgamated in order to sell to
the public. It was considered by the trustees "unfortunate" that Ampthill should have accepted a position
as "expert" in a neighboring city on a matter of gas
lighting.

"They can't smother us,—tell us what to teach!"
Beckwith grumbled over the beer and pretzels.

"No, but they can tell us what not to teach," Clavercin warned.

"Christ, they don't dare! Their money is too rotten
—they'll have to be liberal—so the papers will soft
pedal Larson's methods."

New "trusts" were sprouting daily, new fortunes
being made. The American business world was rushing
madly after bigness, farming "combines" which the
little people, the outsiders, regarded resentfully. "This
dirty beer is made by a combine," They grumbled at
Fleshie's. "The shop itself is run like a trust."

Paradoxically the same leaven was working in their

own ranks, the same feverish desire to pluck riches from the air. Sugden, the cadaverous professor of church history, follower of the races and admirer of athletes, had picked up an "inventor" somewhere, who had a marvelous gas machine. Beckwith first became interested and put up the money to install the man and his machine in a dilapidated brick building somewhere in the steel district. Soon the shares of "Gas and Slag," as the company was called were circulating on the "university bourse" at Fleshie's, changing hands quickly at advancing prices, as Beckwith or Sugden brought in news of progress at the "plant". Then Ampthill appeared with a company to irrigate arid lands along western rivers by hydraulic pumps operated from the flow of the stream. This modernized version of an ancient Egyptian process was named "Buckets". Another short-lived security were the shares of a flying-machine, and later a chubby professor of Anthropology fresh from Yucatan introduced a rubber plantation "San Marcos" to the university bourse, which had the novelty of coöperative cultivation, and a trip to Yucatan. Sanderson specialized in Colorado mining stocks, one of which, "Snowstorm", was popular on the university bourse.

The air was rife with speculation, about the campus as in the murky city. It was known that Aleck Harding (in Economics) had made a sizable fortune by a successful turn in "Carbon", but Harding happened to be married to a rich wife, and her people were supposed to "have let him in on good things". Cable of the Geology Department shortly afterward retired and went to Washington to live, (but not on "Snowstorm!"). . . There was a feverish, restless spirit of dissatisfaction with life as it was, with the flatness, the monotony of Eureka, not only in the university but in the city, and the instinctive need for escape took the form of Aladdin's lamp and paper securities. (The names appealed to Beckwith—Dr. Jack Pot, Gold Pan, the Development Co. of America. Long afterward, finding the faded certificates in an old trunk he burst into strange ironic laughter, expressive of the fantastic dreams of his youth.) This speculation fed their imaginations through the dreary winter months of that first year, gave them a peephole into fulfillments: they discussed gravely what they should do when they "had cashed in". Walter Snow would be off to Rome and the Vatican, Sugden had in mind a ranch in California, Clavercin dreamed of New York. . . . Only a few hundreds of dollars of actual money was involved in the transactions of the university bourse at Flesheimer's: all the rest were notes of hand and elaborately engraved certificates. Ampthill had out six thousand dollars of such notes, more than three years' salary, when the crash came, and all were heavily "extended."

The crash was precipitated when Ampthill persuaded the pompous Aleck Harding to take a thousand shares of "Buckets" off his hands for *cash* at a rise of two hundred per cent. When a few days later Harding discovered that "Buckets" lived only on paper, he tried to induce Ampthill to return his money, and failing to obtain it went to the President. Dr. Harris had already received rumors through Dean Dolittle of the activity of the university bourse; also a Trustee who had had his eye on Ampthill since the latter had attacked the report of his gas company, called the President's attention to "the disgraceful gambling among your professors." Ampthill, to be sure, had completely lost his head, neglecting his classes, trading shares even in the corridors of Founder's Hall. One morning he was summoned hurriedly to the President's office, and thereafter his fate was more or less mysterious. Beckwith had it that Ampthill was to be made a horrible example, not for the neglect of his duties, but because he had aroused the enmity of the Trustees by his activity as "expert". They had been "laying for him" and pounced upon his stock transactions as an excuse. Harding, it was clear, was a yellow dog. The truth was, as Clavercin learned later from Mrs. Crandall, the Trustees were incensed that "one of our professors" should engage in "reprehensible gambling", as they called the dealings of the university bourse at Fleshie's, although a number of them were "long" or "short" of "Carbon" and "Tin Plate." They wished to throw Ampthill out and publish their reasons, they were so righteously shocked, and perhaps Dr. Harris might have yielded to the pressure had it not been for Mrs. Crandall.

"But you can't do that," she said to the President. "It would make a horrid mess; besides Mrs. Ampthill is going to have a baby, poor thing!"

So in the end Ampthill was paroled to a country farm in charge of his wife to recover from a nervous attack, and all calmed down on the surface. But Ampthill never returned to Eureka. Presently the story started up that he had been dropped because of his socialistic teaching. (In that form the story came down in university annals to the present day and recently was incorporated in a diatribe against the American "trust-controlled university", which proves how oddly the truth is mangled by friends as well as foes!). . . .

Mrs. Crandall gave the members of the university bourse a mild warning. "You shouldn't be doing things like that,—you are too old to play marbles for money like this!" Clavercin winced.

"You don't call it playing marbles when Harding makes a pot of money," Beckwith grumbled.

"Nor when Morgan cleans up a few millions," she retorted swiftly, "though in principle it may be the same! . . . . . There are just certain things one can't do if one is a university professor, don't you see?"

"Why be a university professor?" Beckwith gibed. "Much better to be a university trustee."

Mrs. Crandall shook a warning finger at him.

"I know how—dull it often is," she said sympathetically, "how small the salaries are and all that, but the way out doesn't lie through the stock market. You, Beaman, should be saving every penny against your marriage . . . . . and you, Norman, should get married too,—then you would be too busy to play craps!"

Beckwith laughed . . . . . Thereafter the transactions on the university bourse rapidly decreased. The inventor disappeared with his mysterious formula for a cheap gas made from the refuse of steel mills, leaving his university backers numerous small accounts to settle. "Buckets" never got off paper, while the heavier-than-air-machine rose fifty feet, made one erratic glide, and sank forever into the lake. Rubber alone kept alive. That had attracted mature heads of families among the clergy and the faculty, who went on faithfully year after year digging into their meagre savings for the hundred dollar assessments, with a pathetic faith that some day they would enjoy that outing in Yucatan at the expense of the coöperative rubber company, would sit under their own rubber trees and watch the milky juice ooze richly into their individual buckets. . . . Why, Beckwith asked quizzically, is the university professor always put on the sucker list Because, he answered his own question oracularly, he has by nature faith, belief in things unseen.

"I bet if you went through the boxes of the Trustees you would find just as many bum investments," Snow protested.

"Yes," said Clavercin, who had taken his experience seriously to heart, "but you would find some good ones too."

"We should be above such filthy material ends," Beckwith mocked.

"I am going back to the ponies," Sugden averred.

They were having supper cozily in Mrs. Flesheimer's rear parlor. The Flesheimer habit too ran out, hastened by a scandalous dinner that Beckwith gave in honor of Mallory's engagement to Miss Jessica Stowe.

"It is a university Event," he proclaimed, "the truly Eurekan solution of the sex question: educate your wife first. Everybody is giving the happy couple dinners to show their approval. We must do our part!"

Flesheimer was induced to decorate the little arbor in the garden with roses and smilax. A dozen of the younger members of the faculty were invited, also old Thomas Bayberry, who was an admirer of Mallory. Beckwith somehow persuaded the discreet Mallory to put on for the occasion a ridiculous white gown that made him look like a big baby. Thus robed he sat beside his host, whose large blue eyes winked ominously as the men ate stiffly the good food set before them and talked shop. Beckwith ordered another round of cocktails, then Rhine wine, finally champagne. When he rose to greet his guests, tongues had already begun to loosen, and feeble academic jokes to circulate. Beckwith's theme like Dr. Harris's, was the opportunities of Eureka, of which Mallory was making such notable use, and ended with a free version of the Athanasian creed. Bayberry who was seated at the opposite end of the table stared frigidly through his glasses.

"That is blasphemous," he pronounced as Beckwith started on the creed.

"It is the higher criticism," Beckwith corrected, bowing to Bayberry.

"Beckwith is getting drunk," Bayberry pronounced unequivocally, rising from his seat.

"Of course I am getting drunk, as my distinguished colleague has observed. I wish he would do the same."

Bayberry dropped his napkin on the floor, and stalked stiffly out of the arbor. The pebbles crunched under his retreating footsteps. A hush fell momentarily on the party.

"Now that the Puritan has shaken us like the pebbles from his feet, let us resume our festivity. More champagne, Fleshie!"

Clavercin had a fleeting conviction that the path of prudence lay in Bayberry's footsteps, but instead let Flesheimer fill his glass with fresh champagne. After that he was not clear what happened. He had a distorted picture of the guest of the occasion, fleeing before Beckwith and Snow, trying to divest himself of his ceremonial robe, at which the others clutched. Later Beckwith and Sugden were sitting in the garden in the moonlight, giving an impromptu version of the Mallory wooing. After that all was blank.

The party at Flesheimer's resounded on the campus the next morning. Some students had happened into the saloon and peeked into the garden while Beckwith and Sugden were in amorous colloquy, and the married men had told their wives. Beckwith appeared in chapel, very straight and solid, singing loudly in his curious broken barytone, "How firm a foundation ye saints of the Lord". At the close of the brief exercise Dr. Harris took Beckwith into his office; they remained closeted there a long time, while outside a mob of visitors and professors scowled and stormed the secretaries. When Beckwith emerged his face was flushed, and he was repressing a smile.

"Well?" Clavercin queried nervously, expecting nothing less than dismissal.

"The old man is all right. We had quite a talk,— about Munich beer and other things. No more Fleshie's this term, my boy. He wanted to know what was the matter with Eureka,—why we went to Fleshie's and played stocks. I told it to him straight: it's impossible to take this place seriously. He took it quite nicely.

He wants me to help make it serious, offered me a junior deanship."

"Now think of that!" Sugden murmured rapturously.

"I told him I'd consider it. The trouble with our job is its necessary hypocrisy. We are expected to set an example for a couple of thousand young people, who don't give a damn, incidentally, for our example. We are supposed to be religious, upright, God-fearing, chaste, abstemious, and a lot more. We can't be all that. . . . but if we are found out we must be forced to appease the wrath of the community. It's the great game of not getting found out, same as Larson, as I told the old man."

And thus the Flesheimer days ended.

CHAPTER FOUR

I

The squat figure of Dr. Harris on a low bicycle, his baggy trousers clipped tightly around his fat calves, his broad brow above the gold rimmed spectacles bent earnestly over the handlebars, was grotesque. These early, before-breakfast bicycle rides were one of the Eureka President's devices for "getting in touch" with different members of his growing faculty. His secretary sent out the cards of invitation, beginning alphabetically with assistant-professors and working downwards through the list of instructors and teaching fellows. Clavercin came early on the list, thanks to his promotion at the time of his marriage,—which was due, he felt sure, to Mrs. Crandall's kindly insistence. His desire to laugh at the funny figure ahead of him was controlled by a flattered awe at the invitation to accompany the President on this golden October morning.

It was characteristic of the man, part of his general hearty friendliness, something of the drummer's indiscriminate sociability with an eye on possible business. The president would casually introduce a young instructor, or even a student whom he chanced to meet on the station platform, to an eminent citizen, say Samuel Gorridge, the steel man: "Clavercin" (taking him familiarly by the arm), "I want you to know Mr. Samuel Gorridge, president of our Board,—Dr. Clavercin of our department of General Literature," and so forth. President Harris was aware that while this introduction might mean little more to Gorridge than a passing tribute to his local importance, being as he considered himself this young man's employer (having the final say on his appointment, promotion, emoluments), it meant much more to the obscure young man, making him acquainted with this prominent citizen, procuring him possibly,— if he happened to make a good impression,—an invitation to the Gorridge house on the North Boulevard and other agreeable connections, which might prove advantageous to him personally and also to the institution of which he was an humble representative.　Thus a shrewd egoism, mingled with an impulsive kindliness, gave the university President the reputation of being truly "democratic".

The two pedalled industriously into the empty Park, past the few remains of the great Fair.　These crumbling monuments gave the President his conversational clue:

"It is only in America,—only I may say in this most typically American city,—that such a magnificent evidence of civic pride could have been carried to a successful conclusion.　The public spirit of our leading citizens made the World's Fair possible, as it is making our university what it is destined to be,—the greatest in our country!"

Dr. Harris, for all his geniality, which was quite sincere, had a purpose in all his words.　Clavercin understood that he wished to impress upon this recruit from the aristocratic and condescending East the challenge of the new West.　He listened respectfully to the impressive facts that the President was throwing at him over his shoulder while he worked the pedals, about the ready sacrifices made by rich men when a financial panic had threatened the existence of the Fair.　Presently the topic veered to what the same leading citizens had done for the university, what might be expected from them and from "our graduates" in the future.

"Think of the Campanile!" he exclaimed, referring to a recent gift announced at the opening of the autumn term from a milk-paste millionaire.　"Such idealism!

. . . A beautiful beacon to soar above the roofs of the
university buildings, to be seen far out upon the broad
waters of this great lake. Something of pure beauty,"
he stressed for Clavercin's benefit. "You know it is
given in memory of his son, who would have entered the
university had it not been for that untimely boating
accident."

From the Campanile they got to the topic of the many
races of people gathered within the far-reaching city.
This was suggested by the smoking chimneys of the
steel works south of the Park. At the edge of the waste
land, which reached on into the cloudy distance about
the steel chimneys, they got off their wheels to rest.
The president wiped his glasses, adjusted his soft felt
hat, and extended a thick hairy arm from a soiled cuff.

"Have you seen Professor Gartner's remarkable
monograph on the foreign populations of this city? He
finds sixty-seven distinct peoples,—think of it! Sixty-
seven groups coming here from distant lands, each with
its own tongue, its own religious organization, meeting
here and merging into one. . . . .Think of the people
who will live around this great inland sea, the offspring
of these aliens who have come hither in the desire for
better things for themselves and their children! It will
be our opportunity, our duty, to educate this enormous
population. . . a great privilege."

The young professor remembering the pile of student
essays on his desk awaiting correction thought there
might be some limits to this privilege. Nevertheless he
listened respectfully to Harris's panegyric on opportunity,
with a baffling sense of the ridiculous checked by admiration that the words and the gestures of this extraordinary
man so often aroused in him. There could be no doubt
of the sincerity of the emotion which the spectacle of the
great stretch of flat waste land, the moldering ruins of
the fair, the brooding gray lake, and the smoking chimneys of the steel mills gave him. The President of

Eureka saw imaginatively all this raw land peopled by an industrious, contented population, in tens of millions, doing well by themselves, reading books and prosecuting higher studies in their odd moments. Just as the energetic men on his board of Trustees were busy in building and directing these mills and their attendant miles of brick tenements, to make steel for the coming millions, so Dr. Harris was so busy gathering his tribute from them to erect the "plant" for "higher things", building libraries, laboratories, and museums" in which to educate all those millions about to be spawned. It was all part of one process, the cosmic process of growth, and Harris, like Gorridge and Larson, got exhilaration from being part of it. The young professor nurtured in a less glowing atmosphere might have doubts about the ideal, but he recognized that it was this quality of emotional imagination that gave the stocky man wiping his glasses,—without them he had the appearance of a queer blind owl,—and gesticulating, his strong appeal to the rich leaders of an industrial democracy.

"The doctor," as they would say, "could do our job too!"

Presently they pedalled back to the university, passing on the way the new college of education, gift of a neurasthenic old woman and the new commons into which a number of pale youths were streaming for breakfast, and the foundation of that tower of beauty that was to dominate the campus and the city,—the Campanile (variously pronounced, most often as if it were in three words Camp-a-Nile!). Quite pardonable, the young man thought, if the assembling cause of all this took pride grandiosely in his achievements, and planned more blocks of stone and mortar, thinking he was making a university!

"There ought to be a chime of bells in that great tower," Clavercin suggested idly, "to ring out night and morning."

"Fine idea!" Dr. Harris agreed. "We must put in the bells," and Clavercin could see the busy man dictating to Miss Wex, "Memo. a chime of bells for the Campanile—sound Mr. Lexoll (the milk-paste donor) on this." . . .

They parted at the President's house, a new brick affair in much adapted Gothic. A large woman was standing on the porch, the morning newspaper in her hand, looking up the avenue inquiringly. She gave Clavercin a short, blind nod, and remarked to the President, "Your breakfast is waiting for you, doctor!"

The stout little man ducked into the house like a belated schoolboy. Clavercin, realizing that the president would have asked him in for a cup of coffee if he had dared, went his way grinning softly. There was one place at least where this Big Barnum was mere man!

Beyond the President's new house was the Woman's Quadrangle where Mrs. Crandall now reigned like a busy bee. If to some of the members of the faculty, with belated ideas as to woman's sphere, the presence on the campus of this extensive pile of stone solely devoted to the less intellectual sex was an offense, it was a humming hive,—and it would be difficult now to oust the women from the university. Clavercin had to admit to himself that many of the cleverest students in his advanced course on the drama were women, keener and more cultivated than the men. "That's because the best men won't compete with women," as some one said, but Clavercin no longer felt his first instinctive dislike to teaching women. "You are becoming feminized," Beckwith jeered, "like all of us,—it's so easy to put it over women!" Not always!

As he passed the entrance to the Woman's Quadrangle, Mrs. Crandall dashed by in a cab, a bunch of mail in one fist, her eyes rapidly perusing a letter as if she were sucking its contents in one gulp. Already at this early hour she was off for a train to make some engagement several hundred miles away! The young man answered her friendly smile and nod, envying this busy woman who made life so full of drama for herself and others. Over her hurried breakfast she had no doubt already confessed some bewildered girl and set her straight on the track, smoothed out the puckers in an angular graduate's brow over her dissertation, arranged for the necessary credits for another aspirant, and now was on her way to stir the languid imaginations of the Dubuque's Woman's Club over thrilling adventures in the laboratory for their daughters. Like Dr. Harris, her skilful hand was at work in every corner of the institution, patting, mitigating, combining, making possible ways in dark places. She might be superficial as her critics said, too fond of good society, too tactful,—all that,—nevertheless she was anything but flabby, purposeless. Eureka, Clavercin realized again, would have been a very different place, perhaps intolerable, if it had not been for her magical touch. It was rumored that latterly Mrs. Crandall and the President were becoming less intimate, that he disliked her influence with the Trustees and the more important people of the city,— he heard her quoted too often,—and that presently the Dean of Women might be granted that long leave of absence she so richly deserved and—never come back. Clavercin hoped this was gossip, for which Eureka, like all self-contained communities, was a hotbed.

As he passed down the suburban avenue, now properly paved and quite well filled with detached houses, Clavercin recognized the more settled aspect that a few swift years had brought to this slice of prairie wilderness. In these comfortable, roomy brick houses, with little strips of lawn in front, little yard behind, that peculiar institution so often discussed as "the American home" was developing luxuriantly. Not merely for the few prosperous members of the faculty who could afford to live in their own houses, but for professional and business men whose families like the "advantages" and "refinements" of a university neighborhood, as the real estate agents put it. Indeed, the latter outnumbered the former and were rapidly filling in the empty squares. . . . In front of the Fenton's large cream-colored brick house a fat girl of twelve was pushing a small baby carriage.

"See my baby!" she cried out to Clavercin proudly, uncovering the face of a waxy, unhealthy infant. "It isn't really ours, but maybe it will stay with us!"

"Whose baby have you run off with now?" Bayberry asked coming across the street to join them.

"It's the Dexters'," Constance Fenton replied, with a bubbling smile. She tossed back the thick blonde pigtail from her neck and took the baby out of the carriage, in an expert manner, to exhibit it to the two men.

"Its mother's sick, and we are taking care of it, 'cause Mr. Dexter's got too much to do over at the lab'ratory. . . . It hasn't had enough to eat, mother says," she continued breathlessly, kissing the baby's pasty face. "Mrs. Dexter's sick,—she lies in bed all day."

The two men looked away: it was one of the minor scandals of the university that the wife of the professor of anatomy, a very able man, took drugs and was often "not herself". It was rumored indeed that Dexter must find some other place, if he could, "or send his wife away somewhere". The fat girl purred on, "Mother says College people shouldn't have so many babies, but the babies can't help it, poor things, can they?"

"No," the men agreed gravely.

Mrs. Fenton called down from an upper window, "Constance! It's time to feed the baby . . . bring her in!" And she added to the men, "Did you ever! She can't let 'em alone—steals 'em."

"Are you going to college when you grow up?" Bayberry asked the Fenton girl.

"Oh, no, I'd rather have babies," she replied thoughtfully. A university to her was a lot of solemn looking men with books under their arms, a lot of draggled looking women with wan babies.

The two men watched her carefully pull the carriage up the cement steps.

"Another mother for the university," Bayberry chuckled. "She will be wheeling us all in her *baby* carriage one of these days!" He shambled back to the bleak house across the street, nicknamed the Monkery, where he lived with Norman Beckwith and two other bachelors. From the window of his bare study he had watched Constance Fenton, with her thick blonde pigtail and fat legs, busy about the block, first wheeling dolls and now babies.

The Mallorys' new house was on the next corner, a full three-story box with a big white balustrade around the roof. As Clavercin passed, Mrs. Mallory was just leaving the house, a portfolio under her arm, on her way no doubt to the new psychology laboratory where she had a private den. She no longer taught classes: it was not considered quite seemly that a head professor's wife should teach in the university, especially when the family did not need the money, but she had kept up her studies and was said to be conducting some interesting experiments in psychology under the direction of Rudolph Sheimer, a recent "acquisition" from the University of Zurich. Mrs. Mallory gave Clavercin a cool examining gaze, then a slow nod, and briskly set off for the morning's work, joining the stream of day students that were coming up the cross street from the railroad station. At the corner she met Sanderson, also armed with a big bag of papers and books, and the two walked on together. Probably Mallory had gone to his office long ago, being a very active man. It was already noted in university gossip that the Mallorys did not often "appear" together,—they were both very much occupied in a number of ways, and Mrs. Mallory was going to have a child, so the women whispered, although Clavercin could see no evidence of the fact in the trim, erect, slender figure striding along in step with the burly Sanderson.

There was another very coming man, like Mallory, though more inimical to "the culture crowd". Already he had managed to elevate his subject, Geography, to the dignity of a separate department, and now was "putting through" a scheme for a college of "Business Administration," of which he would be the head. As if there were any need of teaching business to the Eurekans! But the idea had appealed to the Trustees and business men of the city as "practical": it elevated their own occupation to the dignity of the learned professions. The same sort of spurious scheme had been urged upon Dr. Harris for a separate department of journalism. American journalism in a university, God save the mark! Yet their competitors were teaching journalism, along with Philosophy, Science, and Mathematics, in obedience to the popular demand for "practical" subjects. If Clavercin could bring himself to favor this converting the university into a conglomeration of trade schools, he might obtain the headship of the department of journalism, more prestige, and a larger salary. It was a sore topic.

He watched the two until having reached the campus Sanderson raised his hat in a sweeping bow to the Dean's wife and made off in the direction of the President's office, striding along like a conqueror. It was long since the days of Flesheimer when Sanderson had been induced occasionally to sip a surreptitious glass of

beer and listen to ribald criticism of Barnum's Show!
Since then he had become editor of a new series of
school geographies that a well-known firm of text-book
publishers were pushing into all the western States, and
had made, so report said, a great deal of money,—on
work done largely by graduate students and assistants.
Many of the faculty, who had not managed to marry
rich women or fit themselves into administrative jobs,
eked out their small salaries by doing text-books. The
manager of a large text-book company lived in the
house next the Mallorys in order to cultivate friend-
ships with the faculty. All this hack work was of
course pure waste for the university, but what could
one do? And still the younger men were criticized if
they did not "produce" something in pure scholarship.
Every term the President's office demanded from all
heads of departments a list of "scholarly publications"
to the credit of their members. These lists were published in the President's annual report, as evidence to
the world that Eureka was contributing vigorously to
higher learning.

Mallory, to be sure, had not made large contributions to the list, but he was "in administration", a sufficient excuse. And Mrs. Mallory was very industrious, having half a dozen items to her credit of articles
published in scientific and semi-scientific journals and
some reviews. But the Mallorys belonged to the fortunate minority in the faculty who had their own houses
and did not have to worry about the size of the salary
cheque.

Clavercin's imagination came back to that trim, alert,
silent figure which had always intrigued him. What
was she really like? He wondered if Mallory knew!
The marriage had taken place the summer before
Clavercin had joined the faculty, at the Stowe's Adiron-
dack camp, and had been properly noted in the newspapers,—"the only daughter of Senator Simeon B.

Stowe of Stoweville, Conn. and Washington, D. C.
(of the Stowe International Thread Co.) with 'Dr.'
Edgar Lane Mallory of the faculty of Eureka University", &c., &c. Clavercin, reading the notices in the
New Hampshire boarding house where he and Louise
were spending their modest honeymoon, wondered why
the young bride had not insisted on having it printed
"Dr. Jessica Stowe of the Sociological Department of
Eureka University". He was sure that if she had had
anything to say about the announcement it would
have been so worded, suppressing any mention of the
Senator and the famous thread works. . . .

Well, Mallory had won the prize: it was obvious from
the first glance that he would,—he was the prize-win-
ning sort. And he had had Mrs. Crandall's efficient
support. "So entirely suitable," Clavercin could hear
her saying genially, this "romance between two scholars", "interested in the same subject, an ideal marriage". Was it? Mallory had given up all professional
work, and Mrs. Mallory was, apparently, transferring
her interest from Sociology to the new department
of experimental psychology that Dr. Sheimer was rapidly
creating,—it was hinted, with some of the Thread
money contributed by Mrs. Mallory. . . .

But it was already late,—Clavercin must gulp a cup of
coffee and hurry back to his morning class. He had promised Mallory to do the text for a musical comedy to be
given as a benefit for the Settlement, and the first
rehearsal was this afternoon. And there was his article
for the next number of the Modern Language Journal.
He had not touched it for a month. It would have to
go over now until the summer vacation, which he hoped
to spend in Europe with Louise. They had planned
this first trip to Europe since they were engaged. It
was the one reward of their profession, these European
vacations, and some day when he was full professor he
could spend a year in Europe on half pay . . . and

then he would do that book on the Mediaeval drama, if some one had not got in ahead of him on the field. Beckwith was in Europe with Walter Snow this winter. Now and then alluring picture cards came from them from out of the way spots, not especially noted for academic renown. If that Rubber Plantation would only begin to pay instead of call for hundred dollar assessments,—or he could manage a text-book or two, like Sanderson. . .

Louise met him at the door, her dark eyes dancing with excitement.

"Oh, Bea, just think! Mrs. Sailer has asked us to-night for dinner and the symphony,—won't it be fun?"

Clavercin frowned dubiously. He had reserved this evening for some special preparation he must make for his "seminar" to-morrow and an overdue book review. But Louise would be so disappointed. He was very much in love with her, and apologetic for the scant diversion he could offer her in Eureka. She was quite pretty, dark, with glints of gold in her chestnut hair, a softly molded white neck. She had already made herself liked in university circles, and, thanks to her vivacious chatter, her "cunning" personality, was attracting invitations from those city people who patronized the university.

It meant, whenever they were asked out like this, either a long ride on the suburban train, then a street car and a walk, or the expense of a hired carriage which was formidable and not to be indulged in every week. The late hours made Clavercin headachy and nervous the following day. They had been going into the city pretty often; whenever he demurred Louise proved to him triumphantly that it was advantageous for him to become known and seen in the company of influential people like the Sailers and the Mudges. There were comparatively few of the faculty who were invited into the city, except of course the Mallorys and Mrs. Crandall. It was a kind of aristocracy worth striving for. She already dreamed of buying a lot on Beechwood Terrace, quite a nicely settled street near the campus, and some day having their own house,—oh, quite small, but *chic*,—where they could ask people, Sundays and for occasional dinners. While he shared to some extent this ambition to be known, to meet interesting and influential people,—and knew that such social opportunities helped unduly in the university,—he had an uneasy feeling that this was not the road to high scholarship and to consideration by real scholars.

On the ground floor in the cheap apartment building where they lived was such a scholar, John Goodwin, head of the German Department, a sallow, bald-headed, middle-aged man, who had married in his later youth a German girl out of the *pension* where he had lived while he was studying for his doctorate. Mrs. Goodwin, who still spoke English with a strong accent, did all the housework, including the washing, and her highest festivity was the family Sunday dinner, to which the Clavercins had once been invited. The dingy apartment, furnished in green plush, smelled of strong cooking and children.

"Impossible!" Louise sniffed when they had escaped. "How can he stand it!"

All the same, Goodwin, as Clavercin well knew, was one of the foremost publicists in the university. The Goodwins went to Europe (second class) almost every year for three months, Mrs. Goodwin spending the time with the children in some remote Saxon hamlet while her husband traveled, attended linguistic congresses, bought books. Of course the Goodwins did not count socially in the university or the city, but scholars knew Goodwin all over the country. And Clavercin felt the humorous contempt of this older man for university professors who "tried to keep up with the bourgeoisie" as he put it. Scholarship was enough for him, and the scholar's lean life. Wisely he had taken the sort of woman who was content to cook and wash, bring children into the world and look after them, and asked nothing better. Was any other sort of wife possible for a scholar?

"What kind of a companion can she be for an educated man?" Louise had commented.

Clavercin, who had felt the affectionate tone of the household, thought that the large Saxon-born lady probably had been just the sort of companion a man needed whose specialty could be understood by only a handful of scholars the world over.

"And, Bea," Louise chirped on, considering the Sailers' invitation settled, "you really must order a new dress suit. I've been trying to get that spot off, and it won't come out. Besides, it's so worn and shabby, like a pauper's."

"We are paupers!" Clavercin responded a little less jovially than usual.

"Oh, not as bad as that," his wife corrected spiritedly. "Wait until you are a head professor and Uncle James Osgood has left me that legacy and we build a house on Beechwood Terrace and give nice parties."

"Wait until . . . oh, hell, I forgot this is the night of the departmental meeting. Caxton spoke to me about it particularly yesterday, wanted to know if it was convenient."

"Oh, Bea-man!" Louise wailed. "I am sure the Mallorys are asked too!"

A crisis threatened, how profound only Clavercin knew.

"You must see Mr. Caxton this morning and make him put the meeting off!"

"Must I?" Clavercin replied, a little tartly. "And what if he won't?"

This social business, which interested his wife so

keenly both amused and annoyed Clavercin. The Harvard tradition was to ignore the richer society of the city, to hold fast to its own pure aristocracy of academic families, but in this new community that was not possible. The President's receptions where the timid wives of the instructors stood about dumbly, waiting to be fed and talked to, were dreary affairs. Mrs. Harris, it was conceded, lacked the social gift, and although Mrs. Crandall tried to help tactfully and to supplement the first lady's efforts jealousies cropped up inevitably. It was felt that the popular dean of women was more interested in the trustees than in the faculty. A few of the "faculty wives" were "invited" by city people. The others had to make their own social life where they could. The Clavercins under Louise's guidance were quite selective, and had formed a small coterie of "possible" university people, like the Aleck Hardings, the Mallorys, Norman Beckwith and the Snows, who saw a good deal of one another. They included some of the city people in the neighborhood, like the Fentons and the Caswells, with a touch of condescension. It was felt that Mrs. Fenton was "pushing", seeking to gain through her acquaintance with university people a recognition she had never been able to win in the city. Her husband was a lawyer who had made latterly considerable money which enabled his family to live in their large cream colored brick house more luxuriously than most faculty families. Mrs. Fenton patronised the university people, and was patronised by those of them who had gained a footing in city society.

"That Mrs. Fenton is too common," Mrs. Harding would say, to which Louise would reply, judiciously, "She is rather obvious, but she has such a good heart," and both ladies would be found at the Fentons the next Sunday evening at supper. After the plethoric feast and the succeeding "music", the Clavercins walked back to their apartment, while Louise discriminatingly conned

over the list of guests. Her husband would remonstrate,
—"If you go to her house, you ought not to talk about
the people you meet there." "How absurd you are,
Beaman. . . I don't have to like all the people I meet
at dinner! . . . That solemn Professor Jorolman, for
instance, and his impossible country wife. Just because
he has been made head of the College of Education.
I don't have to find them interesting, do I?"

"He's as interesting as Fred Mudge." . . .

With the simplification of the idealist Clavercin liked
to believe that social relations represented personal pref-
erences based on discriminating perceptions. One
formed thus an ever widening circle of relationships
that had nothing whatever to do with social ambition.
"We must see more of the university people," he would
say after a tiresome adventure into the city. "Who?"
Louise would promptly demand,—"The Goodwins?"
Proving to him thus that scholarship, professional
ability, character, had little to do with social desir-
ability. He envied Beckwith's free state. Beckwith
might roam and pick acquaintances, friends, where he
would, from the steel mills or the North Boulevard.
Society as such did not exist for him, merely people.
Clavercin thought that was as it should be in the university—it was not concerned with worldy ambitions.

All of which Louise found quaintly unsophisticated.
"Beaman thinks," she confided to Aleck Harding,
"that the university ought to be a monastery. He'd
like that a lot!" and the pompous Aleck laughed loudly.

"Where would your gifts come in?" he asked flat-
teringly.

Nevertheless Clavercin rebelled at the idea of "chas-
ing after society". "I want to see more of my students,"
he protested, "and the neighbors."

"Shall we have in the Satelles?"

The Satelles lived across the way. The families
amicably exchanged courtesies of groceries. Satelle was

in some big bank down town, Mrs. Satelle was prominent in the Arché Club, where women read papers to each other. Clearly the Satelle amalgamation would not do.

So the social question remained an insoluble enigma to Clavercin, while Louise went smilingly on her way making friends that "counted".

CHAPTER FIVE

Most of the classes were held in the factory-like Founder's Hall, up and down whose flights of iron stairs the students tramped in a solid mass each hour from eight-thirty until four. During the morning hours which were more popular, because many of the undergraduates brought their luncheons with their books and went home after their classes, the stairways were so jammed that the professors were jostled in the throng as bareheaded they made their way from office to class. Clavercin was always ruffled by this scramble on the stairs and in the halls, and usually tried to avoid it by getting to his classes either early or late. Occasionally he was caught in the mob and must struggle through the press. The students did not recognize him, and even if they had recognized him they would have jostled just the same, that being the western democratic way. And the women, too! Clavercin could not easily get over his dislike of seeing them chatting familiarly with the men in the corners of the halls, or sitting in the empty class rooms, flirting. He knew that such familiarity between the sexes meant little,—they had been brought up from infancy together, and it was probably a healthier way than the segregation practised in older communities. All the same it offended something romantic in him that he still treasured. . . . In a different way he had been disturbed by the presence in his own classes of so many women students, for his morning class in "Gen. Lit." was popular, especially with women. The women took by prescriptive right all the front benches in the room, while the minority of men slunk into the rear, as if ashamed of exposing their cruder mentality before women in mass. It was difficult to evoke more than a monosyllabic response from the men, even by direct question: they seemed obsessed by a mental diffidence before the other sex, with single members of whom they had just been on such familiar terms. And they felt themselves outnumbered.

The women were not as a rule pretty or even attractive. Clavercin had determined from the start to keep the reactions of the class room and office as sexless as possible. It was not difficult in the majority of cases, for the women were plain and not always tidy. Sometimes a woman would linger after class, and when the others had drifted away would try to bring something into play other than the objective, the impersonal matter between student and instructor. Clavercin had a way of assembling his books and papers while dryly restating the question that effectively suppressed this personal appeal, and quickly he found that he had gained a reputation of being "stiff", even "snobbish". An incredible story went the round of the campus to the effect that Professor Clavercin had asked his women students not to bow to him outside his class because he did not wish to have social relations with them. Mrs. Crandall reported this tale to him with much amusement.

"Of course, my boy, I know you never said anything as silly as that, but you might be a bit less snubby to them. It isn't their fault, poor things, that they are not all as attractive as Jessica or Louise, and they would like to know you,—if you'd let them."

"They can come to my office when I am there, if they need any help," he protested, "just as the men. I don't recognize any difference between the two sexes in the university."

"That is very well! I wish some of the other instructors were as punctilious," and she hinted darkly at a scandal which was rife periodically of the trading of

favors for marks in courses. "That is horrid, of course,
—I mean to get that man some day,—" she mentioned
one of the best known members of the faculty, a married man, who was notorious for his relations with his
women students,—"and have him publicly expelled from
the university. I am watching for him, but he is too
sly!" she said with a determined shake of her head.
"But you don't have to freeze the poor things." She
laughed merrily. "Women are different from men, always will be, in education as elsewhere: they get ideas
differently, apply them differently, more personally,
emotionally."

"I know,—it's just that—"

"Why shouldn't they? Why shouldn't knowledge be
vitalized, applied concretely, worked into the stuff of
life?" she demanded. "Perhaps it is just the positive
element, what you call 'personal', that scholarship has
lacked, has made it something remote from ordinary
life,—and women will help to change all that. And,
poor dears, they need the discipline of objectivity,—
that's what they are coming here for. So you will
both help each other! . . . Only get over that Harvard
idea of yours that women are not for the higher education,—they are for everything, the same as men!
Don't think it beneath your dignity to teach women:
one of these days they will be teaching your sons,—
yes, here in this university and elsewhere. The segregation rule is over, in this world, my man!"

In spite of such strong doctrine, which he might agree
with theoretically, Clavercin, like many of his colleagues,
found a subtle deflection in his professional work, due
to the presence of so many women in the classes he
taught. It was almost intangible. Not, as so often said,
a lowering of mental standard, for most of the women
were as able, even abler, than the men, and were generally of a superior social class, with a more cultivated
background, especially the young women from rich

Jewish families that flocked to the so-called culture courses. The essential difference, so far as he could discover from his own experience and from discussion with his colleagues, was the kind of reaction women gave to what was offered them in class. Unconsciously they sought something more than information, something, as Mrs. Crandall would put it, that they might work directly into their own lives. For that reason women often chose courses that were not highly considered by the faculty, such as the anthropologist's, Moon's, discursive talks on strange peoples and strange ways. They were seeking for something with which to enlarge their consciousness of life, and wherever they found it they responded quickly.

At first when Clavercin entered the filled class-room, mounted the raised platform, removed his coat and hat, and opened his notebook, ranging his reference books on the dusty desk before him, he had experienced a distinct thrill, as of an officer taking command of his ship. His must be the word, the force, to galvanize the dull and wandering minds of fifty-odd young men and women. The sound of his own voice had something hypnotic for him, and as the class sank into a receptive stillness, heads bent over notebooks, hands industriously scribbling, he found himself thinking more lucidly, discovering new meanings in old matter that had hitherto escaped him. As he worked into his subject, seeking those significances, those inner relations it had with the larger aspects of life, he could feel the stillness of note-taking change into a sort of suspense, and was conscious that the men and women before him were too much interested in what he was saying to take notes, were directly absorbing his meaning, completely acquiescent. That was the moment of triumph, with its own subtle thrill, a conscious exercise of power, not unlike what the creative artist or the actor must ex-

perience. "Now," he thought, "I am teaching, I am
creating new consciousness," and the sentences flowed
faster, as in his excitement he rose and came down from
the rostrum, standing with his back against the desk in
order to place his thought more directly into those
open minds in suspense before him. . . . But as the class
exercises became routine, coming four or five times
every week at the same hour, he felt this thrill more
rarely: it was harder to get into the "inspired" mood,
and he was often aware of painfully groping for clues
in a dull mind, and the students either scribbled conscientiously in their notebooks, moved restlessly, or
stared apathetically out of the windows. Then he became irritated, with himself, with them, with the whole
function of teaching, and his voice rasped: he made
mistakes, was overemphatic, and at the conclusion of
the hour he felt drained of every particle of vitality.
Often there was a growing numbness in his mind as the
lecture proceeded in the hot, bad air,—the ventilating
system never worked, and the class room was used
every hour. He hated himself and resented the university! He could hear through the thin partitions similar exercises going on in neighboring class rooms or the
scraping of chairs above or below him as classes on
other floors were dismissed. "Pepper's letting 'em out
fifteen minutes too early,—it's a scandal!" he thought,
and ground his teeth for a last lap. "It's too much
like a day school," he would grumble to Snow or Beckwith, comparing these routine exercises with the meetings in his old University Hall where, before a couple
of hundred young men, some celebrity had appeared like
a priest or a famous actor, and with a detached air
had conducted as it were a religious rite (not wholly
comprehended no doubt by the neophytes) and he
departed, alone, first, his green cloth bag clutched under
one arm, swinging a cane like a dandy, in the direc-

tion of the library or the town, bound for the mysteries of his own solitary studies.

One of Dr. Harris's great ideas for Eureka had been to do away with such exhibitions, to substitute "real teaching" for the university lecture system, that deplorable pumping of so many empty words into so many hundreds of idle minds. In Eureka the classes were supposed never to exceed thirty, and for a time it was possible to keep them small, at least the more advanced ones. But the small class coming almost every day did not necessarily encourage "real teaching", whatever that might mean. More often it induced slackness. And there were so many ways of shirking, known only to the conscientious teacher when he was tired or bored or abstracted. He might save up frugally on the matter prepared so as to have enough for another exercise, or permit some talky student to air his futile ideas wordily while the rest of the class sat by and kept points on the discussion, or set papers.

Nor did he often get that exhilarating stimulus from "keen young minds" that people talked about sloppily. Young minds are not often keen,—rather, cloudy and lethargic, unless prodded by competitive excitement. And his classes were very often mixed, containing candidates for the higher degrees, school teachers, casual listeners from the city, irregulars. The special trouble with his subject was that it attracted these irregulars with a desire for entertainment. This fact gave him a sense of being meretricious, not really "scholarly", and he suspected that he was regarded condescendingly by his fellows in the faculty who were engaged in science or the more "solid" subjects. This suspicion prodded him to fill his lectures with useless references, pedantic displays of scholarship that he realized few of those who listened would ever use. Nor did he himself greatly value this aspect of his subject nor believe that literature should be so treated even in a university

course. The living breath of life, that is what it once
had been, should be to-day if anything, and it was that
he really wanted to give these crude, inexpert youths,
which was exactly what some of them thirsted for,—
"inspiration" they called it. Yet an academic pedantry
made him withold just this element of his subject as
much as possible, a shamed fear of not being "scholarly".

So, often after class he retreated to his office, a cubby-
hole in the embrasure of a pseudo-Gothic window, divided by a shiny varnished partition from other cubby-
holes, in utter depression and exhaustion of spirit, produced by this consciousness of thwarted functioning.
It seemed to him then that a university ought not to
pretend to "teach" literature, any more than life; ought
to confine its activity strictly to the tabulation of facts,
the exploration scientifically of stratified ideas! And
in such moods he growled savagely at the graduate
students lying in wait for him in the outer office in
order to suck from his wearied brain some morsel for
their theses and dissertations. . . . There in his office
he transacted the mass of "paper business" that accumulated every day. It seemed that for every professor
in the university there must be several officials with
stenographers whose sole business it was to bombard
the harassed teacher with questions, reports, abstracts
of minutes, and so forth that the recipient did not
quite dare to chuck unanswered into the waste-basket
and permitted to accumulate in a dusty heap upon
his desk until the end of the term gave him courage
to clean out the rubbish. He cursed the inventor of
"statistics", the cancerous growth of the measuring
habit that tried to apply a yardstick to the most intimate affairs of the spirit. . . . Beckwith was able to
extract a certain amount of humor out of this "paper-
asse", as he called it, framing his replies in mock serious-
ness. "Now would you say that Susie Jones had an
industrious intelligence or an intelligent industry?"

"And to think that in our college one old maid did all this record-keeping, and the President wrote his letters in his own hand,—bully ones too, no 'it seems to me', or 'may I call your attention to the following' stuff!" Clavercin groaned.

It was all part of that factory process—"system" (perhaps the most hated word on Clavercin's private index)—that the university was imitating from the business world. It was the factory symbol that inevitably suggested itself to him whenever he entered this building, with its semi-fireproof construction, its crowded corridors and murmuring class-rooms. He could not get away from the sense of the symbol while he staid in class or office or seminar room. The spare figure of the black-haired instructor in mathematics, Horatio Memnor, who had the adjoining room in the morning hour, emerging with a bundle of neatly folded papers, his dark coat sprinkled with blackboard dust, his long hair greasy and uncut, his trousers bagging, was that of a factory foreman, and the innocent Memnor (who was a conscientious teacher) irritated him unreasonably. He felt that the foppish Sidney Lamb, with his affected intonation, his eye-glass and eternal harping on "form", "what we should give our students is a sense of form", was more nearly right.

Why should education be left to the unkempt, the sallow, the anemic? He knew well enough that it was because Memnor received the same small salary that he had, and even by doing extra work, tutoring and night teaching, he could hardly support the little white-faced woman he had married,—Mrs. Memnor looked exactly like a frightened rabbit,—and his one small child. You couldn't get the graces and the abilities for eighteen hundred a year! It was the poverty of the calling that made it, in a commercial environment like Eureka, America, so inferior. But, as Beckwith pointed out, it had always been poor, originally a function of the church.

One must have an inner sense of superiority, a glow for one's office, a passion for the great objective, learning. A few had that, like old Bayberry, like poor Dexter with his laboratory mice and his morphine wife,—and Memnor too? Perhaps.

Clavercin's afternoon class was better. There was less of a crowd in the big building, a more cloistered air. The students too were different, fewer schoolboys and girls, "lunch-basket students", more of the older, graduate order; for most of the specifically graduate courses, the seminars, were held in the afternoon. The atmosphere was mellower, more what should be expected in a university. . . . Yet, as a rule, the graduate students were not inspiring indviduals. They were usually teachers, seeking the higher degrees in order to improve their position,—rather colorless specimens, too evidently starved in body and spirit in their concentration on the coveted degree. They were more avid, sucking like leeches from the instructor all that he might have within him of advantage to them. Clavercin rose from the two hour period drained, exhausted, sometimes irritated by the pertinacious zeal of some frowsy dull woman who had bored into his mind as she would thumb a library catalogue or extract notes from a reference book. . . . Why could they not wash? Even the bath was a luxury reserved for the leisured class.

At the start of the term there was the business of sorting these advanced students into courses, of trying to fit them with special subjects for "investigation". This Teutonic process, indelibly stamped on the American university now for a full generation, might be efficacious in the sciences where presumably subjects for special examination were exhaustless, but in the humanities it was devastating, producing under forced draft a terrific amount of waste material that moldered on the shelves of university libraries or was ultimately carried out to the dump by the scavenger. For one useful, illuminating piece of "research" sponsored by the university, crowned by the achievement of a higher degree, there must be at least a hundred aimless, dull, utterly arid products, whose sole utility was to train some second-rate mind, fit only for elementary teaching, how to use a card catalogue and other apparatus of scholarship. The very sight of a dissertation or thesis gave Clavercin an attack of mental nausea. Somehow all this applied scholarship was killing the root of the matter it was applied to. American universities that gave so much attention to the teaching and investigating of "literature" were the most unliterary places in the world, most purely barbarous in spirit. There were not a dozen members of the Eureka faculty who could write a well expressed letter, hardly that number who recognized a literary allusion beyond the limits of the popular "Kolumnist" in the *Daily Thunderer*. And yet, employing the jargon of the laboratory, they tried to run the fine essences of spirit through their strainers, classify and label the "results."

The acme of this imbecility appeared in the pompous examinations held toward the close of the term for the candidates for higher degrees who had finally succeeded in finding subjects for "investigation", and after months of harassing effort had produced papers that some instructor would sponsor. At the set time the committee of the faculty designated to examine the candidate assembled in a seminar room, imposingly arrayed in cap and gown, though this bit of academic pomposity was often relaxed, but the candidate must invariably don the costume. If the candidate were a woman, as was often the case, the black gown hid well enough an indifferent dress, the flat cap a mop of loose hair. To Clavercin one of these feminine figures in academic costume always recalled the intentionally comic note of the scene in *The Merchant of Venice* where the learned Portia so glibly puts to rout the pundits of the law. A masquerade, which he could not take seriously. The examiners having ranged themselves around the long table with the chairman at the head, presently the nervous candidate was summoned to the ordeal and graciously permitted to sit. Thereupon one by one the different professors put their questions covering their own fields to the bewildered candidate. This was something of a game, easily recognized. The examining professor desired to show his own *expertise*, to shine and gain prestige in the eyes of his colleagues, and at the same time was desirous that the candidate should not disgrace him by misunderstanding his points or betraying an ignorance of his pet technicalities. So the question must be deftly combined with a mnemonic hint, and if the candidate blundered or hesitated the hint must be made more obvious. Clavercin, observing the professional tactics, often wondered sardonically how many of the examiners could pass an examination if each one were set to quizzing the others,—or indeed could pass their own questions! The farce of the system appeared most fully when the professors who had given courses taken by the candidate happened to be out of residence and their colleagues undertook to examine the candidate on unfamiliar fields. Then the candidate had an easy time, the questions were of a broad simplicity: he might even boldly improvize an answer, trusting to luck that the learned examiner would be hazy on that special matter.

After a couple of hours of this the candidate was excused, allowed to fidget nervously in the gloom of an outer office or hall while the examiners discussed the case and voted to give or to withhold the degree. That moment, when the door closed upon the candidate and the examiners stretched, lighted cigarettes perhaps, and regarded each other, was both comic and humiliating. Clavercin wondered how really intelligent, well trained

men could maintain their gravity or self-respect after
one of these performances. The chairman began, "It
seems to me that the candidate was only superficially
prepared on," or "Miss Smith was evidently very nervous, she did not do full credit to herself in my subject,
but, etc." Clavercin got into the way of voting always
"yes" in every case. It was either that or "no", and
after once being obliged to inform a Miss Smith that
the committee had refused her the degree and having
her collapse on his hands in hysterical sobbing, her
year's grubbing thrown away, while his inner mind knew
that she was no worse informed on these matters than
Miss Jones, her successful predecessor, he decided that
the safer, more humane course was invariably to grant
the degree to any one who had gone through the required ritual. In revenge he amused himself in framing
subtle questions which he blandly and apologetically
proffered, questions that an alert student could easily
answer without much erudition, but which often puzzled his expert colleagues. At last he gave over attending the examinations, explaining frankly to the chairman of his departmental group who had charge of such
matters that he recognized he was not a scholar himself
and felt that he had no business in playing the rôle
before the neophytes of the system. Caxton, the chairman of the group, himself one of the foremost phil-
ologists of the country, for whom Clavercin had profound respect and admiration, received this communication with characteristic liberality.

"I am sorry, Clavercin," he said. "You may not be
a scholar in some senses of the word, but you are a
very useful man in Eureka because you can make your
students understand literature and care for it."

Clavercin reddened boyishly.

"And that's one thing surely a university should do.
As to this degree business I feel very much as you do
about it. But what can we do? The President, as you

know, is all the time pushing us to 'produce'. If we haven't our quota of doctors and masters we'll have our present small budget cut. . . . They want 'results', things they can print in annual reports, show to trustees and rich men, and all that. . . . And the schools want teachers that have a higher degree whether they know anything worth while or not. . . . It's standardization," said the great scholar with a weary frown.

All this useless degree giving business occupied so much of his time that he was years behind in his own work, was overdue, so to speak, on the delivery of promised books, falling behind in the competitive race for publication. What was worse, a fine instrument of a rare perception, such as was Caxton's mind, without any doubt was being dulled in a meaningless routine that any third rate pedant could have done as acceptably.

As the two men stepped out from the empty Hall, where some janitors were sweeping up the day's débris, into the smoky twilight, Clavercin, moved by the older man's kindness, exclaimed bitterly: "I know well enough what I should do if I had the courage. . . . That's the worst of a university: it takes the courage out of you. Like the church—or a government bureau. . . . It gives you a pitiful sort of security, for which you barter your independence, and some soft phrases to drug your soul with!"

Caxton reflectively lighted a cigarette.

"I know," he said. "Yet it is a bigger thing to live uncompromisingly within than merely to get out, don't you think? . . . We need you and Beckwith, men who are not precisely 'scholars'. . . . How is the play getting on?"

"The play? . . . Oh, I had almost forgotten it."

At the further end of the campus the biological laboratories were ablaze with yellow lights, which burned far into the evening. There, at least, in pure science,

Clavercin liked to think, they had students to deal
with that were interested in the subject for itself, not
because it might bring them a job. The teacher also
could be at the same time an investigator: his teaching
and his own intellectual life went hand in hand, as it
should go in all departments of the university. But
the science men, the biologists and pre-medical men, as
well as the chemists and physicists, had their own
troubles, as Clavercin had often heard them relate.
As soon as they had trained a promising student, got
him a small appointment in the laboratory, he was at
once subjected to temptation to sell himself into commercial medicine or business. "I have three applications
for good men in teaching biology, but the jobs only
pay three thousand or less, and I don't know how to
fill them," Dexter told him. "First rate men won't
go to those places, bury themselves', as they call it, in
a laboratory and teaching."

He himself, as Clavercin well knew, had refused the
bait often, saying simply, "I am not a business man.
. . . I am a scholar!"

And he had a tonic scorn for those who "sold themselves" for women and "trash". All the same, if Dexter
had taken more of this "trash" his wife might not
have gone to drugs to still the fatigues and dreariness
of their family life. It was an infernal problem! The
world was finding out every day how it could make
profit out of the labors of scholars and ruthlessly draft-
ing them into the universal processes of gain. Few
could resist. And the worst was that the higher authorities in the university itself aided and abetted the
prostitution, advertising the utility values of the wares
they had to offer. . . .

Clavercin liked to drop in at the little yellow brick
building where Dexter had his private laboratory and
watch the man at work over his long bench. There
was a perpetual smell of animals in the place,—just

now Dexter was experimenting with a new pneumonia
serum and used for this purpose a lot of roosters.
Dexter did not seem to mind the smells.   There at
his bench, often in shirt-sleeves, his pipe in his mouth,
meditatively studying a column of data he had set
down in fine writing, he seemed utterly at peace, removed from all the preoccupations which annoyed
Clavercin, unconscious of the ugliness of his immediate
world, of the pettiness of academic routine,—yes, even
of the squalor of his own home to which presently he
must return, to find his wife in a stupor, his children
unkempt or on the loose, or even the flat shut up,
deserted, as had been the case several times.   Then he
must set forth to find his family, bring the wretched
woman from the spot to which she had wandered.
Clavercin realizing all this had stabs of self-reproach.
He too should rise above the immediate, the appearance of things, and become absorbed in the deeper
current of ideas.   Only the scientists,—and not all of
them by any means,—seemed to have this engrossing
absorption in the world of thought, the single-minded
devotion and pure enthusiasm that religion had once
given men.   Was it because the real man of science
lived more completely aloof from the world as it is
to-day than any other intellectual?   His inner life,
more like that of the Indian sage, profoundly convinced of the unreality of appearances, was absorbed in
the search for an ultimate reality.

"If I were starting again I'd go into science," Clavercin would say to himself, as in another age a distracted man might say, "I'll enter the church."   And
he urged all his students whom he considered had any
mental power and aptitude for thought to spend their
time in the university, not in reading literature and writing, but in trying to understand the process of science,
"so that when you are ready to say something you will
realize more clearly what our world is."

Dexter laid aside his pipe, removed the green shade from his eyes, pushed back his papers, and said slowly, with a little sardonic smile, "It looks as if I had been on the wrong track,—two years' work must go into the discard! . . . . Well, shall we go over to the club and have a game of billiards?"

Without more ado, more emotional explosion, he put out the lights, locked the door, and forgot the futility of his labor. Clavercin regarded Dexter's thick, rather fleshy figure, his livid plain face, with admiration. He was a farmer's son from Wisconsin, and perhaps had acquired from his farmer ancestors this quiet acceptance of the uncertainties of nature with which they had struggled for many generations. . . .

At this hour many of the younger members of the faculty came to the club to play billiards, read the magazines, and write letters. There was a subdued air of relaxation about the somewhat dingy institution, which gave the new members an illusion of clubdom. Around the billiard tables they gossiped a little, talked shop: they were too tired or bored to discuss much else. With the increasing degree of specialization they were cut off from each other in little provinces of thought and interest: knowledge had become an archipelago of small islands instead of a single continent. One popular idea about university life,—that there were "stimulating contacts" among so many exceptional men,—was largely an illusion. Either they were too busy or too narrow in their culture and their interest to give much in general conversation. And the women, who invaded the faculty club as all other departments of the university, hampered free male intercourse. So they played billiards and read the magazines, and at five forty-five hurried off to the domestic hearth, all but the few young men who lived at the club.

CHAPTER SIX

There was one girl in his general class who from the beginning piqued his curiosity. Often as he talked, especially in his more open moods, when the subject touched him personally and he desired to get into the consciousness of the blank faces before him the significance he himself felt, he found his gaze resting on the face of this girl, who usually sat directly beneath him in the front row. Estelle Lambert. She was lithe, light, with a mass of reddish gold hair rippling over a small, well shaped head, a broad low forehead, thin nose, and long hands. She gave the impression of some ripening thing, opening, blooming almost from day to day before his eyes as he watched her. Incidentally he learned that she came from a small town in Texas; this was her third year in the university. Occasionally she came to his office on the fourth floor for a consultation, which was as impersonal, as reserved, as the instructor could make these professional interviews. Yet as she sat beside his desk, the sheets of her written paper between them while he discussed the matter, he was conscious of an extraordinary living quality in the girl. He wanted to ask her personal questions, to satisfy his curiosity about her origin, about herself. Rarely since he had taught in the university had such a vivid consciousness of an individuality come to him from a student. Yet he refrained from stepping over the impersonal line he had established, partly from diffidence, partly from fear of misconception, and partly no doubt from enjoyment of the mystery which the girl's face, her carriage,—the objective

73

sense of her,—offered him. So it went for a term,
a second term, in a continuing course; and again after
an interval she was registered for a third term. Here
he noted an indefinable change in the face and manner
of the girl, a challenge to him, the world, a sullen defiance, and an increasing reserve.

Her mind was as curious to him as her person. She
was, as so many of his students, often crude in expression, nearly illiterate, and naïve,—the child of the small
town with its semi-sophistications. But she was never
common, and occasionally her thinking emitted a glint
of perception that stirred him. Here was a child from
Cascadilla, Texas, who looked out at the universe with
the unblinking gaze of a pioneer, the freshness of a
primitive race. Something, he felt, might be coming
from that sort of product, from an Estelle Lambert.
And then suddenly her papers failed to appear; she cut
the class or slunk in late and took a seat among the
men in the rear. From that more distant place she
regarded him with sombre, savagely cynical eyes,—she
never took notes, and at the close of the hour disappeared in the throng.

One day he sent for her, and when she appeared in
his office demanded curtly, "What's the matter, Miss
Lambert?"

She looked at him blankly.

"At this rate you will fail,—and that is a serious
matter for you. Where is your written work?"

She did not answer, but instead stared blankly at
him. Tears formed and dropped unheeded over the
edge of her eyes to the notebook she held. Clavercin
embarrassed, wheeled in his chair and gazed out of the
window, talking in a cold precise manner, hoping that
she would recover control of herself. This sort of thing,
hysteria, nerves, he had had experience of before, and he
detested the exhibition as one of the inconveniences of
teaching women. When again he turned he met that

same gaze of speechless misery, and behind it he read vaguely a tragedy, something gone wrong. He stopped speaking, then said abruptly,—"Well, tell me!"

Slowly she shook her head, as if to say, "I can't— it's too late."

"You had better ask for leave and go home, he advised. "Drop out for the term."

When thereafter she no longer came to his class he supposed that she had taken his advice. He missed her, and his mind still went back to the painful blankness of her look as the tears rolled over her eyelids. What was the matter? What had blighted that bloom? . . . In most cases he would have forgotten the incident in the turn of the treadmill as something trivial. But with Estelle Lambert he could not forget, and recalling that she had been living in the Women's Hall he went to see Mrs. Crandall.

"What has happened to Estelle Lambert?" he asked. "Did she go home? Some trouble there, I think."

Mrs. Crandall's mobile face sobered instantly.

"I don't think she has left the university. I saw her on the campus the other day. She isn't in the Hall this term. Living in some boarding place in an apartment. I hate those places, but Dr. Harris won't let us build any more women's dormitories, even if we could get the money,—and I think we could. He says the Trustees feel the university is too much of a woman's college as it is, and yet they go on accepting the women. Three-fourths of our women students are now living outside, with no sort of supervision, no decent social life, and I feel responsible for them." She concluded her complaint, and characteristically went back to the immediate matter. "I'll send for Miss Lambert and try to find out what is the trouble. Let me see what courses she is taking this term besides yours."

She sent for the girl's card, and glanced down it, murmuring, "Liddell, Cross, Clavercin, Plant, Plant."

Her face grew more sombre. "Plant, four terms running. . . . a good deal of Plant," she commented meaningly. "I'll let you know, Beaman, what I find out."

Late that afternoon Mrs. Crandall sent a messenger for Clavercin. When he reached her office, she said, "Can you go with me? I may need your help!"

As they got into the cab waiting before the entrance Mrs. Crandall gave an address to the driver, and turning to Clavercin laid a hand on his arm.

"I am terribly afraid . . . we are too late! She hasn't gone home, and she isn't at that place where she has been boarding. She's somewhere in the city. I got an address out of one of her friends, that's where we are going. . . . It's awful to think what she's going through, poor girl!"

Mrs. Crandall belonged to the generation that avoided naming unpleasant facts, although she herself never blinked a necessary fact. Clavercin understood from her broken remarks what she meant him to know, and he was silent, seeing again the lovely girl he had looked at and wondered about all these months. The disturbance that he had divined which had cut across the girl's unfolding was about to be revealed in some tragic event, and yet, and yet, was anything ever fully revealed? Those flaming eyes, that tense figure! How little one could know about another being!

"I had to have some one with me," Mrs. Crandall repeated. "And I thought you and Louise might—possibly—"

"Of course," he said readily, rather dreading the exposure of Estelle Lambert to the sharp, sure judgments of his wife, who was easily censorious.

"I couldn't ask the Mallorys,—for various reasons," Mrs. Crandall explained.

Clavercin wondered if it was because of Mallory's official position in the university or because of Mrs.

Mallory. Plant, he remembered, was a friend of the Mallorys, went there often.

"How this cab crawls!" Mrs. Crandall complained looking out at the unlovely expanse of muddy meadow in the park through which they were passing. It was at the dreariest moment of the year, early March, when even the parks looked forlorn and neglected, uncovered from the winter snows, not yet green with grass. Beyond the park the cab turned northwards in the direction of the city, following one of the interminable avenues that, like the tubes of some gigantic boiler, penetrated the prairie with uncompromising rigidity. Clavercin remarked how even in this new standardized product of an American city with its regular plan, its repetition of a few simple patterns of building, the localities were differentiated. This was a region that he had never penetrated, too far for his strolls and quite distinctive from the commonplace suburban quarter about the university. Once it had been a substantial residential district, with large brick houses surrounded by lawns and a bit of parking space in the good American small town fashion. Now apartment buildings had shoved themselves up between old houses; some of the larger houses had incongruous signs on them of dressmakers, medicine agencies, manicures; some had low extensions for stores built on in front. There were many colored faces on the street. It was a region in transition between living and business.

The cab drew up at last before a large brick house, which even in its dinginess, its mansard-roof ugliness, had an air of having once been of importance in its world. There were no signs on it or evidence of its having been turned into apartments. With the strip of neglected open ground on either side, a rusty iron fence in front, it had a reserved appearance, as if it still tried to keep itself apart from the general decay of its neighbors. Mrs. Crandall opened the cab door before the driver could get down from his seat.

"You had better stay here, Beaman," she said, "until I want you."

She looked up at the forbidding old house and lifting up her skirt she walked resolutely to the door and rang the bell. After a time the door opened, and Mrs. Crandall stepped inside. She was gone a long time, and Clavercin,—whose mind had been in a dull muse over the events of the day, the picture of the fresh loveliness of the Texas girl, her eager mind, the sense of unfolding life she had given him, crossed by perceptions of the ugly sordid street now becoming vague in the March twilight,—began to be uneasy, thinking he should ring the house bell and try to find out what was detaining Mrs. Crandall. Then she appeared, coming in her determined stride down the cement walk, her mobile face set for swift action.

"It's the worst," she said succinctly. "You must go over to the City Hospital . . . it's only a few blocks east, try to find Dr. Cranje,—he's an interne . . . at any rate get some doctor there and an ambulance. I will stay here."

Clavercin without a question set out for the hospital. There were delays, questions, the return to the old house, more waiting. It seemed to Clavercin as if some dreary fate was being run out just off the stage, something that he saw scorchingly, in all its details, as if he were present, but without words, soundlessly, as if it were too bad for words. When finally the door of the brick house opened and the doctor appeared with Mrs. Crandall, holding a swathed form between them, Clavercin directed the cab to move down the block and helped lift the girl into the ambulance.

"No need your coming to the hospital," the doctor advised gruffly, "better not!"

So Mrs. Crandall and Clavercin got into their cab

as the ambulance started in the direction of the city.
Mrs. Crandall was breathing hard, her hands nervously
crumpling a piece of paper on which was scribbled an
address.

"I must telegraph her people," she said. "Tell him
to stop at the nearest office. . . She wouldn't tell—
of course! . . . But I know. I know! . . . Either that
man goes to prison or I leave the university."

Her dark eyes glowed with a fighting fire. Then
after a silence she suddenly exclaimed, "As if that would
do any good now! . . . As if anything will do any good
. . . Oh, my God!"

She shuddered and reached helplessly for Clavercin's
hand. . . .

"Either that man is kicked out of the university—
or I will resign and give my reasons to the newspapers!" she repeated over and over to Clavercin.
The girl had died at the hospital, had not been conscious since she was taken there that March evening.
Her parents had arrived merely to receive her body.
Clavercin and Mrs. Crandall met them at the railroad
station. The woman had something of her daughter's
quick charm, and alertness; the man was more stolid,
obviously less intelligent than his wife, perhaps too
much stunned to comprehend fully what had happened.
Neither one, Clavercin suspected, really wanted to
know the truth, shrank from all inquiry, accepting without question the medical euphemisms that the clever
young interne proffered glibly. . .

"It's best so," Clavercin remarked. "What good
would it do them to hear the truth?"

She shook her head sadly.

"And I don't believe you can get Tom Plant, even if
he were the one. You see we don't know!"

Mrs. Crandall gave him a withering look.

"I know enough," she protested.

Clavercin regretted her vehemence, fearing that in

her passionate resentment she might precipitate a quarrel and weaken her influence in the university. She had already been to Dean Dolittle, who was acting President while Dr. Harris was away. Dolittle had been unsatisfactory, timid about taking any action until the President returned.

"So much harm would be done the institution," he said to Mrs. Crandall, "if we act precipitately in this matter."

He too had questioned the Dean of Women's positive conviction. His attitude was one of unconcealed relief that thus far the newspapers had not got hold of the matter, that it might never get into print.

"He's such a temporizer," Mrs. Crandall said resentfully. "Thank heaven, Harris is not that!"

But when Dr. Harris returned a few weeks later Mrs. Crandall found his sympathies, so quick ordinarily, cold to her. Dolittle had prejudiced the case, implying that Mrs. Crandall had an unreasonable suspicion of "our distinguished colleague", the head of the Maxwell Memorial Laboratory, brother-in-law of a trustee, influential in the city, one of the best known men on the faculty. Of course there had been talk about Tom Plant. It was true that his manners with students were too free, that he encouraged undesirable intimacies; there had been another case, nothing as bad as this; but Mrs. Plant had stood staunchly by him, as she would this time. The best thing to do was to forget the unhappy incident, best for the poor girl's memory, for her parents, for the university and the community. A great deal of morbid interest had been avoided, fortunately. "One must take into consideration the university's position in the community," was the substance of the presidential attitude.

"And not the university's responsibility for the girl?" Mrs. Crandall demanded.

As to that Dr. Harris was vague. It was clear that

pressure had been brought to bear on him before he
met the Dean of Women, more serious pressure than
that of the soft-spoken Dolittle.

"In short," Clavercin laughed sardonically, "the tune
is 'Hush! Hush! Don't let Anybody Know!' "

As he thought of things in terms of plays, he felt that
a comedy might be framed on the situation as he got
it from Mrs. Crandall,—Trustees, Officials, Faculty, all
scuttling from the horrid truth, covering up their cowardice by mumbling phrases about "protecting the good
name of the university", "if it got about that such things
happened here, and so forth", Institutional Cowardice,
he called it.

"I can't see this girl's fate as comedy," Mrs. Crandall replied sombrely.

"Nor do I,—but I see the university as comic when
it tries to act—humanly."

"I am tired," Mrs. Crandall sighed. "Beaman, I
am going away. I have failed, Yes,—you don't have to
say nice things,—I have failed here in what I tried
to do for Eureka, for the education of women, for
women themselves. This isn't the only case. Dr.
Harris no longer listens to me,—he is jealous or suspicious because I have thwarted some of his cheap
plans. . . . Yes, I shall leave at the close of the term,
go to Europe for a while."

Clavercin thought this was nothing more than the
morbid reaction of fatigue which came to all in their
profession, when some slight rebuff takes on huge
significance. He hoped that a few months of travel and
rest, new scenes for her eager eyes, old friends and
memories in England, would restore the balance of her
enthusiastic buoyant spirit. Mrs. Crandall was under
a strain and might be doing a prominent member of
the faculty a great injustice.

But when he happened on Tom Plant, lolling in the
lounging room of the faculty club, sucking a black

cigar in his thick rolling lips, his green eyes just
peering through heavy lids, he felt an over whelming
aversion to the man, who drawled out lazily in a Vir-
ginian accent, "How goes it, Beaman!" Clavercin
glared at Plant without returning his greeting.   A
moment after, he realized how childish his gesture was.
It was merely an instinctive expression of the tumult
within him seeking an outlet in a concentrated aversion.

His mind brooded on different aspects of the case,
on the tragic significance of the multitudinous other
cases like this girl's.   The university after all merely
repeated the attitude of society in general, a shame-
faced, horrified, hush-it-up-in-the-dark attitude.   He
was not clear what society or a university should do
about sex eruptions,   whether anything could be done
effectively.   But at least they might try to be honest
about the thing.   Why had the girl submitted, gone to
that awful fate, in her misery?   Because she had not
dared tell any one who could have helped her.   She
had not dared go home to her parents and face Cascadilla, nor go to Mrs. Crandall and face the university,—nor to anybody!   It was part of the pretense of
the American university that the institution acted as
parent and exercised supervision over the students who
entered it.   And yet when it came to a crisis like this,
after negligently permitting such conditions the university would not accept responsibility, scuttled like
everybody else.   Either the university should disclaim
any responsibility for the lives of the young people
who came to it or it should act as Mrs. Crandall would
have it act, like mother and father.   Either education
must be impersonal or personal,—not both. . . .

"What are you writing these days, Clavercin?" old
Bayberry asked, with kindly interest in the younger man.

"A play about abortion," Clavercin replied.

"What—" Bayberry stammered.

"Yes—abortion—you know what it is, don't you? It's common enough."

"I don't like unpleasant themes," Bayberry remarked coldly. "Why must you young writers choose subjects that nice people don't talk about?"

"Because, I suppose, nice people don't talk about 'em enough."

The play went rapidly, wrote itself in fact.

CHAPTER SEVEN

The news of Edith Crandall's death cabled from London and prominently displayed in the American newspapers with an account of the achievements of her busy life came at the opening of the autumn term. She seemed to possess the dauntless spirit and inexhaustible energy for an endless life, and now a slip on the pavement in front of an omnibus and it was ended. There was on the campus the imposing Woman's Quadrangle, which had been given to the university among the first of its buildings because of her, also the more recent Woman's Commons just being completed. But her real monument lay in the lives of those women throughout the country, who at the magic touch of her enthusiasm and quick sympathy had been stirred to reach for richer fulfillment of themselves. To how many girls in small communities had she first and last brought the illumination of possible escape from a petty environment and an inadequate mating. More than any one of her time Edith Crandall embodied the ideal of equality in educational opportunities—and therefore in life—for men and women. She had never taken part in the political struggle for woman's emancipation. "Let us become better, richer human beings", she had proclaimed insistently, "and all other privileges will be ours. But first we must prove our abilities on men's own ground through the discipline of our minds."

In her youth and early womanhood the college girl was considered a sexless aberration. That was Clavercin's prejudice when he first came to Eureka. A woman

might become learned, but in the process she must
have sacrificed what made her most worth while as a
woman. Mrs. Crandall's mere presence was sufficient
refutation of that condescending view. If not beautiful—her features were too irregular for the magazine-
cover type of feminine loveliness then being stereotyped
by Dana Gibson—her face was singularly attractive, her
mobile mouth and warm brown eyes ever changing
expression as sensitively as the waters in a mountain
lake. As she once told Jessica Mallory she could not
waste precious time on her personal appearance, and
yet no man ever thought of her as unattractive. Her
presence on a platform gave the lie to the silly conception of an educated woman then rife. She was
so gracious, so winning, so gentle, and yet so resolute.
Young women feeling within them the power of independence, yet fearing to endanger their "womanhood"
by competing with men could be reassured by one
look at Edith Crandall. Here was a woman, all woman,
who had been loved by a man, whose marriage had
obviously been happy, and yet she had yielded nothing
of her personal gifts to the accident of having been
born a woman. When she died the significance of her
courageous example had already been absorbed into
American ideas: a girl was no longer considered peculiar
or fit only for the convent because she chose to go to
college like her brothers. Insensibly the sort of femin-
ism for which Edith Crandall had struggled in so many
ways had been won, and more than anybody was
aware at the moment she had become a national figure,
embodying this triumph.

One would hardly have suspected all this at the little
memorial service held a few weeks after her death in
the college hall. Only a few of her intimates on the
faculty and some of the older women students who had
come directly under her influence, several of the younger

trustees and a solitary reporter from the *Thunderer*, were there that October afternoon. The president of the university being absent, Dean Dolittle presided in his place, benignly, deprecatingly. It was evident that officially Eureka wished to minimize the importance of the dead woman now that her presence could no longer bring students or buildings to the institution. Dr. Harris, for all his readiness to use her prestige and her popularity in advertising his university, had never understood her real importance, and of late, obscure, petty jealousies had separated them. Certain elements in the faculty had not ceased to deplore the feminization of the university, as they called it, and attributed to the celebrated dean of women the crime of "making a girls' boarding school out of Eureka." Moreover Mrs. Crandall's intimates were among the unpopular "Harvard gang", and she did not try to disguise her sympathies with them. . . .

So altogether Clavercin felt it was a forlorn occasion, as a tribute to a great person. It reminded him of that last painful episode in which he and Edith Crandall had been concerned, the death of Estelle Lambert. The sheer passion of pity for the girl, she had shown not one word of reproach for her folly! And hatred of the man. . . . "Why are you so sure Plant was the one?" he had asked her, and in reply she had given him an odd, penetrating glance out of those glowing eyes. "It would have to be either you or Plant," she had said, "and I know it could not be you, Beaman!"

"But why so?" he asked, mystified, and she had retorted,—"She wasn't the kind . . . to give herself to anybody! . . . I found some of the verses which she had written recently. They told the whole story. They were remarkable, so like her, crude and fine, old and young at the same time, and so passionately sincere!"

It was a pity, Clavercin reflected, that this sordid little

drama where nothing was to be gained had been Edith
Crandall's last battle in the university; that she had
so recklessly exposed herself to her enemies by seeking
vengeance for the girl. . . . Defeated, she had virtually
abandoned the university into which she had poured
so much enthusiasm, so many days and nights of hard
work, so many passionate aspirations for women and
men. Perhaps she realized that Eureka was not to
become the great university she had hoped to see;
that her own potency in its creation had been exhausted; therefore she had withdrawn. No doubt the
case of Estelle Lambert had a deeper significance for her
than for him: the right of women to compete with
men unhampered by the snares of sex. Thus she had
spoken of the incident to Norman Beckwith whom she
had seen in London before the accident.

"But I think," Beckwith said, "she had grown beyond us. She was restless and needed a fresh field,
something more important than regulating the lives of
women students. She knew that the fight for the
higher education of women had been won. . . . She
ought to have been in politics."

"Yes!" Mallory assented, "how she loved a good
scrap!"

"Few persons are so passionate about life as she
was," Beckwith mused. "Most of them keep their
passions for their petty selves, but Edith Crandall
poured out her passion into causes, and forgot all about
herself!"

"That is true," Jessica Mallory observed. "She was
selfless and she was passionate, an unusual combination."

She spoke impersonally of the dead woman to whom for a
time she had been so close, as though Edith Crandall were
a curious case of psychology that she had observed at
close range. Clavercin remembered her dry comment
on Mrs. Crandall's agitation over Estelle Lambert—
Edith has the crisis psychology badly". . . . Mrs. Mal-

lory carried under her arm her familiar black portfolio, and after the service while the others lingered in the autumn sunshine talking of the dead friend as if she were still living and about to join them with her radiant buoyancy, Jessica slipped away in the direction of her "shop", having devoted all the time she could spare to a futile ceremony. Did she lack all emotional response, or was she afraid of it? Only recently she had become a mother for the second time, and that too had left no mark on the youthful trim figure. She had the same girlish freshness that Clavercin had noted when he first saw her in the president's office. She was impervious to life! Mallory's glance followed her, with a slight frown, until she became merged on the broad main walk in the stream of students, and then he jerked himself back to the present.

"We must think of something as a memorial to Edith Crandall,—something more than a bust or a portrait to hang in the Woman's Hall," he said briskly. "They mustn't forget her, and what she has done for them!" He nodded in the direction of the students, who, as they passed the flag staff in the centre of the campus, glanced curiously at the half-masted flag.

"It has been suggested to call the new woman's commons Crandall Hall some one said!"

They laughed, for all recalled Mrs. Crandall's merry horror over the woman's dining hall.

Bayberry remarked, "She asked me to select those photographs of classical sculpture to hang in the faculty room. She said it would be good for the faculty to have something beautiful to look at. . . . She may not have been a scholar, but she was so much more than that—she was a great person!" the old scholar summed up magnanimously. "We must put some beauty into our gift to her."

"If it had not been for Edith Crandall our lives here would have been—barbarous," Sidney Lamb pronounced plaintively. "She was an inspiration to us all!"

It was Clavercin who added musingly,—"Like a chime of tuneful bells, like those English chimes you hear across green meadows at twilight."

"That's it!" Mallory exclaimed, seizing on the idea and applying it at once. "Chimes! . . . We'll put them into the Campanile where they will ring out night and morning, like her so sweet, so unfaltering, so gay!"

The idea captured their imagination as something simple, not grandiose, a memorial that could not be travestied for promotional schemes. In this way to the thousands who some day would live in this spot Edith Crandall could speak, even if she were unknown to them. . . .

"We won't ask for subscriptions to this," Mallory declared. "We'll merely announce our plan and say that Mrs. Crandall's friends may contribute what they like towards her bells. She hated raising money,—and she had so much of it to do!"

"We'll get the best bells that can be made to-day, and some one who knows how to play them!" Beckwith concluded.

This was the origin of the famous chime of bells that play so softly from the belfry of the slim Campanile above the Eureka campus. The bells arrived in due season and with them an expert British bell-ringer, who distracted the university by his gymnastic agility on the new chimes, until the neighbors complained that they could not sleep because of the frequency of the hours and quarters, with his carillons and peals. The scientists who had their laboratories near the Campanile complained that the tunes distracted their students. So the British bell-ringer was sent back to England, and the care of the chimes was handed over to a divinity student who was earning his way by doing odd jobs. The authorities decreed that the chimes were to be played only twice a day for five minutes, and on

Sundays a little longer. The divinity student learned to pull the bells haltingly and spelled out a few old tunes, two of which became campus favorites,—"Nearer My God to Thee" and "Lead Kindly Light."

So at ten-thirty in the morning, the peculiar hour fixed at Eureka for chapel because it made a convenient break between morning classes, one could hear for a few minutes the chimes stumbling through the familiar tunes. Old Tom Bayberry when he heard the first notes drop hesitantly out of the sky would put down the book he was reading in his lonely library and sit erect in his chair, wiping his glasses, an odd screwed-up look on his homely face; then as the last note died out he would resume his book. . . .

Clavercin, coming exhausted from his late class, with the sense of general futility that is likely to overwhelm the intellectual at that hour, became conscious of the bells and remembered with a quickening of spirit the winsome person so interwoven with the early years of the university; her unfailing gayety, sweetness, courage seemed fused into the soft tones floating in the murky sky. He saw the look on her eager face when he first told her he was to marry Louise and make the venture of poverty.

"My boy, my boy," she had said impulsively laying her hand on his knee, "I am so glad. Don't wait! It is so much easier to face poverty when there are two— if there is love. . . . I found it so!" And she told him of her marriage to the penniless scholar, their struggle, how one good fortune after another came to them unexpectedly. "I consider that my life has been richer, essentially, in all the things which ought to count,—in friends, in beauty, in opportunity for work than the lives of all the moneyed people I have known. Remember always that money doesn't count!" Strange creed for this time and place, and Clavercin beset by the trials of middle life was not always sure of its

truth. But Edith Crandall believed it fervently. . . .
His was but one of the hundreds of the thousands of
human lives she had touched thus intimately, surely,—
students, professors, donors.

"I gave these buildings," the old hardware merchant
Blackstone said at the dedication of the Woman's Commons, "because Edith Crandall was such a woman; it
seemed to me she might make more of her kind out
of our young women." . . .

Did Edith Crandall have any time for self, any personal life whatever? Since she had become a "public
person" with so many engagements on boards and committees, her old friends saw little of her. Edith "has
acquired a taste for lime-light," Jessica Mallory once
commented dryly. But Clavercin felt that Edith Crandall never really forgot anybody. Some spirits, it
seemed, had this extraordinary power of reduplicating
themselves endlessly like living cells, dividing and uniting
in countless combinations, yet retaining always an essential personal quality. . .

They placed a bronze plaque in the entrance of the
Campanile beneath her bells. It showed in relief the
strong face, the coil of thick hair above the low brow.

"The mother spirit of the university!" Bayberry pronounced, as he stood beside Beckwith and Jessica Mallory before the tablet.

"A most inexplicable personality!" Mrs. Mallory
mused in her level, objective voice. "At times she
seemed quite superficial; her mind was certainly not—
orderly. But she arrived swiftly at conclusions in that
haphazard, jumpy way she had that others come to
painstakingly long afterwards—which is what is commonly called genius."

Jessica Mallory, always suspicious of any form of
emotionalism, was trying thus in her own way to render
her tribute of appreciation. But Thomas Bayberry
unconsciously moved a little farther away from her.

He too hated sentimentality, but he disliked hardness
of spirit even more, and he considered the wife of his
beloved Edgar to have been born without what the
older novelists called a heart.

"She was a man of action with a woman's spirit,"
Beckwith said gently. "How she ragged the Doctor!
He used to hate to see her come into his office because
he knew he would have to make good on something.
Promises wouldn't do. He ought, of course, to have
given her an honorary degree when he handed one to
our sainted Founder. . . . Not that she would have
cared much for it!"

"Oh, yes, she would have!" Jessica Mallory averred
confidently.

There was a new dean of women, Miss Gertrude
Porridge, an austere, remote individual supplied by the
Teacher's College, who gave courses in Pedagogy.
Under her domination the Woman's Quadrangle became
sombre. Girls were expelled because they smoked cigarettes, and severely reprimanded for encouraging young
instructors to call upon them. As a consequence the
Woman's Quad was avoided by the younger and prettier
undergraduates. . . . With the passing of Edith
Crandall one period of the university had closed,—its
youth. Crude and makeshift that youth may have
seemed to Clavercin and his kind; nevertheless as they
came to realize in the years that followed there was
something ardent and inspiring in the air those early
days, which the university had never quite lived up to.
Eureka was no longer "Barnum's Show". One no
longer frequented Fleshie's and played penny stocks
on the university bourse, nor heated oneself overmuch
in faculty meetings in the perpetual struggle between
"culture" courses and "practical" courses. Harden
had gone back to his beloved fatherland; Sidney Lamb twittered less frequently in defense of "good
form".

Eureka had become an American university like any other with its yearly grist of graduates, its baseball and football victories, its fraternity houses and "proms", something between a prep school and a laboratory. Clavercin approaching the campus dominated by the imposing Campanile from the suburban station sometimes recalled that first journey and all the agitated fancies which had filled his mind about the future. . . . Well, he was now professor of dramatic literature, hoping some day to have his own department with a little theatre in which to experiment in the writing and staging of plays. Some day. He was married to Louise. . . . And life in general seemed a little less adventurous and exciting than it had that raw spring morning when he forded the yellow mud of the prairie road on his heels in order to preserve the shine on his shoes. Dr. Harris had given up the habit of wearing "congress" boots. The world was moving on—to what?

PART TWO

CHAPTER ONE

The deans occupied one side of the lower floor of Founder's Hall, each dean having a separate cubicle opening from the general office. Lines of students waiting to consult their dean stretched out through the general office into the hall, often making a congestion there especially at the opening of the term. Across the hall was the record office,—the educational banking room of the university,—where were kept those precious "credits" of which a certain number were needed to obtain the coveted degree. Each student on entrance was given a little credit book by his dean in which at a glance he might know how many credits he had accumulated towards his degree, and how many more courses he must enter there before arrival. It was all very systematic, like a savings bank, as worked out by Mallory in the first years of the university. As each course had the same credit value, the students insensibly came to think of their education in terms of "units" and "credits", so many units for admission, so many credits for a degree, and the instructor when confronted by the plea of a delinquent student,—"I lack half a unit," realised that his function was primarily to supply credits and hesitated before handicapping a student in his life quest because of a personal doubt as to his proficiency in a certain subject. Courses varied widely in their educational content, as did the minds of the instructors who gave them, their standards of accomplishment, and the care with which they imposed their standards—and yet all counted the same in the educational banking office. Inevitably the student came to have a cynical indifference as to the content of any given course and a cynical appreciation of the instructor's weaknesses. Getting a degree with the minimum risk and amount of effort was a game like any other. It was the business of the deans to apply the rules of the game as decreed by the faculty and to adjust the individual to the banking system. The Harris idea was to give the student a great deal of individual attention, and hence the increasing number of deans. Apart from the Senior Deans with Abel Dolittle at the head as Dean of the University and Mallory as Dean of the Graduate School, there was a tribe of junior deans of whom Norman Beckwith was one, the most popular, the least academic. . . .

Clavercin making his way through the crowded hall caught sight of Beckwith at the end of a long queue of waiting students, course book and pencil in hand, figuring out the necessary credits to be obtained, trying to fit the student into the current program of instruction, an immense broadsheet that lay on his desk. Beckwith's peculiarly arched eyebrows worked up and down as he scanned the crowded program of courses for some empty hole into which he might insert the case, thus rounding out the required credits. Suddenly, having detected a possible combination, his pencil darted down on the spot on the map of all human knowledge before him, and he turned triumphantly to the student,—"That's your chance, Professor Dodson, Geography 13, at eight-thirty," Clavercin could hear Beckwith announce. . . .

He knew that Beckwith had as little respect as himself for the involved system of educational banking whose proper functioning it was his business to administer. Indeed long years of contact with the machine had taught Beckwith most of its weak spots. He knew the instructors who shirked, those who talked piffle to their classes and catered to the athletes, those who were illiterate or mean spirited or merely dull. Better than any man in the university he could justly estimate the comparative worth of the hundreds of items on the university menu, and many times he had been able skilfully to steer a promising boy or girl away from weak or meretricious courses into something that might enlist their best efforts. He knew the pretentiousness of the whole fabric and the mechanical routine of it. Why did he stick to the job? It was miserably paid, a few hundred dollars a year for long hours of exhausting office work. It had been a rare bit of executive insight on the part of Dr. Harris making the "bad boy of the faculty" as Mrs. Crandall had once called Beckwith a junior dean. It had put him under bonds to keep the peace, for one thing, and even Dolittle who had disapproved of his selection had to admit that under Beckwith the junior deanship was the most efficient office in the university. Beckwith had an unquenchable youth in him that reached out to the youth around him and responded to them. "He don't talk bunk", "He's all right", "He knows what he is talking about", they said in their vernacular, and rarely tried to lie to "Becky". They knew as youth easily divines such things that their Dean did not take the university too seriously and was not in favor with the higher officials such as Dolittle. His general course in European history was one of the most popular in the university because of Beckwith's unconventional frankness and personal comment on current events. The more intelligent students suspected that the professor of mediaeval history was a radical or a "socialist" as the liberal minded were then called, and that added a spice to his instruction. When he arrived in his lecture hall, his arms full of papers and books, his smooth shaven face with the rugged cheekbones rosy from the exertion of running across the campus, and tossed his shapeless cap into a corner, squaring his shoulders for the fifty minutes' lecture, there was always a pleasant stir of anticipation in the crowded room. One never knew what might happen in Becky's classes. Those judicious cormorants, the graduate students, reported well of him. He was the most generous man in the department with his time and his scholarship, and if erratic and obviously biased by his social views he was none the less sound. "Beckwith knows his field," they said, "though he publishes little—too busy with too many things." So they ransacked his brain and took what they wanted there. The learned papers which might have brought him academic fame and position were thus compiled by others, as theses and dissertations, and Beckwith remarked,—"Well, I might never get around to that myself!" The peculiar jealousy, or miserliness, of the academic mind he was wholly without. Provided something worth while, of significance in any field, got done, it mattered little to Beckwith who did it. In this as in other respects he had the communal mind, which is more interested in the thing done than in the doer of it. His friends like Walter Snow and Caxton complained that, "Beckwith wasted himself," on trivial things like the junior deanship and his settlement classes. They did not realise, perhaps, that the very spirit which they prized in the man of tireless enterprise and generosity necessitated waste. Life was too interesting to Norman Beckwith to be niggardly with it anywhere.

Ruggedly built, Beckwith had probably never felt fatigue in his life and did not have to save himself nervously and mentally as so many of the intellectual type must. From the musty atmosphere of his dean's office he could plunge into the stale air of his lecture hall, pour himself out abundantly for the period and then rush off to the city to some long evening engagement. After midnight he would return to the bare chamber which happened for the time to house him—it

made little difference where or how ugly it might be—
seize the few hours of rest he needed to rise fresh for
another full day.

"He functions all day at full speed, "Snow said of
him, "and what is more he never needs a rest. He
is woven of steel cords!"

Which was only part of Beckwith's secret, the obvious
part, as Clavercin felt. The quality in him which made
the junior deanship tolerable, indeed nourishing while
to another its routine drudgery would have been killing
was due to something more than physical endurance.
Beckwith could nourish himself on coarser fare than
another, do with fewer hours of sleep, stand cold without warm clothing, and he could feed his spirit with
robust comedy where another would starve. . . . Jessica Mallory, who did not feel drawn to Beckwith,
shrewdly estimated the source of his inexhaustible
energy. "He never once thought about himself in his
whole life," she said, "Not that such a habit is praise-
worthy. He is an 'extravert', that is all," using one
of the newer terms of her science.

"I wish we had more such extraverts in the university," Mallory replied, He had an almost tender feeling
for his younger colleague, born of long, dreary official
business enlivened by Beckwith's jesting habit. . . .

So there he sat "functioning" as a junior dean with
a long queue of men students waiting their turn for
attention. Imaginatively one might see that queue
extended into the indefinite distance of past and future.
with all the patterns of young lives that had sat in it.
Already—and Norman Beckwith was not yet forty—
his students were numbered by the thousands, scattered
up and down the states, teaching, in business, each
"functioning" in his turn. Now and then when he was
on a journey some half familiar young man in Pullman
or smoking car would stare at Beckwith for a few
moments, then approach him with the formula,—"I

suppose you don't remember me, Professor Beckwith, but" . . . to which the dean's beaming reply would be, "But I do remember you, Simeon Strasky—how goes it?" Often before the queue formed outside his door some moustached young man would step in authoritatively and ask the indulgence of the machine for some erring brother with an "I know, Dean you will treat him fair." Such recognitions, gaining in volume year by year, were Norman Beckwith's reward for the hours spent in that ill-ventilated den of a dean's office, listening to the naïve troubles of the new crop of first year "men", trying to straighten out some muddled schedule of courses with the aid of the jumbo program of courses on his desk. They counted for him far more than the few hundred dollars added to his salary (which he would allow to slip swiftly through his disdainful fingers either in a riotous dinner or a gilded speculation!).

Yet that was not all the secret of his clinging to the deanship, to his professorship. The call of paternity had an indefinable share in it. Having no children of his own, too busy and too nomadic in his habits to adopt any, he compensated himself as so many teachers do, with this secondary paternity of hundreds and thousands of young lives, whom he counselled, disciplined, and encouraged. "I have a large flock," he would say," mostly poor stuff I am afraid, but a few thoroughbreds among 'em. That's what a university can give one, if you have the taste for it, a lot of interesting children whose bills you are not expected to pay!"

Possibly he felt it more important to spread his influence into the coming generations through his students than through articles and books, "which somebody would have to do over after me," as he said. "It's the only way in which such a place as Eureka can be made over, or such a world as ours, by corrupting the young. I've corrupted a number of thousands by this time, I hope, so that they will be a little less complacent, a little less arrogant, than their fathers. . . . Of course Sandy" (Sanderson, dean of Business Administration, occupied the next cubicle to Beckwith) "is corrupting his thousands too, and a lot of my students fall for his cheap counting house stuff. . . . But in the end if there ever were a revolution some good boys will remember Becky told them there had been one before and might be another some day and not to get scared."

This was said in an expansive hour at Snow's lakeside bungalow, which had soberly taken the place of Flesheimer's as an occasional rendezvous. Perched on a steep sandy bluff beside an old wind driven pine, the tiny wooden box of a house with three rooms was hardly more than a shack which Walter Snow and his wife, a painter, had rented from a fisherman and had cleaned and patched. It served as an escape from the growing tyranny of the smoky city whose leaden pall crept yearly farther and farther into the flat prairie. Around the city there were a number of country clubs, to which comfortable citizens resorted for rest and recreation. A few of the faculty, like Aleck Harding, had memberships in one of these clubs, but for the majority the expense was prohibitive. They must join the army of vagrant "hikers" who filled the Saturday trains, clothed in nondescript garments, with canvas sacks on their backs, in search of fresh air and a clear sky. At the end of the lake beyond the zone of the steel mills, where the northerly winds had heaped mountains of sand, was a notable region of sandy farms, tiny lakes, and grape orchards. Here every holiday came hundreds of trampers, wandering over the beaches and dunes, building drift-wood fires, cooking their food and sleeping in the open. This nomadic population had no country houses, golf clubs, winter refuges in the

south and west: they were tied to the office treadmill
and the cramped rooms of some flat building in the city.
With these hikers the university people partly associ-
ated, their economic status being very nearly the same,
yet except for a few artists and musicians among the
vagrants there was little real intimacy between the two
groups.

Something in his occupation set apart the college professor and his family both from the ordinary wage-
earner and the successful capitalist, so that they were
really at home only with their own kind. They had
a wider perspective of life's possibilities than either, a
gentler tradition of culture, and less initiative, perhaps.
For the professor there was always at the close of every
academic year the vision of European wanderings, to be
repeated or begun. "When we go to Europe", or
"Next time I am over," they said to one another, recognising thus the home of their spirits. Snow's professional work took him to Spain; Beckwith managed every
other summer a few weeks in Switzerland.

Thus after disposing of the university situation of
Jorolman's encroachments in the Teachers' College
and Sanderson's pretensions in Business Administration,
and the pressure to create a College of Journalism, to
which Clavercin was passionately opposed, they left
the shop and let their minds roam more happily over
the approaching summer vacations which they all three
hoped to spend in Europe. There, they fondly believed,
ideas counted, learning had an honorable and assured
position, not dependent on the patronage of wealth, not
compelled to "make good" in the American way by
Teachers' Colleges, Business Schools, Schools of Journalism, all the meretricious devices by which such
"educators" as Dr. Harris wheedled millions from what
President Roosevelt had called "predatory wealth".
Of course as Beckwith aptly observed learning like art
had always been parasitic, but after a long tradition

the two had established themselves in European civilization so securely that their parasitic origins had been forgotten: they had an honorable and secure place of their own so that they attracted the best minds, the freest spirits. Obviously the American university had no such prestige, now less than ever when industry was bidding so heavily for the keenest intelligences. Even the professions like medicine and law were constantly wiling away the ablest young men from the faculty. . . .

"The fellow who bored out my nose, the other day," Snow remarked, throwing a bit of driftwood on the dying beach fire, "used to be Dexter's assistant— now he's making forty thousand a year in that suite of offices in the Gas Building."

Each felt that in some way he had been trapped by an illusion, when he had entered what Clavercin called "the pleasant walks of Academe,"—a dream of something that did not exist in America or if it had once existed faintly in the older colleges of the East had been choked by the rapid growth of national wealth.

"Look at our master!" Snow cried, pointing to the flaming stacks of the steel city.

CHAPTER TWO

Nobody in the university—or outside of it for that matter—knew much about Jessica Mallory, which was what she preferred. Not even her husband nor her children. She was as much of an "extravert" as Norman Beckwith, with whom she had nothing else in common. While Beckwith became more absorbed in the life around him, Jessica more and more withdrew association from it, and accentuated her differentiation, her individuality. A woman and exquisitely dainty, feminine in person, she disliked women, preferred men and their minds. Deriding all conventions, especially those that tyrannously restricted women in their relations with men, she fulfilled the orthodox rôles of wife and mother acceptably, having had three healthy children, well cared for. She had never paraded her maternity, but had never forgotten the obligation. Now that her children were old enough to be at school she left them largely alone, to make their own characters. A passionate individualist, exacting respect for her own individuality, she scrupulously respected the individuality of others, even that of a small child. She refused to be classified, identified, submerged in any function, maternal, matrimonial, or professional. Her cool aloofness of attitude seemed to say, "Yes, I happen to be a woman, and I hope an attractive one. I am married and a mother—but what of it? I am more than all that—I am myself, free in spirit to undertake any engagement that I may happen to choose." No formula, rule, prescription made by others should hem in her life. . . .

She had small regard for noisy protestants, talky

radicals, who vaunted their revolts in order presumably to give themselves courage. Silence, Jessica had found to be the most effective means of expressing oneself, of obtaining one's own way. The expressive people gave themselves away, weakened their prestige, and their revolts usually evaporated in words. Silence puzzled all opponents. Jessica's capacity for silence was immense, and it increased with the years. Behind that hedge of silence she listened and observed, safe and amused, drawing shrewd conclusions, making what she called "the indirect approach" to her objectives whatever they might be. Realising that this is a psychological world, she looked for the concealed, the hidden cause, ignoring the obvious. Moreover she was an opportunist. Now this, now that might be done: the only fixed quantity was the inner thought. Some people called her sly, but like most comment this contained less than a half truth.

As a girl in conflict with her people, whose ideas were entirely of their own class, Edith Crandall had caught her up in the whirl of her buoyant enthusiasms and almost made her into an assistant dean of women in Eureka. Having exhausted the Crandall ideal—enthusiasm for the education of women—Jessica engaged with Edgar Mallory in applied sociology, until its vague emotional basis lost validity for her. She referred later to this time as her "militant period", when she was all for causes of one kind or another, settlement work, serving on committees, working for woman's suffrage, incidentally having children and writing those books on social organization which afterwards she regarded indifferently as mere compilations of other people's ideas. Meanwhile her husband was being drawn more and more into the administration of the university, which appealed to her even less than settlement work. To her cool mind there was nothing sacred in any institution. The sentimental loyalties which the university was supposed to arouse left her cold. Eureka was merely a collection of buildings, apparatus, and men like another, less complete and less interesting than some others. Intellectually and culturally she felt some disdain for Dr. Harris and his impromptu university, which impaired a mocking chill to her intercourse with her husband's colleagues. "She feels superior to us because she is rich", they said unjustly. What had annoyed her had been the refusal of the trustees to have her continue her teaching in the university after her marriage. That ban had roused all her militancy as a member of the lesser sex. "As if having a husband and children had anything to do with my own work!" As a scholar she knew that she was abler, more distinguished because of her many publications, than any member of her department, than most of the faculty. The fact that she was a woman, married to a university official prevented her from attaining her rightful position.

That exclusion was indirectly the cause of her abandoning sociology altogether for psychology. That and the advent of Rudolph Sheimer. Sheimer was a German Swiss, who had studied in Jung's laboratory and had come to Eureka to teach medicine in the new medical school Dr. Harris was then engaged in forming, on paper. Finding the medical school still nebulous he had given a course of lectures at the university on the new experimental psychology which Jessica attended. She found his ideas suggestive, and together they planned a department of experimental psychology, which Jessica largely supported from her own means. Sheimer was a thoroughly trained German scientist with an unconcealed contempt for American superficiality. He was arrogant, dominating, entertaining, and conceited. His method with Jessica was a composite of German domineering and of the subtle flattery of considering her the only person in the university whom he could deal with as an equal. He rapidly demolished in her eyes what credit the general studies she had made in sociology still retained for her.

"Very good!" he would say with a curl of his expressive long upper lip. "Weiniger stuff. But what do you know about the facts? You haven't sufficient data. You are repeating like all the rest unproved assumptions, myths,—what do we know about society? Begin with a study of the individual. . . . This is mere book stuff."

Jessica was ready to believe him. Already her thorough, proving mind, which never deceived itself, had grown tired of stale verbal generalizations. She had the pertinacity, the energy to pursue any line of investigation that promised results. Sheimer convinced her that the facile triumphs which her papers and books had obtained hitherto were illusory. "Popular journalism". He pointed out to her the endless vista of science, the patient, minute research for something fundamental. . . . So when the new department was opened in an apartment building hastily converted into class rooms and laboratories, Jessica took possession of a room on the upper floor to which she gradually transferred all her papers and books from the little study she had hitherto occupied in the University Avenue house, and there she could be found at almost any hour of the day or evening sitting bent over an immense table, tabulating, annotating, writing in her fine firm hand.

She was absorbed, genuinely happy, on the right road at last, the road that would lead to basic discoveries, putting stone squarely upon stone in the great structure of science. Not merely adding to the noisy volume of printed words! Sheimer, whose office was opposite Jessica's, discussed with her every detail of installation and instruction, deferring to her not merely as patroness but as colleague. Instead of going to the faculty club, several long blocks away for luncheon, Jessica, who

had early formed the sandwich habit as most economical
of time, would spread out her sandwiches with a piece
of candy and an apple on the broad desk and heat some
cocoa over a gas jet in the closet. Presently Sheimer
would come in from his office, and the two would
munch negligently talking meanwhile of current tasks.
It was the most intimate intellectual relation that Jessica ever had experienced and the most exhilarating.
Sheimer not only had a sharp, eager mind, thoroughly
trained, but he was ambitious and a terrific worker.
He dressed for a laboratory worker rather foppishly,
with an attention to head, feet, and hands that the
American university instructor rarely displayed. His
somewhat narrow head was beautifully modelled. He
had rapidly run through the personnel of the university, rejecting most of the faculty as negligible, even
notable members. He taught Jessica the scorn of the
pure scientist for the dilettante, the advertiser, the
populariser, respect for the obscure and the plodding.
Not until long afterwards if ever did Jessica become
thoroughly aware of the influence which Rudolph
Sheimer had had over her mind and soul. His was the
hand that opened a ready door in her spirit. He demolished whatever traces of mysticism there might be
lingering from her ancestry. "Sentimental," and "literary" were his two most familiar sneers. She had
always been doubtful about popular appreciation, and
became more so from contact with Edgar Mallory's
facile touch, his oratorical manner. So she quickly
acquired the scientist's scorn of "cheap" achievements,
and intolerantly considered any popular success as
meretricious. In place of what he took away the Swiss
psychologist taught her the concepts of a new religion,
the only religion as he maintained that could possibly
satisfy the modern intelligence, the religion of science.
This religion like its great predecessors imposed humility,
self-abnegation, devotion, ardor. Its zealots were scat-

tered over the four corners of the earth and recognised
one another instantly by secret signs impossible to com-
municate to an outsider. As with other religions, science
must suffer from the charlatan, the self-seeker, the ex-
ploiter, but as with other religions the true practitioner
had an inner and infallible test by means of which he
could detect and reject the spurious. As with any religion seriously embraced and ardently prosecuted it
insensibly changed for its *devote* all previous values.
Jessica had never sought the usual worldly prizes,
social position, and material comforts, but now she became almost eccentric and ascetic in her habits, withdrawing more and more into her "work". In place of
the social relations which Edgar Mallory prized and
constantly increased, she substituted a small group of
scientists, picked from the university and from the
Eureka Medical school which had been loosely affiliated
with the university. Every week or so "the bunch"
as Jessica called them met for luncheon at a small
Italian restaurant in the city and exchanged goods.
Jessica now contributed little papers, notes, and reviews
to the departmental journal which Sheimer had started
with a liberal subsidy from herself instead of compiling
books or an occasional semi-popular article for one of
the "more serious" magazines. Only a handful of persons throughout the world would read these technical
monographs, but they would be experts, keen to criti-
cise her ideas or to utilize them in their own researches.
"Grains of sand", as Sheimer with an unexpected poetic
insight called them. He himself was accumulating similar grains of sand which ultimately might be worked
into a large design for mapping the psychological reactions of grouped individuals, Jessica found in her husband's office a new interest, beginning a long series of
experiments to determine the mentality of students,
their inherent capacities. Mallory, who was always
generously encouraging towards all Jessica's intellectual

pursuits, described her present undertaking to Beckwith. "It will do away with deans," he said. "An
examining board of psychologists will run over all candidates for entrance and sort 'em out, then look 'em
over every few months to see if they are playing true
to form. No more educational misfits, Norman! What
do you think of that?"

Beckwith smiled indulgently. He did not think much
of such a mechanical plan. It sounded to him like
the sort of thing Mrs. Mallory would go in for. . . .

She took it very seriously, having appointments all
day long with the students sent to her office by the
deans. Then she induced the hiring and firing department of a large factory to let her experiment with their
personnel. Some of her "results" were considered almost uncanny. Articles on the "mentality tests" being
worked out in the Eureka laboratory began to appear
even in the daily newspapers. Sheimer's name was
connected with the new experiments, rarely Jessica's,
but that made little difference to her. Had she not
become a hand-maiden in the noble temple of science?
Ready to submerge her personality wholly in the "problem"!

She tried her method on the children. Simeon, who
was in an eastern boarding school, passed the "test"
brilliantly. Sheimer marked his paper and gave him
ninety-five percent. This gratified Jessica rather un-
accountably. Edgar slyly exchanged papers with Valery,
the daughter, who received but fifty-four percent. They
kept the joke to themselves for a time, and when it
leaked out Jessica did not take it precisely as a joke.
She admitted that there were occasional errors in her
"method", which as she became more expert in her
mastery of the technique she expected to eradicate.
Meanwhile she practised her "technique" on all whom
she could persuade, the servants, guests at the rare
dinner-parties she still attended, even chance travellers

on the train when she journeyed. With the progress of her work she developed a professional jargon and talked in terms of "reactions", and "tests", classifying according to her mechanical formulae all characters, accumulating a set of hypotheses or preconceptions which he did not seem to realize were far from "scientific".

"It would be a good thing if all the faculty had to take our intelligence tests," she suggested to her husband, hoping that he would coöperate with her in putting this experiment through.

"And base promotions on the results?" Mallory queried ironically. "I am afraid that would not be popular, and they might attribute some of the results to my influence."

"Oh, we could arrange to have the papers marked by outsiders."

Mallory looked at his wife in amusement.

"Everybody hasn't quite your faith in intelligence tests," he said gently. "Intelligence is a variable term, like all human qualities. It evades mechanical analysis, like art and passion," he added with a sudden meaning.

Jessica dropped the subject as she was accustomed to do when Edgar became "literary" and talked about the soul. Such phrases might mean something to him, she was generous enough to recognize, like his semi-religious expressions about service and public spirit and the rest of the social service patter. But they meant nothing to her. She gathered up her papers, arranged them neatly in her black portfolio, hunted for a special pair of glasses and fountain pen and set forth presently for the laboratory. Edgar had a luncheon engagement in the city where he would speak. Joan, the younger girl, had already set out for the Teachers' College School where she would spend her day until four o'clock. Jessica complacently reflected that modern customs disposed of one's family for a large part of the time, so

that each might be pleasantly occupied in his or her
own affairs, and not dependent on each other for entertainment or assistance. That prevented "staleness",
Jessica's special aversion. Her rôle in the family now
that the three children no longer needed personal care
and supervision was to provide for them all (including
Edgar) sufficient suitable engagements. Modern family
life should be fluid and crowded, each member of the
family so absorbed in his or her own special engagements that he had little or no time for the others.
Then on those rare occasions, as on holidays, when they
were gathered together each would have something of
the novelty of a stranger to offer to the others, each
would contribute as Jessica put it. . . . Once when she
defended this plan of family life to the proprietor of
the THUNDERER with whom she was dining, that
downright gentleman, whose hair was close cropped
giving his smooth face the expression of an ex-convict,
remarked bluntly,—

"Yes, I know all about that. That was the plan
my family tried out on me. They didn't want to be
bothered with me I suppose, and so put me into a
boarding school at twelve, summers at a camp on the
Maine coast, then college—and let me spend the vacations as I liked. Well, it worked so well that I can
get along now without them quite easily, thank you,
with my job, a club or two for spare hours. Oh, it
works all right, if you want it."

Jessica dropped the subject, conscious that in some
way she had blundered onto a sore spot in the newspaper man's mentality.

"Probably he has made for himself some romantic notion of family life as compensation for all that he
fancies he lost in his youth because his mother and
sisters didn't coddle him enough", she reflected. She
failed to carry on the idea to its conclusion, that his
thwarted youth might account for the pale little wife,

on the other side of the table, and also for the peculiar
brutality of the THUNDERER since the young proprietor had taken hold of its management.   Like its
owner it had become the notorious thug of journalism. . . .

Jessica was really happy when she had entered her
"den" on the top floor of the psychological laboratory,
turned off the sizzling steam heat, removed her papers
and sandwiches from her portfolio, and taking up a
favorite fountain pen in her little fingers settled herself
at her broad desk among the piles of pamphlets, test
sheets, books.   Then she emitted a sigh of content over
the prospect of ten uninterrupted, absorbing hours of
work. . . . Somehow, she felt, she had beaten life!

CHAPTER THREE

When Clavercin saw the letters of flaming gas spelling out the name of his play,—WHY? in dancing yellow light several blocks off in the crowded street, he had a strange sense of unreality, and shrank unconsciously from the coming exposure of himself when the curtain went up on this piece he had labored over so long, changed and rewritten at the behest of several managers, who had been attracted by its unusual subject and stark treatment. Hitherto it had been returned to him with civil notes and the payment, finally, of the forfeit money, the managers being unwilling when it came to the point to risk their money on "such a raw subject". Its appearance, in the end, had come about almost by accident, when he had given up hope of getting it produced and his friends had almost ceased making polite inquiries about the fate of his play. Brieux's *Les a varies* had been put on the preceding season and to the surprise of Broadway had been fairly successful. With the peculiar Broadway logic, the managers argued that if the American public could stand for venereal disease in a play they might go even abortion and get a thrill from it. So when the romantic piffle of, "A Thousand Nights", had broken down completely in Eureka after its first week, the actor manager Horatio Bullion had despairingly resolved to take a chance with "the professor's abortion play", and had summoned Clavercin from his bed after midnight by telephone. That had been five days before. Clavercin had almost forgotten that at the suggestion of Maida Grant, one of Louise's newer city friends, he had sent his

play to Bullion, who knew Maida as pretty nearly all
the world did. . . .

Clavercin returning from a hasty supper to the theatre
where he had lived the last five days had a sense of
complete unreality, symbolized by the flaring gas
word,—WHY? It no longer seemed to be his play
that he was about to witness. Long ago the story of
the unfortunate girl in his class, which had given him
the incentive to write the play, had become less vivid,
less momentous, less poignant, in the way of actuality.
She had died. Edith Crandall had died, alas!—she
would have been so vividly interested in this success—
and even Tom Plant had resigned from the university,
finding a government post in Washington more congenial. Every one but himself had forgotten Estelle
Lambert and her fate, and he had long since forgotten
his thrill of horror over the thing. He tried to convince himself that it was best so, that if his play contained the essence of anguish he had felt and tried to
embody in it, it would appeal to the persons streaming
past him on the city pavement. God knew, it should
make them pause and think—it was close enough to
them.

He had been so harassed with all the details of hasty
production, with the effort to save something of the
simple diction of his play, something of the unrhetorical,
unsentimental directness of it that he had not had
time to consider what its success might mean. At the
time when he wrote it he had been much influenced
by the younger European playwrights especially Strind-
berg and Wedekind and had adopted their simple uncom-
plicated structure in the telling of his tale. Bullion
fearing that there was too little "theatre" in the piece
had wanted him to incorporate a stale plot, containing
a noble youth and a lustful lady as foil to the central
theme, and had actually composed a few irrelevant
speeches which gave one of his women an opportunity

to stay on the stage a few minutes longer than her part required . . . Clavercin who had often felt cramped in the academic atmosphere realized as he had never had the opportunity to do before that there were other sorts of limitations outside the university, which might be even more galling than the academic ones. He had wanted that afternoon to withdraw his play, and if it had not been for the mortification of Louise who had widely heralded "Beaman's play" among her friends, he might have tried to do so. Instead he had dulled his scruples by the thought, "If it only goes and makes some money! Then another time I shall be more independent and can dictate to the managers, not let them mangle my piece like this." Thus he had made the compromise with his workman's conscience, with his memory of Estelle Lambert's tragedy. Composed without a thought of compromise in pure passion, WHY? was now being produced by a nervous, skeptical manager as a desperate chance, and Clavercin himself was aiding and assisting in the prostitution of his piece in the hope of—escaping from the university. That he realized was the sum of the situation, as wearily he came from behind the scenes for the last time and waited for the curtain to go up on his play. . .

At least, he reflected, if it did not bring him an immediate release from the monotony of teaching boys and girls some elementary notions about literature, from correcting their tiresome productions, and attending to the petty details of departmental routine, it should enhance his prestige in the university so that he could demand action on that promised experimental theatre for his play course. It was no longer as easy as it had once been to excite Dr. Harris by an alluring new educational scheme. All the president's energies were going into the plan for the new medical school, which according to campus rumor was hanging fire. And the trustees were restive about the deficit, scrutinizing those long lists of appointments and promotions, which formed the meat of the President's spring reports. Latterly there had been no new appointments or promotions in Clavercin's departmental group; instead there were resignations as the more fortunate younger men found opportunities of going elsewhere. . . There was an air of hard times about the campus!

These reflections coursed through the playwright's mind as he scanned the audience which was gradually filtering into the tunnel-like auditorium of the small theatre. On the judgment of these chance comers from the street depended so much for him! Of course this first night audience was not the real test for the staying quality of his play because it was so largely composed of friends and people presumably prejudiced in its favor. There had been little time in which to advertise the production, but Louise had loyally risen to the crisis with enthusiasm and gone up and down Eureka forming a claque which was considerable in size and distinguished in social quality. She had demanded a box for herself and the small party she was entertaining at dinner, the Mudges and the Grants and Norman Beckwith. Clavercin refused peremptorily to sit in the box and be stared at. The curtain went up while the audience was still assembling and the sharpness of the picture was blurred by the sound of banging seats and the tramp of feet so that nobody got clearly the background of a small home in Cascadilla, Texas, one of the best things in the play and necessary for its unity. Clavercin had not yet acquired the technique of saying nothing for the first ten minutes of his piece in order to allow the audience to seat itself, take off its coat and hat and look around at its leisure, without being distracted by the business on the stage, sure that it was missing nothing. . . . Clavercin frowned at the rustle and bustle, as he did in his class room over late arrivals. It was an impertinence. The worst offenders were Louise's box party which arrived a half hour late and distracted the audience's attention by its efforts to find the box and seat itself. Clavercin suspected his wife of enjoying the publicity of her appearance, of arranging it in fact. "That's Mrs. Clavercin, the author's wife, and the thin grey-haired man is Horace Mudge, of the Eureka National, one of the university trustees, you know, and the big woman next him is Mrs. Maida Grant, the leader of the charity ball, you know, always in the papers," etc. . . . Meanwhile the curtain dropped on the first scene in a shower of mild hand claps.

The next scene was a snowy afternoon on the college campus, in the corner made by the Woman's Hall. It was one of the best sets in the piece, of which the scenery perforce was hastily scrabbled together, and the audience recognised it genially. Here the story encountered a difficulty that the inexperienced playwright had not foreseen. His imagination focussed on the girl whose opening bloom he had watched from the elevation of his instructor's platform, he had conceived her advent at the university with all the freshness, impressionability and ardor of eager youth. Bullion's leading lady was a nice enough young person, quite sympathetic with "the professor's ideas" during rehearsals, catching his conception he had thought better than any of the company. But in this second scene she failed utterly to give out this conception if she really recognised it. The girl in WHY? from Cascadilla, Texas, was just opening in bud and though Mailie Fortescue was by no means tough or old, there could be no doubt that she had bloomed several times, and what was worse she had lost all memory of any previous state. She played the part pertly, (what was later called flapperishly), with an eye obviously out for the male. Clavercin was confounded by the utterly false note the young woman could give a few simple words and gestures. Was it possible that virginity could never be imitated on the stage? That

might account for the unpopularity of virginal characters
in contemporary plays. The women in them were as a
rule undeniably experienced, and their "virtue," still such
an asset theatrically, was a hard won triumph against
experience and temptation! How could Mailie Fortescue
cope with the next scenes where his virginal heroine gave
herself ecstatically and simply to the male with the
fervid self-forgetfulness that only the inexperienced could
have? Which, of course, was the point of the play, the
core of its tragedy!

Horatio Bullion had insisted on a lot of irrelevant
college stuff to fill out this campus scene, husky youths
in sweaters with big letters, spindly professors, a woman
dean, "local color" he called it, and Clavercin had
yielded to his desire, aware that the audience (even the
faculty members among them) would expect this conventional padding. And the actor-manager was proved
to be right, for it was by all odds the most successful
scene in the play, especially the conclusion where Mailie
had an encounter with the beefy, sweatered foot-ball
hero, (the virtuous youth injected at the actor-manager's
insistence). She played this bit with a boisterous coyness
that won the heart of the audience. If she had only
given herself to the half-back there and then, the audience would have readily condoned her error.

The applause after this scene was so hearty that
Bullion felt Clavercin should answer in person the good-
natured calls for "Author, author," shouted here and
there in the gallery by his students. Clavercin supposed
he might have to make a speech at the end of the play,
if it arrived at the last curtain without serious misadventure and had thought of some things he wanted to
say about contemporary plays and subjects, the university and the drama, etc. But once set loose in front of
the curtain, with the footlights glaring up at his feet and
half blinding him and the strange pit of unfamiliar faces
receding into the distance before him, he lost connection

with all these ideas,—or their inapplicability overwhelmed him. So instead he uttered the inevitable platitudes, half jocose and half wheedling. What he wanted to say was, "Damn you, this isn't the piece I wrote—it's a burlesque which this actor-manager fellow thinks is all that you can understand and probably he is right—but it isn't my play by a long shot, damn you!" What he heard himself saying in the end was something about the necessity of presenting actual situations on the stage if we wanted to create a vigorous, native drama, and so forth. What Louise called "academic patter." The audience seemed to expect it "from the professor" and listened respectfully enough. Bullion filled in the rest of the time while the set was being changed by a character-istic speech, flattering and jovial, with a few round phrases at the end about the "high intelligence of American audiences, outside the metropolis," "the loyalty and pride of Eureka in their great university and its faculty," etc.

Clavercin lost the opening of the third scene because Bullion, encouraged by the amiable reception of the first scenes and by his own little speech, sent for the author and demanded an immediate contract, on extremely favorable terms, not only for WHY?, but an option on Clavercin's next play. Clavercin demurred, wanted time to consider the contract and consult a lawyer. (He had been warned that some such trick might be played—it was the custom of the profession.) Bullion blustered and refused roundly to let the play continue after the present scene unless Clavercin signed the paper he held out. In disgust and a subconscious indifference Clavercin dashed down his name and without a word went back to the theatre. . . . It was the scene where the girl first realises her plight. Mailie played it like the sleep walking scene from Lady Macbeth. The audience was very still, puzzled, and at the end there was almost no applause. They were uncomfortable, sensing danger and not know-

ing exactly from what quarter it might hit them. . . .
In the next scene, at the house of the abortionist, this
uneasiness expressed itself in giggles and laughter, a
nervous laughter as if they were protecting themselves
from something the author had improperly let themselves
in for. . . . Clavercin's eye fell on the front box, where
Louise sat with her friends. Louise's face was very red.
Mudge who sat next her looked glum, forbidding, as
though he were conscious of a bad smell. He was an
elder in the First Presbyterian Church, where they
taught infant damnation. Probably by this time Louise
wished she had not taken a box. . . .

Before the last curtain Clavercin had fled from the
theatre, entirely forgetting his engagement for supper at
a hotel with Louise and her party, Bullion, Mailie
Fortescue, Beckwith, Snow, and some other friends. . . .
It wasn't his play, he kept repeating to himself as he
wandered down the glaring street under other flaming
signs of other theatrical offerings, wondering whether
they covered the same hypocritical travesty of life that
WHY? had become. . . . It wasn't his play! Not the play
that he had written from pictures seared into his soul.
It was Bullion's play, Mailie Fortescue's play, the American public's play, the little they wanted to see of life,
that distorted, emasculated little. . . . More than ever he
desired to start a theatre at the university where it
would not be necessary to consider any of these. And
more than ever he burned to write plays, felt that he
had the power in him, to set forth the dance of life as
he saw it, in clear-etched pictures. Not once that night
in his long wanderings through desolate streets did he
consider the impression his play might have made on his
friends, on the newspapers, the university. . . . When
towards morning he returned to the little house in Beechwood Terrace he found the door shut between his room
and Louise's. . . .

When he came down the next morning to breakfast

Louise was already reading the notice of WHY? in the THUNDERER that had just come. Her cheeks still flamed, and she replied to his greeting distantly. When she had finished with the notice she dropped the paper on the floor and went off on some errand. Clavercin wondered what his wife really thought of his play or whether she had any definite reaction to it apart from the scandal it quickly created.

The newspaper notices varied from the scoffing, sneering article in the THUNDER to the forthright indignation of the *Hearst* paper, that said among other inanities, "The sweet, girlish purity of Mailie Fortescue could not put across Professor Clavercin's dull filth." The pious *Post* thought that if Eureka University held up such sordid and debased ideals of literary art to its students parents should consider boycotting the home institution. "This is a fit case for police censorship," was the conclusion. The THUNDERER in characteristic fashion followed up its dramatic review with a front page article the next morning, headed by a cut of "the professor dramatist," which purported to be an interview with a number of his colleagues including Susan Porridge, dean of women, who indignantly repudiated the idea that abortion was a common incident among female students of Eureka, and excoriated the play, which incidentally she had not seen. Also there were comments by "prominent students", all of whom expressed outrage that "the fair name of their alma mater had been tarnished by the inescapable inference that the squalid story of Professor Clavercin's play had been taken from the university." And there were suggestions that the professor of dramatic literature had "descended to moral scavenging to give a sensational interest to an otherwise dull piece," etc.

Beckwith greeted Clavercin with a broad, commiserating grin when they met. "Don't mind the mud," he counselled generously. "It's just our American way of taking everything personally. It's the same old vulgar curiosity. . . . And it will advertise your play. Let 'em keep it up, the worse the better for you. . . . I liked the play, its honesty," he concluded, a little hesitantly. "Of course it was obvious the company could not do it, did not know what they were doing. I doubt if you could find actors in this country sufficiently intelligent and well trained to do such a play."

In spite of Beckwith's friendly tone, Clavercin felt that there were reservations beneath: he had not convinced even his best friend. And as friends spoke to him or ignored the matter that day he felt the same reservations, as if they thought,—why stir so much mud unless you can put over something big and thrilling!. . . . He avoided the theatre that second night. He was told that there was a poor audience, apathetic except as before in the tragic passages where they laughed uncomfortably or indignantly flounced out of the theatre. Much the same the third night, and Clavercin nerved himself for the announcement that WHY? had been withdrawn when something unexpected happened: the police took a hand and ordered the theatre closed just before the Thursday matinee. Horatio Bullion who had been gloomily cursing himself for becoming involved with a "professor's play" (while giving out solemn interviews about the sacredness of pure art and the necessity of educating the public to objective and European standards of dramatic work), saw his chance and grabbed it. He induced some judge to grant a writ of injunction against the police and before the evening performance made a fighting speech in defense of WHY? and the uncensored drama. All the dubious lines which had been expurgated after the first performance were restored to the text and the actors were told to play the risky parts strong. The result was a tumult, which increased the next night. Bullion was in high feather and when Clavercin sought him out to advise withdrawing his play, he spoke so solemnly of the duty to fight for the untrammeled expression of art that the author felt ashamed of his own pusillanimity. "We'll take this case to the supreme court and meanwhile we'll play WHY? from New York to San Francisco," he proclaimed, "and let the people judge what is decent and what is not!" So for another few evenings the small Lakeside theatre was jammed with a crowd curious to see the professor's play about a girl student, who got into trouble with a member of the faculty. Popular opinion was vague whether the seducer was the author himself or one of the deans. "Some prominent member of the faculty," it was said.

All this was gall to the author! His first play achieving a *success de scandale*. And such a mean little personal, local scandal at that! Clearer than ever he saw that a creator could not work freely within the narrow walls of a modern university, even as loose and inchoate a university as Eureka. The gossip, the personalities, the conventions of a restricted group such as a university fostered were and always had been and probably always would be inimical to the freedom necessary for the creative artist. If the noise about WHY? blew him some money he would use it, he promised himself, to cut loose from this hampering academic environment.

Meanwhile he went about his university engagements, met his classes and attended committee meetings, trying not to flinch before prying, gossipy eyes, that revealed what his students, his colleagues, even his friends were thinking. He had committed an indiscretion, an impropriety almost unpardonable, first in dealing with a subject that the community had always covered with a conspiracy of silence, and even worse had connected it with the university.

"Fouled his own nest," the prim Sanderson was reported to have said contemptuously.

His enemies, and underlings in his own department who envied him his position and hoped to advance on his ruin, exultantly awaited "the end of Clavercin and the **Harvard** idea," as they put it. Some of the trustees wanted drastic action taken with the author of WHY?. Oddly enough as he learned much later it was the small-minded senior dean, Abel Dolittle, who prevented the feeling against him coming to a head in a demand for his resignation.

"That would just add fuel to the flame and make the scandal worse," Dolittle counselled. "Wait! The racket will die out in a few weeks, and later we may find ways of ridding ourselves of the man."

The Dean was right about the publicity noise. Before the injunction reached a final hearing in the court, the play had ceased to attract the crowd which had come from curiosity and could find nothing satisfying in the simple tragedy. So it left Eureka where it had had its one notorious week and died shortly afterwards. There was nothing in WHY? sufficiently sensational or nasty to attract. The big, substantial American audience wants cheerful plays to which it can take its wives and sweethearts, without being made uncomfortable. . . . So the question of the merit of Clavercin's little tragedy was never really settled. It dropped too soon into the limbo of failures. The following season Horatio Bullion was starring with Mailie Fortescue in a saccharine idyl of young womanhood called, "June". The actor-manager remembered vividly his experience with "the serious drama," and whenever the topic came up as it did perennially of "improving the American stage," the portly Bullion would emit a few bitter curses and recount his misadventure with "the college professor's abortion play." "And that's enough of this high brow stuff for me!"

So Clavercin did not climb to fame and freedom on the wings of WHY?.

CHAPTER FOUR

The disaster of WHY? might have had more serious consequences personally for its author had it not been for the fact that it happened at a time of stress and strain in the university. Institutions like individuals have their times of expansion and contraction, the ebb as well as the flood of their spiritual being, and this was unmistakably a period of ebb in Eureka. The list of donations, which next to promotions and appointments was the part of the president's annual report most eagerly awaited by faculty and public, had latterly been padded with such items as books and apparatus, special gifts of a hundred or a thousand dollars or so, no millions, for over a year not even a respectable hundred thousand or a dormitory. The growing deficit worried the trustees, who were primarily business men. In his militant days, Dr. Harris used to proclaim that a deficit should be considered an asset for a great university because a balanced budget cannot arouse the sympathies of the benefactor. And he proved his theory by his successful campaigns in the city to "clean off the deficit" (on the strength of which he immediately started a new deficit!)

Latterly it was being whispered about in "well informed circles" that the original fount of wood pulp was drying up. Not that the Larson millions had become exhausted, all that wealth springing from the forests of the new land, ground into pulp and spread out for breakfast before teeming millions—that was inexhaustible, so long as wood was to be found and print paper was in demand! But somehow Aladdin had lost his magic touch; the last time he had approached the Founder with a glowing scheme he had been turned coldly over to intermediaries, cold business secretaries, ex-missionaries, lawyers and the like, who scanned the university president's program with the same acid realism they would apply to any other business undertaking, mumbling terms like "turn-over", "cost sheet", and "overhead". They even hinted in their report to the Founder that this greedy suckling of his beneficence might profitably be left to "fill in" and become solid without more millions or fend for itself with the public.

Meanwhile there still hung in the new office of the President in the Administration Building that airy architectural extravangaza, the Plan of Eureka, growing a little yellow and dusty with age, with few of the old gaps freshly inked. The great centre oval was still open for some crowning gift, like a chapel or a library. The Law School, a modest structure in English gothic with restrained flying buttresses had been the last building to be added. The Teachers' College was cut off in the middle with a temporary wall that the architect had gracefully disguised by some trees (which did not exist). Sanderson's satrapy, the expanding Business College, was still bulging out of the old gymnasium which was somehow held together by new props and girders, waiting until a millionaire graduate should recognise his indebtedness to Eureka. There was yet to come the Engineering School, the Arts' School, the Medical School, with its own hospital, clinics, laboratories.

They must have this medical school soon. The biologists were grumbling and crying for it. Many of the ambitious young men working in the laboratories had been lured to the university in the expectation of opportunities to be provided by the new Eureka Post Graduate Medical School that Dr. Harris had persuasively dangled before them. And they were teaching undergraduates in a paper pre-medical course, how to use test tubes and make analyses! . . . So the President studying the fading Plan on the wall opposite his littered desk set his jaws once more and confronted his Board with an elaborate "Plan for the coördination of medical research in Eureka", ending with a scheme for the post graduate school near the campus. "Coördination" and "affiliation" were his two pet names for paper programs. The Trustees looked suspiciously at the thick "Plan" and asked,—

"Where are we to find the money?"

"Times are bad, getting worse, in spite of the republican victory last fall!" said the one member who did not belong to the orthodox party.

"We have been through worse times than these," the President reminded the Board. "The money will come if we show the right spirit, confidence in the future of this great country, in Eureka, in the university, in ourselves!"

This was the optimistic note that had always lured the spirits of these men, who felt that it was the right way to think. . . . Using once more the hypnotic voice and glance that had wiled so many dollars from canny business men, the President continued his appeal:

"We must not slacken in our endeavors to give Eureka a complete university, rounded out with all departments. . . . There hasn't been a new building for over a year, gentlemen."

"Let's leave something for the next generation to do," a cavilling trustee objected.

"The next generation will find plenty to do building on our foundations," the President retorted readily.

He could not wait on time. What it had taken centuries and many generations of men heretofore to accomplish, slow accretion of a shell, must grow beneath his touch in a few short years. His dream was pressing him, and something already whispered to his spirit that he might not live to see the Plan wholly inked in, with buildings roofed and pinnacles boldly soaring into the sky. . . . In the end the Board reluctantly consented

to the Medical Program, as they usually did to Dr.
Harris' projects.

"But you must do it all yourself," they warned him,
"and no building until we have the money in hand!"
By this time they thought they knew their man. . .
The President's face which of late had become softer
and more sallow tightened in the old gesture of inexor-
able will.

"Trust me, gentlemen!" he pleaded.

"Universities," the objecting member of the Board
remarked as a last jibe, "are not just buildings and
programs—they are men!"

"But we must have the facilities to attract good men,"
Dr. Harris responded suavely. . . .

Who was it said that a university consisted of scholars rather than buildings? A saying that had often
plagued Dr. Harris. Some old fellow like Bacon or
Emerson had got it off, who did not know the world.
All the same the remark touched a raw spot in the
university president. Harden had long ago retired to
Germany, there to inveigh characteristically against
superficial American methods. The distinguished phy-
siologist, Silas Love, had also resigned, euphemism for
quit in disgust. Axon, the great chemist, had gone to a
nerve cure and might never come back to active work.
(But his name still counted in the catalogue!) . . . The
strong young men were dropping away, decoyed
by offers from other institutions, who looked over
"Barnum's Show" at their leisure and knowingly picked
a man here and there. It was easier to detach men from
the faculty than it had been in the early years when
hopes were high and promises running freely. The
President of the University was conscious of this spirit
of discontent in his faculty, of the grumbling at himself,
of doubt about his magic powers. He must perform a
fresh, a greater miracle than ever to reclaim the waver-
ing loyalties of the university.

So summoning the sturdy Miss Wex, his most expert stenographer, the university president set forth for California where the Founder was spending the winter months in the midst of an orange grove. In Miss Wex's capacious portfolio were the neatly typed pages of the Report on Medical Affairs in Eureka, which set forth the lamentable inadequacy, the dire need of the existing schools of medicine in and about Eureka, together with neatly tabulated statistics of population, doctors, laboratory equipment and so forth, which was like so much ready ammunition that the irrepressible general hopes not to be obliged to use.

There was delay in reaching the ranch where the ex-lumberman was wintering beneath his orange trees, an inexplicable delay,—an interval which Dr. Harris and Miss Wex must spend in a Los Angeles hotel, going over their data. When finally admitted to the orange grove and the presence of the Founder, seated beneath a glossy tree laden with golden balls, Dr. Harris found an impalpable barrier preventing him from approaching the old man in the intimate way of former interviews. The Founder insisted upon talking oranges and climate, and when finally Dr. Harris inserted a few words about Eureka and the proposed medical school the old lumberman listened glumly a little while, then interrupted querulously,—"I am too old to begin new enterprises. I leave all those matters to my Office. Don't you want to try one of my oranges?" and with a skinny hand he proffered a large, red, thick-skinned orange to the university president.

Not another word could be extracted from the Founder. The mouth of the purse had closed tight. Sadly, silently, Dr. Harris and the faithful Wex retraced their way, not to Eureka, but clear across the continent to Washington, D. C., where there had been established modestly in an old brick house, the office of the Larson Estate. It was on this melancholy journey from coast to coast that Miss Wex first noted symptoms of serious illness in her employer. Entering the compartment where they worked one morning as the train was crossing the arid plateau of Arizona she found Dr. Harris staring glassily out of the window at the bold outlines of some sandstone cliffs in the distance. His sallow face was almost lifeless and one pudgy hand clutched at his breast. Presently he came to himself, and remarking in a faint voice, at the same time pointing to the mountains, "They were not made in a day, Miss Wex." He resumed his dictation. "He must have been having an attack then," Miss Wex later reported. . . .

At Washington that brilliant scheme by which all the existing little medical enterprises about Eureka should be amalgamated into one great medical "trust" to be located next the university campus was submitted to a meticulous scrutiny that took some time. The standing and the assets of the component schools—so persuasively tabulated in the "data'"—were examined with the same cold caution that bankers would apply to a proposed combination of business enterprises, each asset weighed and marked off. "We do not find your scheme attractive," the officers of the Larson Estate said in conclusion. "Besides there are several good schools out there, one run by the State University—why duplicate that?" Dr. Harris who had been waiting the decision in Eureka knew that it meant the people in Washington had lost confidence in him, would never entrust him with the millions necessary to complete the great Plan. He promptly announced that the new medical school had been postponed "temporarily" because of the high cost of building, and departed presently on another mysterious errand whither not even the faithful Miss Wex was allowed to know.

But the facts about the aborted miracle leaked as they will where so many eager minds are interested in finding them out or ready to offer a plausible theory.

Walter Snow, who had an intimacy with some underling in the University Treasurer's Office, usually obtained a fairly authentic version of these matters which
he retailed to his circle embellished in his Gascon manner of exaggeration and hearty humor.

"The old man was let down badly this time," he
reported. "It was the old trust game you see, and
those Washington sharps in the Larson office know that
game in and out. So when Harris gave them his pros-
pectus of the new medical school, they put their ac-
countants to work, examined all the data with a micro-
scope, got a line on the assets and found they wouldn't
bring ten cents on the dollar as listed. You know how
they do those things! So they told the old man flat,—
'Nothing doing! No medical school this Christmas, nor
anything else in your stocking! Live on your income,
my boy!' They say it gave the old man a stroke, and
he's had to go to a hospital somewhere in the east. . . .
And what's more they've sent out a bunch of appraisers
to go over the books of the university and find out where
all the money has gone the past dozen years. Yes! A
fact. They are over there now in the administration
building,—you can see them any morning poking into
this and that, from the janitor's cleaning cloths to
Dexter's mice and roosters! They've got that ex-parson
Treasurer of ours on the run!" So on and so forth, as
men will amiably gossip about the mysterious powers
which control their destiny.

If his hearers did not take Snow's tale literally or the
other rumors flying thickly over the broad campus of
the university these days, at least they interpreted them
as metaphors thinly disguising truth and were worried.
The Founder turning a cold shoulder on Dr. Harris,
interposing between himself and the university promoter
the cold impersonality of a corporation, "founded not
for gain," though it might be! No new millions, no
new buildings. Nothing. . . . And the miracle-worker

ill, some said dying, already delegating most of his duties to Abel Dolittle, the discreet senior dean. These were indeed dreary days for Eureka. The biologists and laboratory men especially felt bitter, their bubble burst of a great medical centre wherein they might have expanded magnificently.

"Eureka is nothing but a day school," they growled disgustedly and looked eastwards. . . .

"Ah, Clavey," Norman Beckwith, who was in the way of hearing administration rumors commented to Clavercin, softening as was his way a bitter truth with a laugh, "it's bad business when they begin closing your second mortgage bonds. The old man has put out too many obligations, and they are beginning to fall due." Beckwith mused on his figure, tenderly, for he had an affection for the President, as did all those who worked with him. "Be sure, Clavey, that you can meet your bonds when they fall due some years hence!"

Clavercin smiled wryly, suspecting an allusion to his ill-fated play about which he was still sensitive. The President was experiencing like himself the swift descent of the curtain upon a dream, and it was not pleasant. One's dreams, he felt, should not be dependent for their conversion into reality upon uncertainties like donors and publics. All this as he walked homewards for luncheon to the Beechwood Terrace house, which found expression later after a long silence between him and Louise, like this,—

"How would you like to pull up here and move to New York? . . . . The university seems rather going to pot—Harris ill, no promotions, nothing in sight!"

"And what would you do in New York, Beaman?" she demanded pointedly. . . . "Just as we are settled and beginning to know people! . . . Let's wait another year and see what happens!"

Yet for the President of Eureka sitting haggard in his big swivel chair behind the push buttons, contemplating inwardly those piled up obligations about to fall due, there was one consolation these days: the university was attracting students. The campus outside was fairly thronged with students, especially during the morning hours, and they crowded the sidewalks of the neighborhood. The letting down of the entrance bars had worked; also the Harris democratization of learning through night and day classes in city centres, and the famous summer school. Dean Dolittle and his nimble assistants could figure out more than ten thousand names in some way registered on the rolls of the University, if for no more than attendance on an entertaining evening lecture course. Ten thousand! In those first days how that round figure would have inflamed the president's imagination! All these aspiring minds coming to Eureka for the feast that he with the Founder's help had spread before them would have impelled him to new marvels of architectural achievement. But now with a dragging weight of care he listened to the Dean's report of crowded classes, insufficient instruction in different departments, the necessity for enlarged facilities in dormitories and commons,—all the applied detail of numbers,—and stroked his sallow face. It had worked, his passionate proselytizing: they were streaming towards Eureka, thousands of those "seekers for opportunity" whom he had so often invoked. And what was he going to do with them?

The university football team had won the championship of the west for three successive seasons, thanks to the highly paid coach. The fraternities were growing, putting up new houses or buying out the professors who found their homes near the campus too expensive to maintain on their salaries. Eureka, thanks to all this, was now reckoned among the "Big Six" of American universities. It was no longer referred to even in the THUNDERER as "Barnum's Show" or "The Harris School." On holiday afternoons the streets in the neighborhood of the campus were lined with carriages and the new-fangled automobile, which brought crowds to the football game going on within the cement fortress set apart for athletics. Other thousands tramped up the street from the suburban station, bearing pennants and the usual paraphernalia of collegiate sport. The cheers, like savage roars from an ancient circus, where animals fought, greeted the professors' ears as they emerged from their seminar rooms or the library towards twilight. The many windowed walls of the biological laboratories which offered excellent box seats for the show going on across the way were filled by students and laboratory assistants—Yes, Eureka had abundantly arrived in the American sense, with all the palpable evidences of being "a great university". To these students, children of the miles of flat buildings and suburban homes with neat grass plots or fertile prairie farms, Eureka was a fact, something to be proud of. They were not conscious of its physical incompleteness as a university, nor of the spiritual canker at its root. There were always teachers in the class rooms, an ample schedule of routine tasks to be performed in order to obtain the "points" necessary to get a degree. There were "marks" and "tests" and "Dean's cards" and "flunks" and "Proms" and "cane rushes" and finally degrees—all the traditional ritual of "college" in the American mind. What more could one expect?—They themselves were making the "life" of the place, moulding Eureka and its faculty, its Board of Trustees, and its benefactors, to suit their own conception of what a university should be, a sort of superior day school where one performed the rites of knowledge for a few hours each day and the much more elaborate rites of sport and society the rest of the time, with some sort of "good job" at the far end of the vista and those "happy memories" that "old grads" are supposed to cherish so warmly. *Vive la jeunesse!*

To them it mattered little that the president's soaring

plan had been arrested midway; that the great postgraduate medical school so often heralded and described,
its future site pointed out to visiting relatives, still existed only on thin sheets of typed paper; that the young
men who taught them "Math" or "English" or "Physics"
were of an inferior quality to their predecessors, who had
moved away somewhere; that the "older profs" whom
they rarely met in the lower classes nursed grievances
because of broken promises, bore grudges against colleagues who had more successfully "pulled the old man's
leg" for promotion or "facilities"; that it was whispered
about that the president himself, traditionally a great
man, had some mortal disease which might strike him
down any day,—or more sinisterly that the rumor of
disease was a mere blind to prepare for his removal from
the presidency! Nobody really knew the facts even
among the faculty, unless it were the discreet senior
dean, who was called on so frequently to act as president
these days. Possibly Edgar Mallory, that efficient
protege of Dr. Harris, next to Dolittle in the succession,
might know more than his good sense would permit him
to divulge of what was happening beneath the apparent
calm of academic life.

CHAPTER FIVE

No wonder that the shrewd Mallory, cognizant of all this and much more, was deeply preoccupied at the Thanksgiving Day football match with the State University team. He attended all the important athletic games in his official capacity, and sat in the president's box in the centre of the grand stand observed by all. To-day Jessica had been prevailed upon to leave her den in the psychology laboratory and to sit beside him with their daughter, Valery, a leggy child, promising to be tall like her mother. It was a fine day, not too chill for the season, and Jessica Mallory seemed to enjoy the brooding air of the prairie autumn, the gay colors in the crowded arena, the effervescence of youth all around her. Sitting wrapped in mouse-colored furs, her gold hair straying from beneath a fur cap, she looked too young to be the mother of the twelve year old girl beside her. She seemed quite detached not only from the little girl and from her husband, but from the college scene itself, beholding it always as a spectator, who keeps strictly to herself the impressions life made.

"There is Mr. Cyrus Mudge below on the front row; he is bowing to us," Mallory reminded his wife. Edgar had the prominent citizen's alert eye for discovering in any gathering the right people to bow to. Jessica without turning her head kept on smiling at the spectacle of the brawny figures of the state university players now parading across the field. Mudge might be the most important member of the Board,—that meant nothing to her. Her husband knew that her indifference was neither personal nor spiteful: the Mudges did not interest her.

And he realized with a sudden twinge that it would not interest her if. . . . anything happened to Dr. Harris and her husband was called to the presidency of Eureka. To become thus the wife of a university president would bore Jessica dreadfully: she would either ignore the fact altogether or perform her part perfunctorily. Thus sombrely brooding over an intricate pattern of possibilities Edgar Mallory lost all consciousness of the scene and applauded mechanically when the home team appeared in the arena. No doubt people were saying that he had married a rich woman, at least comfortably rich, which would be distinctly in his favor over all his university rivals, but that his wife had taken no part whatever in the social life of the university, holding herself aloof in her laboratory from the faculty wives and their "functions"—would be very much against him. Even were she as negligible as good Mrs. Harris,—but whatever might be said of Jessica Mallory she was never negligible. And she had made it quite plain these years of their marriage that in marrying the ambitious junior dean of the university she had not married the university. That was what Mallory was thinking about as he applauded mechanically the first rush of Eureka's famous centre. He did not care for sports, regarded their prominence in the university as a necessary bore and evil that no clever executive would dare to suppress because they brought so much prestige to the institution. They must be controlled, indirectly, judiciously. To-day there was little applauding to be done because Eureka was losing. The first rough outburst of glee over the centre rush's initial performance soon gave way to a dead silence in the grand stand, broken occasionally by the lusty shouts from the opposite benches, which made up in heartiness for what they lacked in volume. Eureka was losing!

"I thought those country boys looked beefier than

ours," Jessica remarked at the close of the first half when conversation was renewed in the grand stand.

"Our team is overtrained. Too many games this season."

"You'll have to import some of those heavyweights," Jessica jeered good-humoredly. Among his other official capacities Edgar was chairman of the Eureka Athletic Board. There was a recurrent scandal, with charges and countercharges between universities, with their faculties involved in the undignified wrangle, this decoying of promising athletic material from other colleges and preparatory schools. Mallory had recently prepared a whitewashing report on this matter, which gave point to his wife's jeer. What she did not know and what made it worse was that the one bright star of the Eureka team, the beefy centre, was allowed to play in this game solely through executive clemency, He had failed in his carefully chosen courses and should have been automatically dropped from all athletics, according to regulations. But. . but! Often the President himself took a hand in these matters, and across the credentials of some promising "athletic material" was inscribed,— "conditions waived by order of the president."

As the second half of the game proceded heavily towards defeat, the junior dean's face grew more sombre. "She must change that tone," he was thinking. "She must realize how it interferes with my legitimate ambitions for our future." The possessive 'our' had an unsubstantial appearance even in thought. "I must tell her frankly what the situation is," and his brooding mind went off to another maze of perplexity. "If it shouldn't be the presidency of Eureka, why there are other places!" he thought. His restless mind had turned over the "university field" quite thoroughly: Dakota was looking for a young man to push it into prominence,—too small; California was periodically in the market for a president—too far away; Cornell? Penn-

sylvania? There were objections to all even if he should
be considered "available." No doubt the right place
would come in time,—he must not seem eager! In fact
he was not grossly ambitious. But if one had the administrative talent, as undeniably he had, one desired
the "larger field" in which to exercise this talent, as in
any other calling. That was natural. Of course with
his background, he thought of it even to himself in
terms of "service", "usefulness to his fellow-men", and all
the other evangelical cant, which was not then so offensive as it became later. Edgar Mallory believed sincerely in ambition, progress, the struggle of noble minds
to achieve, and Eureka seemed, except for the presidency, a blind alley for him.

In a final raucous burst of enthusiasm from the
"Staters" crowd and a thick gloom on the home benches,
the game closed, almost in the dark. Jessica had shown
signs of restlessness the last half, but in the president's
box they were too conspicuous for her to make an escape. Even she had to sit it through. But now, her
husband knew well enough, she would try to slip away
at the gate in the crowd, to return to her laboratory
workshop where supping on a cup of cocoa and some
biscuits which she kept handy in her locker she would
work far into the evening, abstracted, absorbed in some
new, fascinating theory of human behavior. She had
done the family act graciously enough at the midday
dinner to which had been asked some of the students,
a stray instructor or two. This midday dinner, which
Mallory liked to have on holidays and Sundays, taxed
his wife's endurance. He knew it was better to let her
recover from it by herself; otherwise she might have a
glum attack. . . . But to-day the matter was too urgent.
So when he saw her sidling through the crowd in the
direction of Dr. Rudolph Sheimer who was waiting by
the gate he said imperatively,—

"Jessica, will you come over to the house for a few minutes? I have something important to tell you!"

With a slight frown Jessica composed herself to the inevitable. Sheimer, who observed her deflection in the direction of the Mallory house, waved a hand above the press, his white face breaking into a little intelligent smile. Mrs. Clavercin who had the Mudges with her came purring up to Jessica.

"Oh, Jessica," she said, "won't you and your husband come in for a cup of tea? With the Mudges you know, and the Cappers!"

Jessica Mallory, who did not like Louise Clavercin, although she found her more interesting than the average faculty wife, shook her head, without giving excuse or regret. (That was her way, which earned her in some quarters the reputation of having bad manners. Beckwith maintained that the Dean's wife had "no manners," but a manner—a subtle, but valid distinction). She followed her husband in ill humor thinking, "She wanted me because of Edgar, to show him off as an intimate, my husband." And she divided her dislike between the objectionable "status" position and Louise Clavercin's obvious social manoeuvre. She did not mind her pushing, artful ways—she, too, could plot on occasion, but she despised the obviousness and pettiness of the game as played by women like Louise Clavercin. As soon as their door had closed upon them, Jessica demanded,—

"What is it?"

She stood in the hall as if expecting to escape as soon as she had received his important communication.

"Come in here!"

He spoke more peremptorily than was his custom, because his nerves had been rasped by the variety of his preoccupations. . . . He switched on the lights in the comfortable living room where the remains of a wood fire were pleasantly smouldering on the hearth, then drew down the shades so that the stream of spectators still filing past the house might not observe them.

"Do sit down!" He fussed for a few moments with the fire, then said abruptly, "Jessica, Dr. Harris is a very sick man!"

Mrs. Mallory waited: it could not be to tell her this, which was no longer news in the Eureka world, that he had insisted on dragging her away from her work back to the house.

"He has angina. I got it from Dolittle who had it from Dr. Sparhawk. Sparhawk was with him at the hospital, for the examination."

"He hasn't looked well for some time," Jessica commented blankly.

"He's a very sick man! They want him to drop everything and go somewhere, abroad, but he won't, of course, not until he gets the medical school, and I am afraid from what Mudge told me the other day there isn't any chance of that."

"Why not?"

The new medical school interested Jessica because so many of her friends in the laboratories were counting on it. Even the psychologists expected to come in on psychiatric clinics.

"Larson isn't likely to do much for a dying man," Mallory remarked significantly.

Jessica lighted a cigarette and smoked thoughtfully.

"That's rather brutal."

"Well, they aren't too well pleased with the way things are going in Eureka, the deficits and all that. It's business! There'll be another president in Eureka before long, and he may have different ideas of what is best for the university."

Jessica smoked.

"It lies between me and Sanderson!" Mallory exclaimed, at last.

Jessica, who began to comprehend, said appraisingly,—

"You'd make a good president, Edgar. I hope you will get it if you want it."

Mallory realized ironically the implication of the last remark: in his wife's opinion a college president was a fussy, pretentious, usually ignorant sort of bore. If she had regarded her husband as a scholar, she would not have said that. He must come closer to his thought.

"Of course I want it! It would alter our life though I am not sure you would like the position."

"What position? I am not going to be president of Eureka!"

"The position of the wife of a university president."

Jessica reflected on this.

"I don't see why it should make such a great difference," she said at last. "You wouldn't expect me to give dinners and stand in line at receptions, much—and to fuss about a lot of duddy trustees and benefactors, would you, Edgar?"

"It is a prominent position in the community. There are certain inescapable obligations, social and of other sorts," he replied evasively.

Jessica broke into a peal of her light laughter, which was more ironic appreciation than humor.

"Mrs. Harris seems to have escaped them!"

"Mrs. Harris!"

Both recognized the humor of the comparison.

"I am afraid my taking the presidency of the university might curtail your freedom," Mallory observed dryly.

"Well, you aren't president yet," she said practically.

"I hope to be some day! Here or elsewhere. Can't you coöperate in this matter, which is of such vital concern to our future?"

"To *your* future," she corrected crisply.

"I should think in such matters we could hardly make the distinction."

Jessica let that drop flatly. They had been into it before both theoretically and practically. Edgar must know exactly what she thought of the "these twain one" theory of marriage. She had no wish to embark on an arid discussion of the respective rights and duties of husband and wife. To date they had got along by avoiding a too intimate definition of the terms on which they lived. Edgar had recognized from the start that the only way to hold the intellectual woman whom he had wooed and won was to make a display of his liberality, his modernity, (as he had in his courtship when they were both interested in social "movements", settlements and the like.) He considered that he had been a very lenient husband, not in the least "possessive" or "monopolistic", two of Jessica's special aversions. He had encouraged and welcomed her achievements in scholarship, including her deflection to Sheimer's department of experimental psychology,—indeed was proud of having such a distinguished woman for his wife. She had her own independent career like a man, which he respected, and so far as could be done he had freed her from the objectionable round of social activity which their position in the university and city involved. He liked these dinners and luncheons and house parties, as he liked speechmaking and all pleasant social exchanges. They seemed to him human and right. For husband and wife they formed the natural expression of a harmonious dual life. But realizing how they fatigued Jessica, how she resented sacrificing her working hours or an evening merely to "gossip" as she called it—still more resented "tagging" after a husband!—he had artfully built up a screen between her and their little public, expressed in the formula,—"Mrs. Mallory is at her laboratory," or "Jessica has an article she is finishing," as his missionary father might have said, "The wife is at the sewing circle this evening," or in another stratum of society the man would have said, "My wife has gone abroad for a few weeks to be with her sister." There was something distinguished even for the husband in having a wife who published articles that were translated and commented upon in serious foreign reviews, whose signature "Jessica Stowe" (professionally she had dropped "Mallory" as a private "tag") was quite as well known as his own, in a different circle. But there were limits to his masculine tolerance. After all they had entered into the universal contract of coöperative living (modern style for, "the sacred bonds of matrimony") which meant more than merely abiding under the same roof and having three children together. Just as he respected her individual work and encouraged it, relieving her from the household responsibilities that more ordinary wives cheerfully performed, so she must respect the ambition of his life and help him to achieve it, as a woman could help in so many delicate ways. If not that, at least she must not act in such a way as to interfere with the realization of that ambition. Which, he felt with a slight sense of grievance, was what Jessica was doing.

Jessica removed her coat and settled back in her favorite low chair, a sign that she recognized the importance of the occasion, to him, and had given over all hope of escape for that evening. She had been aware that for some little time something had been on her husband's mind, a rising cloud of dissatisfaction which she had felt intangibly and had ignored as long as possible. This was as good a time as any to have it out, to let him air his grievance, and if it had a valid cause (as she did not yet admit) to see what they could do about it—pleasantly. She settled herself, but as was her habit she let "the other fellow" do the talking.

"You aren't an ordinary woman, Jessica," Edgar Mallory began conciliatorily, "and I think I have always recognized that,—have given you much more freedom than a wife usually has in a stable marriage."

Jessica did not accept any of these terms, but she knew by this time that however modern Edgar Mallory might be in administrative policies and general enlightenment, he still thought in the old "categories", as she called it, about sex and matrimony and women. So she merely smiled to herself.

"At times I have feared that our lives were growing apart, that we were both too busy perhaps to create the sort of home life that endures, that is best for children."

(Jessica who had been waiting for "the children" note smiled again to herself.)

. . ."But it could not be helped, considering your occupations and mine. Now, however, we have come to a point where outwardly at least our lives must coalesce to a much greater degree than hitherto. You would not like to leave Eureka, would you?" he demanded abruptly.

"Why, I hadn't thought about it. I am very well pleased here," Jessica replied, thinking of the laboratory, the conveniences for her work, of Rudolph Sheimer's stimulating help. "Have you any change in mind?"

"Nothing specific," Mallory said hastily, "but I could not be content to remain at Eureka all my life in the position of Junior Dean. There are better opportunities."

"I suppose if you wanted to leave the university—"

"That's just it!" he pounced on his opening. "When it comes to the point you recognize the bond, the obligation of community living!"

It was an unfortunate word. Jessica interrupted wearily,—

"Don't let's get into all that, Edgar! I want you to have what you want, of course, just as I want certain things for myself, my work, undisturbed. I'd like you to be president of Eureka if you want that, but I can't get out and electioneer for you as the dutiful English wife does!"

"No, but you might easily—"

"Look at it squarely, Edgar! There's nothing I could do to make you president of the university,—that is, that I could do with any content to myself. The fact is that I am more of a hinderance than a help to you in this

ambition, my being here as your wife and non-coöperating
as you feel. Suppose, then, I eliminate myself altogether?"

"How?" Mallory asked with a swift dread.

"Oh, just spend the next year abroad. You know I
have a chance to work under Jung in Zurich. I really
would like to do that. Those fellows are doing most in
psychology these days. That would give you a perfectly
free hand. No doubt my mother could be induced to
spend the winter here, now that Brother Alf has finally
got himself a wife who promises to be permanent, for a
little while. Mother dotes on public appearances as
much as I dislike 'em. . . .And that arrangement will
prove to the world that we are not divorcing each other,"
she added slyly. She felt that this last point would win.

Edgar Mallory frowned as he considered the proposal
hastily from many angles.

"That's possible," he admitted at last.

"Think it over! You will see it is the best way. I
know that you'd like me to hang about and play your
game as Louise Clavercin could, get close to the right
people, take part in university functions and all that.
I can't. I am not that sort of woman,—it's too much of
a nuisance. Now instead of having me here on the
scene to explain away always, you will have a perfectly
free hand. You might make up to Louise a bit and work
her in somehow as a substitute. She'd dote on that, and
she would do it awfully well!"

Jessica laughed with a silvery tinkle, and as if she considered the matter settled satisfactorily she took a book
and went upstairs to her room. She felt sure that Edgar
would accept this solution, for the present. The idea of
Zurich had been in her mind before, vaguely, but she
had waited for the opportune occasion, and now it had
come. She settled herself to read with growing satisfaction over the way she had managed the situation. She
was conscious of Edgar's dissatisfaction. She was really

not the sort of wife for him,—that was obvious. And yet he would be the first to deny such a statement. Like so many human beings he clung tenaciously to what was not good for him. Besides Edgar had the romantic idea about love, that men and women never changed in their affections and if they did that they ought to disguise it from each other. . . . He believed that by taking thought she could make herself over into the sort of wife he wanted,—the Louise Clavercin sort. That was quite absurd, and she had no intention of attempting such a sacrificial operation. The best she could do, and he must content himself with that, was not to stand in his way. Nor he in hers! After all this was the compromise that most marriages ultimately arrived at, sooner or later. Marriage, she had already diagnosed, was a most imperfect human institution, at least for people of strong individuality.

When she told Rudolph Sheimer casually on the morrow that she was thinking of spending the next winter in Zurich, his pale face flushed suddenly, then as quickly lapsed into its usual passivity.

"Good idea!" he said. "One gets stale after a while working out here!"

Jessica thought that one got stale in more ways than in work.

"Why don't you ask for a leave of absence and come over too?" she suggested.

"I might."

"That would be pleasant," Jessica said evenly.

CHAPTER SIX

When the doctors said "angina", Harris did not wince,
—perhaps he had known it all along. All he asked was,
—"How long?" and when told that it depended in part
on how he treated himself, that he had better take a
long rest and go to Europe or California for the winter,
he closed his lips tightly with the stubborn look that his
secretaries knew so well. He had other plans and set
about at once to compass them. He must see Larson.

The last meeting with the Founder in the California
orange grove had been the most humiliating experience
of his life, and he had no mind to repeat it. Now,
however, it was another matter! With death clutching
at him, it was no longer a question of a medical school
or an art school, of that grandiose dream of a vast
popular institution made out of the fabulous wealth that
the old lumberman had stripped from the forests of a
continent. That had been as little an egotistic dream of
his own aggrandizement as had been the lumberman's
accumulations for his own personal comfort. Both were
forces, one to strip and the other to create afresh; both
converting matter to some end which neither was very
clear about. "I want," Larson had said in the few grave
words he had spoken when he received the doctorate of
learned laws, "to make my wealth fertile in new lives,
and therefore I am dedicating it to education!" And
Alonzo Harris might as honestly say, "I have not sought
the renown of creating Eureka university so much as to
make the way of learning possible for the many who
desire it!". . . And now the time had passed for anything
personal. It never entered his mind to use his sentence

his large, loose, exuberant way. And for each need his quick mind, still fully alert, found the solution. The Geology Building promised old Noble: for that Rosenfield, the west side clothing man should furnish the funds. He had promised Tom Bayberry, for years, a separate department of Archeology and the funds for an exploratory expedition, which the Trustees had blocked as another deep hole for a deficit. But now Bayberry should have his dream fulfilled,—Gorridge had half promised the necessary amount for an expedition, so that Bayberry could sail away before it was too late to dig some beauty out of the ancient sands of Africa. So it went, each case, each separate personal longing, each drama of the academic soul, remembered and so far as possible set on the way of accomplishment. Much of this thoughtful plotting did not appear until after his death. "Keep this letter for future reference," his communications concluded often. Like all university heads Dr. Harris had been repeatedly called a liar. Nobody ever called him that, afterwards.

"He must have spent those months when he was dying remembering all he had forgotten from the beginning, every promise he had made or allowed others to make themselves," Beckwith remarked, opening his letter from the President's Office which said briefly,—"Your leave of absence on pay has been arranged for, to begin, etc." Clavercin too was given a leave of absence in which to write, as well as his delayed professorship. But the Dexter case was the most notable. The Dexter situation had become an open scandal. His wife had been arrested in a large city store, shop-lifting, and Dexter had had the humiliation of appearing in the police court and paying her fine. After reading the account of this incident in the THUNDERER (which gave it a conspicuous place because of Dexter's prominence in his profession) one of the trustees, Cyrus Mudge, a very correct person, spoke to the president about the Dexter scandal.

"We can't have that sort of thing going on in the university," Mudge said reprovingly. "It's a public disgrace. . . . He should have been let out long ago,— before this happened."

"What institution would take him?"

The trustee shrugged his shoulder.

"It would smash Dexter for life. Are we not somewhat responsible ourselves, Mr. Mudge?" Dr. Harris inquired blandly.

"How?"

"You know what Dexter's salary is?"

"I do not see the connection."

"Twenty-four hundred dollars a year. Two hundred dollars a month, and he has had this woman and three children to support. . . . She was sick, overworked I suppose after the last one came and took to drugs. Yes, Dexter told me the whole story. . . . He has struggled to keep her with him because of the children. She is not an attractive woman. . . . He has gone home time and again to find her in a stupor and the children hungry, cared for by neighbors—Well, that isn't a life for one of the best men of research we have, is it?"

"The university can't stand that sort of thing," the trustee commented primly, disgust in his voice.

"An institution like the university can stand anything, but a man can't," the President of Eureka replied solemnly. "If we send Dexter away, it is the end for him."

"It's a horrid scandal; the students know, everybody knows," the trustee fumed.

"It's a crime on Dexter, that's what it is!" Dr. Harris retorted with a quick flush on his pallid face.

The two men looked at each other for a few moments; then Harris took the word from the other's mouth.

"I am going to send for Dexter and see if we can't get this woman into an asylum in the country, and I am going to raise his salary to four thousand dollars,

"Dolittle!"

"They scoffed at the idea. Eureka in the hands of the soft-spoken suave, efficient Senior Dean, who had once been superintendent of schools in some place like Dubuque!

"Yes," Snow insisted. "Dolittle has been acting president the past year. He has the reins in his hands and has come close to the trustees. They think he is a safe man, far safer than Harris ever was. They got scared of Harris: he carried them too fast. Now they want to sit back and breathe and not have to meet deficits. . . . What do they know about a university? They want the books to balance and show a margin of profit, with students coming and going like sausages from a machine. Donothing is their sausage man!"

Glumly they separated beneath the Campanile, each going his own way, trying to imagine the application of Dolittle to his own private plot, to the university. Clavercin thought, "Dolittle was scandalized by my play. Now I'll never have that theatre and a chance to build up something in my play-writing work. I might as well leave the university, if only Louise—" and his mind went off wearily into a maze. Caxton, who thought simply in terms of scholarship, foresaw niggardliness, the cutting off of appropriations, small enough now for books and men, more routine teaching performed by inferior teachers, less research, production, problems solved. . . . Dexter, sadder than the others, felt a personal loss. "With all the boost Harris gave me, I must make good—it's my last chance! Dolittle would like to see me out of the university. I must make good." Beckwith from years of dealing with the Senior Dean understood Dolittle best of all. He knew the smallness, the commonness of his spirit and foresaw the little indirect ways he would take once president to make the university as common as himself, commercial, popular, catering to the prosperous classes. "It will be like the republican machine," he mused, "smooth, unscrupulous, without fineness. And the students will feel that, will become like that. Success in the saddle! Better even Sanderson and his adding machines. What power to be given to one man! There is no political boss in the country, no head of a great corporation who has the autocratic power over an institution that an American university president has—to mould and mar!" And half consciously he imagined what might be done with the inchoate university that Harris had left behind him, if one had the power! As he was temperamentally a radical he thought of student goverment, and faculty control, a cluster of earnest men surrounded by a body of eager youth, shaping a community that should be in contrast with the world outside rather than imitative of it. Unaware that in his day dream of the possible university he was substituting another form of autocracy for the philistine autocracy of a Dolittle. "Well, it ought to be Mallory," he concluded. . . .

Meanwhile the chimes in the Campanile having completed for the tenth time "Lead Kindly Light" were playing softly, "Rest in peace". It was as if the gallant spirit of Edith Crandall was calling softly through the air to the restless, striving spirit of the dead man. "We have both done what we could, each in his or her way, and now it is for others to take up the work we shaped the best we could and make of it in their guise what they can. This campus and these buildings, these lives young and old gathered here are more than what they seemed to us. Our part in them is done. One begins, friend, but never finishes anything. Your university will become something neither you nor I can see!"

PART THREE

CHAPTER ONE

Samuel Gorridge, first president of the board of trustees of the university no longer made steel. The company which he had inherited from his father had long since been absorbed into one of the bigger steel companies, leaving him free in middle life to do as he pleased, towards himself and his neighbors. He was a tall, thin, grave man, with a chronic indigestion. Although not a university graduate—his father Isaac, instead of sending his son to college, had put him into the steel works, with the true pioneer's disdain for learning—he was essentially more cultivated and more sympathetic with professors than the college men on the board. Those older members of the faculty who knew the president of the board felt that in some respects he understood what a university should be better than Dr. Harris. Because of his own thwarted youth he had an exaggerated respect for learning, and by reading, travel, and association with specialists he was in fact better educated than most university graduates, before whom he was always strangely humble. Once as a young man happening to be in Mexico on a business errand he had become interested in remains of Aztec pottery being turned up at Teotihuaxan and had stayed there as long as he could, returning to Eureka with his bag stuffed full of strange little figures of ancient gods, that strangely roused his imagination. If he could have done what he most wanted to do then, he would have become an archeologist and explored Aztec remains all his life. Instead he made steel under the dark pall of smoke ever growing thicker and broader over Eureka.

163

Years later after the death of his father when he had
become president of the university board he took his
family on one of those luxurious cruises to the Mediterranean designed for timid Americans who have no
language but their own. At Mityline where the steamer
put in for a day some German scholars were excavating.
Old memories were revived in Samuel Gorridge at sight
of the mutilated fragments, still covered with mould,
and in Athens and other places he bought quite recklessly a large number of "antiques" to which he added
from time to time by purchases from responsible dealers.
This collection was dear to his heart; he thought of
giving it ultimately to the university whenever there
should be a museum to house it properly. Meanwhile
it was placed temporarily on exhibition in the reading
room of the library and Thomas Bayberry was asked
to prepare a suitable catalogue for the collection. Here
was Bayberry's chance if he had been able to realize it.
Perhaps he did realize it, but something stern within
him prevented him from improving judiciously his opportunity. He put away from him the temptation to
utilize the rich man's hobby by encouraging him to
pour some of the profits of steel into a classical museum
of which Thomas Bayberry would be the curator with
sufficient funds to make world advertised expeditions
and discoveries in the Mediterranean homeland of
ancient beauty. Instead, he permitted his scholar
prejudice against amateurs, (mere academic snobbery),
to stiffen his critical spirit and it did not take him
long once he had peered at the Tanagra figurines through
his thick lenses to decide that the little images like so
many he had examined were clever fakes, containing
hardly a remnant of actual antiquity. This point established to the satisfaction of his scrupulous mind, instead
of making a catalogue he wrote a brief report, exposing
specifically the fraud that had been perpetrated on the
rich amateur.

"I don't suppose he'll like it," Bayberry said to himself with a dry smile as he sealed and stamped his report. "Nobody likes being taken in, though in this matter it is no disgrace."

Gorridge did not like the Bayberry report on his figurines, which the old scholar had taken no pains to soften. In a way he felt that it was an impertinence. The professor of classical archeology had not been asked for his opinion on the genuineness of the figurines. He had been asked to write some historical and descriptive notes on the collection, useful and entertaining for the layman. Gorridge preferred to take the opinion of other experts (including the responsible dealers who had sold him his figurines) and they had all pronounced the collection "superb". He said nothing to Bayberry, however, his sense of dignity imposing silence, and the figurines were duly installed in a case in the library. Thomas Bayberry improved this opportunity by using the Gorridge collection as laboratory material for his advanced students, pointing out to them the dangers of amateur judgment on highly technical matters. Naturally some of these remarks reached the ears of the president of the board: the figurines disappeared from their case and all talk of a university museum of classical archeology was dropped at the same time. Instead, a chair of American Archeology was presently endowed by Gorridge, and funds supplied so that the young hustler, who was called to fill it, might undertake elaborate excavations in Mexico. Much was made in the newspapers of the Eureka Archeological Expedition. In a series of illustrated articles supplied by Ezra Gulick, the young hustler, local pride and patriotism was appealed to tactfully. It was emphasized that a peculiarly American university like Eureka desired naturally to explore the remains of the primitive American cultures, which it was hinted broadly might prove equal if not superior to the ancient cultures of Europe and Asia

Minor, already so much exploited.   Gulick was nothing
if not patriotic! . . .

Old Bayberry reading in his SUNDAY THUNDERER
these florid accounts of the importance and the beauty of
Maya civilization about to be revealed wrinkled his eyebrows quizzically.   He belonged to the race of scholars
that did not advertise its results—in advance—in the
newspapers, but everybody was doing it now, proffering
their wares to the ignorant public with the showman's
insistence.   No doubt this sort of thing pleased the
president of the board, having his name linked so closely
with a widely advertised American enterprise.   It especially pained Bayberry to have the uncultivated young
hustler, who knew only American archeology, assume
so complacently the equality of his subject with classical
archeology.   "There is such a thing, after all," he said,
"as beauty and no science can ever take its place."

All of which accounts briefly for the fact that Dr.
Harris's dying gesture on Bayberry's behalf missed
fire, in large part.   The board did not consider it ad-
visable to embark on two archeological enterprises of
such magnitude at the same time.   The mere name
"American" plus the support of Samuel Gorridge was
enough to make them prefer the Yucatan expedition.
So it came about that the summer after Dr. Harris's
death Thomas Bayberry set forth as usual alone to
make his annual pilgrimage to the shrines of his worship
in Europe.   After a brief visit to a certain spot on the
coast of Africa where he had dreamed of directing the
energies of enthusiastic young Americans in uncovering
an ancient city, he drifted across the Mediterranean to
Sicily and quaintly equipped with a black silk umbrella
and a pith helmet was resting beside a prostrate column
at Girgenti when two other travelers approached the
lonely temple, a man and a woman.   They paused at
some distance from the ruin, gazed upon it silently,
and then the woman after a brief word to her com-

panion proceeded alone in the direction of the shore, striding lightly over the flower strewn field.

"Like a modern Europa," Bayberry observed with a chuckle.

The man thus abandoned prowled closer to where Bayberry was sitting and finally discovered him.

"A hot day," the stranger remarked, wiping the perspiration from his long white face. "Not much hotter than it would be at Eureka, Dr. Sheimer," Bayberry replied with a little laugh. "You don't remember me. . . Bayberry, classical archeology. I used to see you at my friend Mallory's."

"Oh, of course, Dr. Bayberry!" Sheimer stammered in surprise.

"Just 'professor', please," Bayberry corrected.

"Didn't expect to find you here," the Swiss remarked.

"No? But it is my field, rather more than yours."

"A vacation trip . . . we . ." and Sheimer stopped abruptly, looking more closely at the old archeologist, as if to discover how much he had recognized before he should commit himself.

"Your companion seems to have taken the better part," Bayberry chuckled, with a slight gesture to the distant sea.

"She's gone for a bath," Sheimer admitted

Thomas Bayberry discreetly turned his gaze upwards to the standing pillars of the temple, although the curving line of foam marking the famous "wine-dark" sea beyond the point was all of a mile distant. . . . There was an uncomfortable silence while the two men sought some common ground, broken by Bayberry's remark,—

"Are you interested in Greek remains?"

"I used to spend my summers when I was at the University of Berlin in wandering about the Mediterranean," the psychologist replied. "I thought then I should go in for archeology!"

The ground thus being broken Bayberry proceded to discant in his modest fashion on the beauties and peculiarities of the temple whose remains lay around them. Having discovered an intelligent listener Bayberry reverted to his pedagogic habit, and time sped while the two men examined pillars, and architraves, measured distances and reconstructed the ancient temple on its promontory above the "wine-dark sea". Suddenly Sheimer straightened up and scanned the sea-beach, muttering, "I wonder what can have happened to her!"

"It must be nearly noon," Bayberry observed, "and I had better go for luncheon. . . . Good-bye, *doctor* Sheimer! Glad to have run across you. . . perhaps we'll resume our conversation sometime in Eureka?"

"I'm not going back there," the Swiss said glumly.

"Ah!" . . . .

As they stood there facing the sea a lovely apparition came up over the crest of the little hill, a flower-laden young woman, accompanied by a retinue of small boys. She came rapidly over the slope, holding in her arms a great mass of flowers, with tendrils wound about her head. Bayberry, knowing that he ought to leave, lingered in fascination, a smile pleasantly breaking his long lips. Any form of beauty magnetised him, and the picture of the flower-laden woman coming across the smiling flower-strewn field towards the temple was entrancing.

"Hello!" she called. Her lips were curved in a happy smile like a joyous girl, as if she were eager to announce some triumph. "It was great!" and then recognising the second figure she paused, and the smile died from her lips.

Thomas Bayberry also became suddenly grave.

"Why, why," he stammered, "Mrs. Mallory!"

"Yes," Sheimer admitted curtly and started to walk rapidly towards Jessica who had slowly resumed her

progress, a slight frown gathering on her glowing face.
Bayberry after a moment's hesitation grasped his umbrella and walked away in the direction of the road to
the hillside town, now gleaming under a blazing midday
sun. He passed a motor car with a chauffeur asleep
in the rear seat, and had begun the ascent of the hilly
road leading to his hotel when he heard in his rear the
roar and rumble of a motor in action and presently
was overtaken by the lumbering car, which forced him
to one side of the road. Jessica evidently had not taken
much time with the old temple. . . . As Bayberry, his
umbrella over his head, was trying to bury himself in
the hedge the car came abruptly to a stop and Jessica's
clear voice reached his ears,—"Mr. Bayberry won't
you get in!"

"Thanks," the archeologist replied gruffly. "It's not
far to the inn—I prefer to walk."

"Oh," said Jessica slowly, without acceptance of the
refusal. "We are going up there too for luncheon. . . .
You had better get in!"

Somehow Bayberry obeyed and not only rode to the
inn in the motor but lunched on the vine-shaded terrace
with Sheimer and Mrs. Mallory. Jessica throughout the
meal was as much at her ease, as unconcerned, as if they
had been lunching in the faculty club on the campus of
Eureka. She told with girlish gusto the story of the
adventure on the sea-beach. . .

"They didn't want to let me go into the water. They
thought it wasn't healthy to take sea-baths, but I persuaded 'em with my Italian. . . There was a wedding
going on and they took me in and gave me cakes and
wine and one of the young men had been in New York—
he explained everything. See—these were some of the
bride's flowers!" and she pointed to the white wreath
about her head.

There was something so simple and joyous in the ripple
of laughter that ended her recital that Thomas Bayberry

already warmed by the fiery Sicilian wine and comforted
by the succulent food relaxed and for the time forgot the
irritating question,—"What is Edgar's wife doing here
with this Sheimer fellow?". . . .For these golden quarter
hours of sun and warmth Jessica's relation with his colleague and friend, with the whole laborious American
world of convention and order, faded from his mind and
she became the symbol of a joyous, young goddess sporting along the wine-dark sea below and playing at a
wedding feast with garlands in her hair and flowers
beneath her feet.   The frank smile she turned upon
Bayberry seemed to recognise the metamorphosis that
she was working.   And indeed to a less imaginative
spirit than Bayberry's this glowing, elusive, virginal
woman would not have appeared to be the same being
as the wife of the Senior Dean, the head of a Eureka
household, nor the demure, scholarly figure wending her
way with a bulky portfolio under an arm to and from
the psychology laboratory.   A different being altogether!
Such transformations, Bayberry might reflect, were not
unknown in this marvellous sun-drenched land loved of
gods and men. . .   So for a few golden hours while
Rudolph Sheimer having well drunken and ate sank into
a sullen silence of repletion and discontent, his long white
face perspiring freely.

When Jessica deliberately fastened a cigarette into an
amber holder and began to smoke, the charm was broken
for Bayberry, however.   Young goddesses sporting by the
wine-dark sea did not smoke and though he knew that
Mrs. Mallory in common with many women had the
habit, it always affected him unpleasantly.   He rose from
his seat with his usual abruptness and demanded of the
waiter his bill.   Jessica observing him through her
tawny eyes remarked languidly,—

"And why are you hurrying?"

"It is pretty nearly time for my train," the archeologist replied, "I am on my way to Syracuse."

"Syracuse?" Jessica mused caressingly. "That's the place where they kept the Greek prisoners in a quarry, isn't it?"

"The Latomiae," said Bayberry briefly, paying his bill.

"And there's a Greek theatre there? . . . I'd like to go to Syracuse," Jessica sighed, "and have another bath in that divine water."

Bayberry, pocketing his change, made no remark, while Sheimer looked fixedly at Jessica from half-closed eyes.

"If we are to make Palermo tonight we had better be off," he remarked at last warningly. Bayberry turned to leave the room, as though to indicate that what the two might do was no concern of his. He had not crossed the threshold before Jessica's silvery voice overtook him,—

"Oh, Mr. Bayberry," she called, "I'd like to go to Syracuse too. Won't you come with me in the car?"

Bayberry stopped, and Jessica carefully extracting the remains of the cigarette from the holder replaced the holder in a little gold case on her watch chain and rose from the table as if that matter was settled. Then Sheimer bestirred himself.

"You are not going to Syracuse!" he exclaimed. . . "It's at the other end of the island, and there is no good hotel there."

Jessica looked at him blandly as a child might regard an older person who spoke another language.

"You need not go," she said amiably, evenly. "But I am going with Mr. Bayberry who will tell me all the old stories of the Greeks.". . . and without another look at the bewildered face of the Swiss passed out of the room into the sunny courtyard where the lumbering car stood waiting. Bayberry waiting outside in the sunshine could not see the look of blank amazement, surmounted by rage, which covered the face of the man inside, but the vibrations of the two voices hinted at many things, which Thomas Bayberry was too much the old-fashioned gentleman to consider. . .

"I shall be very glad to go to Syracuse with you," he said, the smile coming back to his old wizened face, "and tell you all the stories I know on the way."

Jessica sighed a little as she settled herself in her corner of the car and murmured,—"This is very pleasant. We'll see a lot of lovely things, won't we?" and as the old car got noisily into motion she added, "I just had a cable from Edgar. He's being sent over to London on some sort of educational conference next month. . . Can one get a steamer from Sicily to London, do you know?"

"I can find out," Bayberry replied matter-of-factly.

"I hope so—I hate long railroad journeys," Jessica said with another sigh, settling herself still deeper into her seat.

CHAPTER TWO

This was Thomas Bayberry's summer with women. Usually his European trips were of the most austere, not to say colorless character: he moved from one small pension near a gallery or museum to another and his social life was bounded by the chance encounters of pension tables. But the Syracuse expedition began a delightful fortnight during which the lumbering motor car and its somnolent driver that Jessica had engaged covered all that was accessible of the lovely island, and certain Arabic fastnesses in the mountains the two travelers attained by mule back. For whenever Bayberry suggested going on his way Jessica, who found his rich scholarship sharpened by the passion of beauty highly stimulating, wiled him onwards by reminding him of a spot not far away to which he had alluded. "We must see that," she would say, and old Thomas, one of the most positive of souls, so rigid and blunt in his notions of what he would or would not do, always acquiesced, without a protest. Jessica did not want to be alone and clutched the archeologist with her small deft hand. As scholars they interested each other, and yet it was not Jessica's scholarship that rewarded Bayberry, rather the winsomeness, the gentle appeal of this other being born in the sea waves of Sicily that lulled to sleep all his prejudices and preconceptions. . . . Jessica took many sea baths along the rocky coasts while Bayberry sat in the car conversing with the chauffeur or looking over the guidebook, and often she wandered fearlessly alone at night into the hamlets and open country. Bayberry well knowing the dangers of the Sicilian country never protested.

"She needs to be alone," he said to himself, for having spent most of his life in a partial solitude he respected the solitudes of another.

Both were completely impersonal, objective. It never entered Bayberry's head to speculate on the Sheimer episode or to refer to it in any way. Jessica divined in her companion this scrupulous quality of non-interference and liked him because of it. "I wonder," she mused, "why such a kindly person never married! I suppose because he thinks he is so homely that no woman could care for him. He has none of the usual male egotisms." And she thought of Sheimer's excessive confidence which had disagreeably protruded itself as soon as they had left New York, his assumptions and demands and expectations. To which she had given the final check at the inn in Girgenti. "I am too much of a man myself, perhaps," she thought, "ever to satisfy the ordinary man—I am not ready to surrender my individuality at his bidding and be absorbed wholly into him!"

So instead of the conventional lovers' pilgrimage through the beauty spots of Italy which Rudolph Sheimer had somewhat vulgarly imagined when Jessica Mallory consented to his suggestion of a vacation in the south from their labors in Jung's laboratory, Thomas Bayberry learnedly and knowingly conducted the lady, in the lumbering car, for a fortnight, and when they finally parted at Naples where Jessica found a ship for England they both had a high regard for each other "He is more nearly the gentleman than I ever thought a man could be," Jessica commented to herself, "altogether a very nice sort of person—and most instructive. Few persons have taught me as much about things as Thomas Bayberry. He has taught me how to find beauty in more places than temples and galleries."

Sitting on deck as the steamer left the great bay, tranquilly smoking a cigarette, she enjoyed the scene and even more she enjoyed the mood of self-mastery which she had gained. In some subtle way a milestone in her life had been passed: henceforth nobody and nothing would be strong enough to upset her poise, to destroy her calm. . . . In London there would be Edgar, who would be very much occupied, and the elder boy whom he had brought over. Jessica might take the boy to Stockholm with her where in September she was to attend a congress of psychologists. Sheimer would doubtless be at the congress, as he had a paper, on which she had helped him to deliver. Jessica smiled placidly. She would as soon meet Rudolph Sheimer there as any one else! . . .

Thomas Bayberry continuing his pilgrimage alone, more alone after Jessica Mallory's companionship than ever, arrived in Rome in mid-September. There in the gallery of the Vatican before the writhing Laocoön he met his neighbor Constance Fenton, fanning her fair, florid face with a catalogue.

"Terrible, isn't it?" she gurgled to the old archeologist. "It's like most things in Europe. They're terrible—unhappy. It makes me want to be back in dear old Eureka, with all the babies playing out in the backyard. We don't have such agonies over there!" and she challenged Bayberry out of her soft eyes. Bayberry chuckled audibly. If Jessica Mallory had stimulated him to display before her all the treasures of his learning, of his life-long hunt for beauty, Constance Fenton's state of mind was more restful: it would be impossible to disturb the solid placidity of her soul. . . . So he chuckled as she recounted the campus gossip— she had just left Eureka for a four weeks "tour".

The Flynns had moved into her house and were looking after her children. Everybody said that Dolittle would be made president of the university in the autumn when the trustees returned from their vacations. "He's such a safe kind of man, you know," Constance quoted, "won't do anything reckless like poor Dr. Harris . . . and he's promised me light and heat from the university power plant if I can raise the funds for enlarging the nursery. Of course I am for him! . . . I am sorry, though, that Edgar Mallory didn't get it—he's so attractive. But everybody says Jessica went off with that Sheimer man. And they couldn't make Edgar president of the university with his wife over in Switzerland with—"

"I don't see that has anything to do with it," Bayberry interrupted bluntly, "his wife's studying in Switzerland. . . You know I don't like to hear my friends gossiped about."

"I like Jessica well enough," Constance hastened to add, "but she's queer; I do wish for the sake of her husband she wouldn't be so queer."

Bayberry thinking of the secret places in human beings sighed and let the topic drop. He was sorry that Edgar, whom he greatly admired, was not to be the next president of Eureka, and he was sorrier that the gossips assigned as a cause for his failure in this ambition the character of his wife. He did not pretend to himself that he knew the intricacies of Jessica's character, but after his recent intimacy with her he was less ready than ever to condemn her. Well, a man with all the qualifications for public work that Mallory had shown would not stay long in an inferior position, no matter how queer his wife might be, in the eyes of the public. Edgar would no doubt be called away from Eureka, and Bayberry sighed again at this thought. He would so much like a stable world of friends, and the crowded world into which he was living from a past generation threatened to be less stable and lonelier than he had thought possible. . . .

"Come with me to Ajaccio this afternoon," he suggested to Constance after they had exhausted the

Laocoön and the remaining "starred" sculptures, which
Constance conscientiously thumbing the catalogue insisted on appraising. . . ."I'll show you plenty of babies
out there!"

So in a rickety carriage drawn by an emaciated horse
they penetrated the little hill town and Bayberry re-
deemed his promise to Constance. They were surrounded
by a mob of healthy brown children. Constance whose
limited Italian got no farther than "Bambini, bambini,"
with an occasional "caro", or "carina mia" sat down on
the church steps a youngester in either hand. Bayberry
watching her from a little distance thought how much
more of a person she seemed sitting there on the dusty
church steps, a child on either knee than she had been
confronting the celebrated Laocoön. Paradoxically the
placid maternal girl, whom he could remember as a fat
child mothering all the babies she could lay a hand on
in the neighborhood, was a very integral part of the
university, and belonged in Eureka far more than Jessica,
the learned, or Abel Dolittle, for instance. The university, in simple substance, was a place for rearing the
youth of the world, and Constance Fenton began the
process a little farther back even than the elementary
division of the Teachers' College. Her pedagogy was of
the instinctive sort, tempered by the knowledge she had
acquired of sanitation, hygiene, and kindred matters, but
her aim was what the university ought to try for,—the
development of the normal human being, correction of
the abuses that life had already handicapped the child
with, and in her own placid, warmly loving self provide a
constant solvent for growth.

"I'd like to take a dozen of these heavenly little
rascals back with me," Constance exclaimed. "But the
little Swedes and Dutchies in the nursery would call them
Dagoes, I suppose. They're better off here in all their
dirt than they would be in any Eureka backyard" . . .

The two completed Constance's "tour" together, doing

Florence, Milan, Venice (in a stewing heat) and the Italian lakes. Bayberry was much interested in the serious effort of Constance not to omit anything in her itinerary. She had come after foreign glamour, and she pursued it relentlessly. With a sigh of relief she settled herself in the Ostend express from Switzerland, her task accomplished, and murmured, "Well, I am glad I was born in Eureka!" Bayberry laughed with his peculiar suppressed chuckle. "Why so?" he asked.

"It seems so normal," Constance sighed. "You university people are always talking of getting to Europe, as if it were a heaven, and my city friends, the women I mean, are longing to 'run over' here, to get away from husbands I suppose. . . So I've heard about Europe all my life as some dream place. . . Well, it's just crowded and dirty and a lot more like Eureka than one would suspect!" he concluded triumphantly. "I'm glad I came, of course, to see what it is like, the old buildings, museums and cafes. But I don't want to live with it: I want to live where there's a future, more future than past—and that's Eureka, U.S.A."

Bayberry's laughter died out into thoughts he could not share with Constance, who had settled back in her corner with a copy of *Figaro*. . . . It was true that as Constance said faculty people were likely to sigh for Europe as for their home land. Perhaps it was time that American universities recovered from the glamour that the older continent had always had for them and lived more in their own present and future. The European tradition was not the American tradition, and although scholarship was supposed to be international, Americans, like himself, might overestimate the European contribution. As for the other kinds of Americans who looked to Europe for entertainment and indulgence Thomas Bayberry had small concern. They belonged to the negligible fringe of sophisticated fashion.

"Yes, Constance," he said at the conclusion of his

meditation, "we'll go home and be better Eurekeans because of our wanderings. . . But you must admit they have a few things here we can't turn out yet."

"What?"

"Laocoöns."

Constance made a face. . .

At the Bloomsbury hotel where they stayed in London they found a number of university people enjoying a last look at Westminster and the Museum before departing for their homes. Among them were Edgar Mallory and his son waiting for Jessica, who had not yet returned from Stockholm.

"I do think the way she flits off by herself!" Constance Fenton remarked to Bayberry.

"It's her professional engagements," Bayberry said defensively, wrinkling his nose.

"If I were a man, I'd want a little less professional reputation and a little more domesticity."

"Ah, Constance, you and I are archaic, I'm afraid."

Jessica caught the boat at Southampton.

CHAPTER THREE

They called it the Wind Bag. It grew out of those
desultory hours spent in the little arbor in the rear of
Flesheimer's saloon, where Beckwith, Clavercin, Snow,
and occasionally others gathered,—Caxton whose steely
mind penetrated every subject, the poet Don Garland,
who early wandered away and became almost a great
poet. Later they took in Harding, the ponderous, the
pompous, the assured, whose solid judgment and wide
contact with life blended with the effervescent wine
of Snow's Gascon wit, Beckwith's idealism, Clavercin's
aestheticism. They talked of everything in their eager
fresh minds except shop, which was tacitly barred,—
of socialism and trusts, of scholarship and poetry, of that
ideal university which existed only in their dreams.
Time passed, the group broke up, merged into other
lives, but every now and then when three of them met
by accident the desire rose instinctively for talk, the
wayward talk of men at the end of the day's work
after they have eaten and drunk well, talk far into the
morning. "Let us have a Wind Bag," one would say
to another. "Good! Where?" "At my place—we've
a good cook now."

So having been in abeyance for more than a year
the Wind Bag was dining at Clavercin's one of those
first warm spring evenings which came to Eureka as
elsewhere with teasing suggestions of green fields and
trickling streams. The long windows to the tiny terrace were open, admitting the roar of the enveloping
city. The special occasion for this Wind Bag was the
chance visit to Eureka of Aleck Harding, who after

serving as private secretary to a cabinet officer in the last administration had recently become a vice-president in a New York trust company. He was a trifle balder, a trifle heavier, than when he had addressed the faculty authoritatively or drunk Flesheimer's beer with hearty gusto, and his clothes were more noticeably finished.

"Well, what are you fellows doing with Dolittle as president of the university?" he asked in that slightly condescending manner that always made Clavercin itch to kick him under the table. "Ho, ho, to think of old Abel Donothing as president!"

This sneer at their misfortune affected the group unpleasantly.

"At least," Dexter observed, "the university is getting students, more than it can properly take care of."

"And there is some good material in the graduate school," Caxton added, "but most of the money goes into the business college, to make bank presidents!"

Harding laughed at the thrust.

"The trouble with your job," he generalised in his most irritating manner, as if he were giving a final diagnosis, "is that after all it is just school-teaching: you are always dealing with immature minds, your inferiors, even in the graduate courses."

(As if Harding himself had not taught political economy for ten years to mixed classes of undergraduates, escaping from "the job" by the simple device of marrying into one of the rich families in the city whose men boosted him along to his present position!)

"What are the sort of minds you dealt with in Washington?" Beckwith interposed. "So much more mature and intelligent than university students?"

"In the outside world," Harding insisted in his heavy, imposing voice, "men may not be exceptionally brilliant or learned, but the things they are working for count, are of life interest, not theory. And that makes a great difference!"

"Evidently!" Beckwith admitted, but his irony escaped Harding's flat mind.

"Their decisions count! That's what makes mature minds. Here nothing counts very much. An instructor can slop along doing poor work, and if he isn't too rotten he gets by and so the students realising that what they are doing does not bear directly on what is coming, work half-heartedly. Not until they reach the professional schools or business do they begin to wake up!"

"It sounds like Dolittle and Sanderson when they want to put over some new piece of trade machinery," Clavercin remarked.

"I speak as a man of experience, Clavey," Harding retorted. "That is the reason why our universities have so little influence on American life. You are theorists, immuned in your cloisters, lulled to sleep by chimes. Teachers of boys and girls. Until you show that the university is dealing with things that affect people's daily lives, you will be run by Dolittles and yourselves be rated socially in the white collar class!"

The coarse frankness of this attack on his former profession started a long and animated windbag. Each man thus touched on a tender point reacted promptly in defense of himself, of the institution which with all its obvious limitations he must believe in as he believed in life itself. Yet each knew the kernel of truth in this popular estimate of the university career. Those in it labored under what later was called an inferiority complex. . . Harding feeling his ground firm beneath him continued, expanding his chest, leaning back as though to say,—"Here is the proof of my words!" . . .

"No, gentlemen, I am not condemning you as individuals nor commending the present cultural state of our country, the position of inferiority that our universities occupy in the social plan. I am merely stating it as a fact and asking you as persons most intimately concerned with it why it should be so. . . . So long, I tell you, as you can't make yourselves felt, you will be bossed by Dolittles and you will work all your lives for a few thousand dollars a year while men inferior to you in intellectual power make fortunes. You are competing with yourselves in a little secluded corner of the universe! Get out!" he concluded dogmatically, with a flourish of his cigar.

"And to think he was once a professor himself!" Clavercin groaned.

"It was just because I realised all this in time, Clavey, that I got out before it was too late," he said in his big brother manner.

"If we were all as clever, we should be doing the same?" Clavercin asked, thinking of the pale, neurasthenic Mrs. Harding.

"No, we are all hopelessly inferior!" Snow laughed. "You are not giving the world what it is willing to pay well for."

"I accept that," Beckwith said in a more serious tone than the others. "We do not wish to give this world what it cares to pay for! And when we betray our profession and try to play the world's game, as you put it, like Sanderson for example or Dolittle, we seem to ourselves a little ridiculous, Harding, a little base and inferior, also."

This thrust reached through the banker's thick complacency.

"Then you should not complain if the world lets you go your own way and starve!" he retorted sullenly.

"We were not complaining, were we?" Beckwith asked sweetly. "You put the question,—what is the matter with the American university and answered that it was not delivering the goods wanted."

Caxton joined.

"Beckwith is right. We have no ambition to compete with what our socialists call the *bourgeoisie*, at least not most of us!" he grinned at the extraordinarily good *entrecôte* that had just been put before him—Louise Clavercin certainly had a good cook! . . . "And we seem ridiculous when we try it. But we must live in the world as we find it, reasonably free from anxieties, and that is becoming impossible on our present salaries, without wasting our time in commercial work which takes our energies from our real contribution to life. For we believe that we have a function to perform in the community as valuable, as important, let us say as banking or steel-making or politics! And we believe that the community does not always recognise what is best for it, how much it really needs our contribution".

"Make 'em recognise it!" Harding snapped back.

"And that function," Caxton persisted in his unpassionate, dry voice, "is a good deal more than keeping a sort of higher boarding school for the children of the well-to-do, where they can play about harmlessly for four adolescent years. It is to preserve and increase knowledge."

"And to train good minds for leadership," Beckwith added.

"All very good," Harding accepted confidently. "But leadership means character, and that is made through strife, in the world," and he quoted as he had at every Wind Bag that Clavercin remembered, the verse from Goethe to that effect "As for knowledge there are other places where it is preserved and increased. . . The American university is a hybrid between a preparatory school for the professions and a research laboratory. The men in it are paid like school-teachers and laboratory workers, and will be until you prove that you are necessary."

"It sounds like Dolittle's inner thought—serving the

community what it thinks it wants as cheaply as possible."

All laughed, for the cheeseparing methods of the new executive had become a common joke.

"He is building up a surplus," Snow said. "Whoever heard of a respectable university with a surplus in its budget? It's like the steel corporation."

"The old man's palsy is growing on him," Dexter remarked. "He can't go on forever sitting on the lid and saying 'no, no,' to any suggestion for improvement in this best of all worlds."

Harding, who had been smoking with dubious sniffs one of the large cigars Clavercin had specially ordered from the university club in honor of the banker's presence, now cleared his throat, with the air of one who after listening to the testimony is ready to deliver judgment.

"You all speak in terms of the competitive society in which we are living and thus indirectly concede my point. Caxton wants higher salaries, more books, leisure for research. Dexter here, I take it, wants much the same, more laboratories, more assistants and better paid ones, more time for his own research. Clavey probably wants the university to build him a theatre and run it, and also endow him so that he can write more horrifying sex plays."

This last was aimed at the three days' notoriety caused by WHY? Clavercin's abortion play, of which the sensation had not entirely disappeared. As Clavercin took no notice of this allusion to his ill-fated play, Harding continued in his most impressive manner:

"So each one of you is concerned like everybody else in boosting the goods in his own stall at the fair, trying as we all try to make our own wares attractive to others and thereby enlarge our business, our own prestige, our standing in the community. In this process the university in no way differs from any other social enterprise. If you cannot make your goods sell themselves as they say in business, you must not blame the public who will not buy them, but yourselves for offering an undesired commodity or offering it unattractively."

He paused to light a fresh cigar, which this time he drew from a limp-leather gold-rimmed case, adorned with a delicate monogram. The company watched him silently while he lighted this cigar, smelled it appreciatively, and relaxed. There was nothing more to be said. The cigar, the monogrammed cigar case, the finely cut sleeve of the banker's coat were palpable symbols to all of what Harding had sought in life, material achievements rather than the intangibilities for which they were leading cramped existences.

"Your world needs us more than it knows," Beckwith insisted. "Some day it will come to us seeking."

"Make them know it then!" Harding exclaimed skeptically.

"But not on your terms," Beckwith said.

"On any terms you can get over," Harding came back. "The trouble with you fellows in the universities is that you won't accept the world as it is. You are all idealists at heart and this is a realistic world. . . . You despise the Sandersons and Donothings who do understand their world and cater to it, and yet you expect it to support you in an elegant and learned leisure.". . .

"An elegant and learned leisure!" a woman's voice mocked from the terrace outside, and Louise Clavercin appeared in the window followed by Jessica Mallory, the Flynns, and others. They had been dining with Constance Fenton and inspecting the new university creche, which she had made out of her father's old brick house.

"So that's what he thinks our life is like, does he? I don't see much leisure in it; the learning I take for

granted, though every professor seems to consider that
most of his colleagues are not 'real scholars', and as
for our elegance I suppose that is a joke, isn't it?"

"Ah, Louise, come in here and tell these fellows they
are a lot of day-dreamers and loafers, grouching because
they can't live like millionaires."

"Why, weren't you satisfied with your dinner"?
Louise asked insinuatingly.

"It was delicious—you are an epicure, Louise!"
Harding roared. "You don't belong with this oatmeal
and gruel crowd."

"And of course if they were real men," she gurgled
amiably, "they'd give up their school-teaching, as you
call it and make money—or marry it like you, Aleck."

"Of course they would!" he accepted frankly.

And so the last Wind Bag broke up in the usual
piffle and sallies of dubious wit that characterised
university society when it met in double sex. Louise's
good dinner combined with Harding's coarse complacency had killed the Wind Bag. . . The company drifted
into the living room, which originally had been decorated in gold and black, setting off the dusky coloring
of its hostess, but was now dulled after a few years
exposure to Eureka grime. They chatted desultorily,
seated about the fire in couples. Harding drew Louise
to one side and devoted himself to her, while Clavercin
having replenished the glasses and stirred the fire stood
to one side, observing his guests. He was conscious
of his wife's vivacity, which made her look younger
than she was. She was exerting herself to entertain
the pompous, successful banker, whom in former years
she had derided. Clavercin did not believe she liked
the man any better now, but she liked success and
found the almost universal lack of its evidence in university circles painful. That was what made her accept
so avidly all the invitations that came their way from
city people, made her exert herself rather obviously

to please them with her lively chatter. Many of their houses were tiresome, stuffy places where there was too much rich food and a boisterous merriment sustained on alcohol. Clavercin disliked these city parties more and more, and resented the rôle of parasite which Louise's taste for them thrust on him. Also the reciprocating entertainments in his own house when Louise invited in such of his colleagues as she thought most presentable to meet her city friends, who occasionally motored down to the university as to an arctic adventure. He did not know what he would substitute for this form of society; the university people undiluted bored him almost as much as they did Louise. As for that electric "artistic" circle of musicians and painters and writers, which in his younger days he had dreamed of discovering, it did not exist in Eureka, if anywhere in America. The more successful of the artist tribe tried to identify themselves with the rich city people, like the portrait painter Jug, the amiable sculptor Pitch, who was busily filling the parks with his marble masonry on a contract, and the others existed in feeble coteries less exhilarating than that of the university people.

On the first night of Clavercin's play the little downtown theatre had been packed with these city friends, prepared to applaud him warmly into fame. The one most painful experience of his entire life had been the realization of their disappointment, first silent mystification, then laughter, inept laughter at some of the most tragic passages in the play. At first he had been angry with their crass stupidity, then had realized that they were laughing nervously because they were uncomfortable when it had dawned on them what was happening to the girl on the stage. His was one of those disagreeable situations that the "healthy-minded" American resents as in some way denying the very postulates of his existence.

Louise had never been the same since the night of the

play, on which she had counted for her own triumph before her friends. It had opened her eyes to the fact that her dear Beaman might not possess the kind of talent that succeeds on Broadway. There were now two children to consider, the older one just entering high school in the Teachers' College. Naturally Louise thought more and more in terms of her children's future and of family stability. . . .

She was having a quite earnest conversation with Harding, in the niche beyond the fireplace to which they had withdrawn. Probably Louise was pumping the banker about investments, getting his advice: she was always asking the more prosperous men whom she met whether this or that was "a good buy," in the hope of somehow rolling Uncle Blair's small inheritance into the desirable hundreds of thousands. To Beaman this "piker" stock marketing habit of women these days was intensely distasteful because it was so closely linked with their sex play. No man would take the trouble to put a woman into really good things unless his interest were stimulated by some display of her charms. Harding had always been a little épris of Louise in his elephantine, strictly moral way, and was now emphasizing his words with tense gestures, while Louise nodded respectfully.

Clavercin who still loved his wife, when not hurt by her occasional selfishness, still found her desirable, had a quick perception while he watched the two that Louise no longer loved him completely if she ever had. She would have been happier with a different sort of man, with the Harding sort perhaps, who would be doing things she recognized as worth while in the world and above all would enable her to exploit her own social talent more brilliantly. No doubt Harding also would have profited by marrying Louise because he needed somebody more vital than his neurasthenic wife to smooth off his boorishness, which still remained an obstacle to his worldly success. Both Harding and Louise were of the same unmistakable breed, *arrivistes*, hearty believers in the "game" and keen players of it. Neither belonged in a university, even a university so little exacting as Eureka was.

Clavercin saw all this with painful clarity.

Once when he was in Rome, Bayberry had taken him to call on old Madame Seltzan, the austere wife of the gay sculptor well known during two generations for his relations with various women. Dressed in a long gray robe like a piece of seamless sacking, a wisp of gray hair knotted on the top of her large bony head, Madame Seltzan was engaged in looking through the ledger of a hospital, one of her many charities. She was a Tolstoian, and when the conversation came to the great Russian the old woman's face lighted with an almost youthful radiance.

"I knew him very well for many years," she told Clavercin, "and his wife too. They were neighbors." Then with the dispassionateness of a familiar revery she added, "Yes, Tolstoi and I should have married long ago, and Seltzan should have married Madame Tolstoi. They would have perfectly suited each other! . . and Tolstoi would not have had to wander off like that at the end and die in a railroad station!" The old woman's simple gesture completed the story of wasted opportunity, of her realization what she might have given the Christian theorist, while the other pair were rejoicing together in the sparkle of worldly life.

Was it always like that, human misfits? Or would it have happened as Madame Seltzan thought? Human beings might need in order to make their unions enduring some secret antinomy. Who could tell! There was Jessica Mallory. University gossip had it that she and Rudolph Sheimer had been together the winter both had spent in Jung's laboratory in Zurich, and it would seem that they could be more useful to each other, working on common problems, than the Mallorys ever could be. All

the same, Mrs. Mallory had returned to Eureka this
year, her vacation ended, and had calmly resumed her
domesticity with her own work in the laboratory, while
the German-Swiss had stayed over there. . . She was
seated a little apart from the chatting groups, smoking a
cigarette in a long holder, with that air of detached yet
interested observation of the scene that was characteristic of her. Suddenly Clavercin crossed the room and
repeated to her the Russian woman's remark about
Tolstoi. Jessica listened with a deepening smile on her
fine lips, and at the conclusion emitted a low "Huh!", a
sort of Indian grunt of appreciation.

"Both couples had gone stale," she commented.

"And if they had married the other, they wouldn't
have gone stale?"

"No telling! . . . It isn't the people so much as the
institution. Marriage usually goes stale one way or
another," she pronounced dogmatically.

"Necessarily?" Clavercin said wistfully.

"Oh, more or less. They exhaust after a time what
each has to offer the other in the way of stimulus."

"And they can't renew?"

She made a little gesture as though to call his attention to the couples chatting animatedly in this room, all
of whom would presently depart and trudge homewards,
yawning, silent, each repressed into self. . . .

"Mallory still in Washington?" some one asked Jessica.

"So far as I know," she answered tranquilly and
drawing a scarf over her thin shoulders rose to leave in
her usual abrupt manner.

Since Dolittle's accession to the presidency of Eureka,
Mallory, who had been offered the position of senior
Dean, had found one reason or another for absenting
himself from the university. It was hinted that the
Larson estate having converted itself into a giant
philanthropic trust with headquarters in Washington
was being run by the competent Mallory. At any rate

he spent most of his time in Washington, and people were wondering how long the Mallorys would keep open their house opposite the campus. The three children were all parcelled out at different boarding schools, and collected for vacations either in Washington or in Eureka. This scattered family hearth seemed to work in its way,—Jessica's way.

"Good-night," Jessica nodded collectively to the room and disappeared through the blue curtains followed by Clavercin. "No thanks! Don't trouble . . . only a few steps around the corner."

So she went her way alone, fading quickly into the darkness, her little boot-heels clicking smartly on the pavement. Odd creature! So pretty, almost girlish still, so self-sufficient! Was she simply inhuman? Clavercin suspected that she was not, but no observer would ever discover what went on within her hidden being. Probably the only thing she passionately cared for was her work, her investigations and theories and publications. In this respect she was more like the men he knew, like Caxton or that dry compendium of irrelevant knowledge in his own department, Paul Rymer. Such beings got what nourishment they needed through printed words, ideas, abstractions. Yet Jessica Mallory had made one of the few discriminating remarks about Clavercin's play, WHY?.

"It's too honest,—truth has to be more veiled for most people," she had said.

The party was breaking up. The Flynns went off with Constance Fenton and old Bayberry, chaffing Constance over her creche. Pretty Mrs. Flynn, who was the daughter of a missionary and used to begging, had helped Constance in raising the necessary endowment. "We got five thousand dollars and the heat and light from the university," Constance told Clavercin triumphantly, "and Mr. Bayberry has promised to give five hundred, though he hasn't any babies to be looked after!" "Come, Connie," Tom Flynn urged, "don't hold up a man like that in his own doorway at midnight!" The Flynns who had nothing at all except a meagre salary managed to look after more stray and forlorn persons in the university than anybody else. They had four children of their own. Bayberry had given Constance five hundred dollars, while he and Louise were hesitating over fifty! These people were the very salt of the community in kindliness and generosity—they were neither ambitious nor critical of life. They conformed and went along, and found it all good. What made it possible to be like that?

Last of all Harding left, saying as he donned the celebrated fur coat and silk hat,—

"Clavey I'm telling Louise you must bring her to N'York next year. Get out into the world, man, and see something besides books and students." He patted Clavercin patronizingly on the shoulder.

"That's just what I have been saying to him for years!" Louise cried glibly.

The university chimes were playing the nightly hymn. Since the accession of Dolittle the repertoire had been enlarged, and now through the misty dark was sounding softly the refrain of, "Now let thy servant depart in peace." The Clavercins stood on the steps listening to the sweet bells, until Louise yawning turned back to the living room and began collecting the empty glasses.

"What did you mean by what you said to Aleck Harding—that you have been urging me to give up Eureka?"

"Haven't I always said I was ready any time you felt it was best?"

"No! You have been proving to me how necessary it is to stay on in Eureka and earn more money."

His dislike of Harding's crude materialism and condescension, his appreciation of the sweet quality of the

Flynns, of Bayberry and Constance Fenton, the chimes with their special appeal to his youthful vision of a life not devoted to self-seeking, a life peaceful, serene, ruffled,—all mingled in his irritation with his wife. Just as after another painful struggle he had convinced himself that his true work lay here, trying to enlarge the vision of such raw youth as came his way, Louise was again fretting the nerve of his thwarted ambition.

"Oh don't let's go all over that again," she said wearily, in her bored after-the-party air. "If you are ready to give up teaching in the university and can make a decent living for your family by your writing, I shall be only too glad to do a wife's part and help you," she said stiltedly, adding as an after-thought, "but you will have to write something different from WHY? if you want to make good on Broadway."

Then she went to her room and Clavercin went to his study on the third floor, thinking of Jessica Mallory's dictum on the staleness of marriage. Louise, he felt, held to their marriage because of the two children, because of the social risk of breaking it, rather than from any faith in him or enthusiasm for his interests. She was much more adapted to the Eureka world than he, accepting it with its limited ideals and obeying its dictates. Unfortunately like so many other women she had made her choice of mate too early, taking a professional man of slender earning power and now in the glare of middle age was confronted without illusions by all the cramping facts of a small income, thwarting constantly her instincts. Quite inevitable, Clavercin thought as he lifted one of the bulky manuscripts from the pile on his desk and began to turn its dull pages, that she should be attracted to the more burly, the more dominating men whom she met in the city, like Harding. They might not appeal to her aesthetically as much as he could, but to the practical woman in her with children to launch they must appeal. And for him some other woman, without that eternal feminine instinct for congregating socially, for building and enlarging the nest, so that her own importance could be felt, would be preferable. Somebody who cared for ideas, perceptions, somebody like Jessica Mallory. And the figure of the old woman in the gray sacking, her gaunt face glowing in vision of what might have been if life had been lived with another teased him.

However, as the last notes of the chimes died, he pulled himself together. He must try to see Dolittle and find out whether there was any prospect of a salary increase another year, or of the university's building that theatre Dr. Harris had promised him. If not, it was not too late to go down into the open arena outside the university and battle there in the competitive world. Jessica Mallory, that fierce individualist, would smile sarcastically at his thus leaving such a decision to the fitful will of one palsied old man. Or to the expectation of a wife for security and position!

CHAPTER FOUR

A steel engraving of the martyred president, William
McKinley, now hung in the president's office beside the
portrait of the Founder and opposite the oil painting
of Dr. Harris in cap and gown, whose round face with
tightly gripped jaw cast a challenge at the others.
Dolittle had once encountered McKinley at some
political convention held in Eureka and the Ohio states-
man's suave appearance and benign courtesy had deeply
impressed the college dean. To Abel Dolittle, William
McKinley was "the great American of our era." His
manners he patterned on the McKinley model, his administrative methods on those of Pliny Lucus, president of the Public Utility Corporation that held Eureka
in its embrace—for its own good.

Under the inspiration of these two great Americans
(although Pliny hailed from Canada) the presidential
suite had been withdrawn from the public eye at the end
of a maze of corridors not easily penetrated. There
President Dolittle, a little shrunken, gray-haired man,
whose face and hands already trembled slightly from
incipient palsy sat behind the broad desk, no longer
disorderly with piles of unanswered correspondence
and notebooks, and received in a chilly isolation the
occasional caller who got through the guard of stenographers and secretaries. Even the outer office was
no longer the humming hive it had been in the old
days, with scraps of heated conversations heard across
partitions, telegrams flying in and out, the incessant
ringing of telephone bells. The worn, middle-aged Miss
Wex had been replaced by a fresh faced young woman

whose correct attire and soft voice were in the best corporation style. A suave young man from the department of public speaking took many of the president's burdens from his shoulders, showing visitors the library, the Campanile, the new gymnasium, and commons. He wore a small silk hat and tight frock coat, and was nicknamed the "Little President" because he was supposed to be in training for the succession. His burly wife assisted Mrs. Dolittle at her monthly receptions, "standing in line" and passing on the guests with a soft word of explanation to the hostess. Under the secretary's watchful eye everything in the outer office went smoothly after the fashion of the best new business administration properly "filed", "organized", "correlated", and "delegated", so that to the superficial eye the university ran itself.

Dolittle had arrived, rather late but securely. A new order of things had come with him to Eureka. Instead of haste and aspiration and red ink balances, there was the efficient functioning of a well oiled machine where high school boys and girls entered at one end and dropped out at the other as "our graduates" arrayed in caps and gowns with rolls of parchment in their hands. Whether the university in its zeal for economy cheapened its process, Dolittle considered to be no one's affair, provided it turned out a satisfactory product, and by satisfactory the president meant something that would sell. He detested as he frequently said "the critical spirit", the noisy habit of confessing one's shortcomings in public. One should boost and boast, not knock or kick. He liked as instructors smooth young men with soft voices, who dressed neatly in the best ready-to-wear styles and avoided all "unfortunate complications" either with women or politics. His influence with the local republican machine was sufficient to procure for the university some valuable privileges, such as closing up a city street in order to erect a

central heating and lighting plant, whose tall yellow stack
was to become the enduring monument of his administration. From his big swivel chair behind the presidential desk he could watch this soaring creation shoot
upwards day by day. This sight gave him, perhaps,
the most acute sense of accomplishment of his long life.
He was just seventy when the cloud of black smoke
first poured from the throat of the stack (in contra-
vention of a city ordinance) rivalling the steel chimneys
farther south.

Dolittle disliked the head of the department of
political science because this lively young man had de-
fied the old machine and had the temerity to run for
office as an independent. "It is a bad thing for the
university to be identified with radicals and reformers
and unstable people of that sort," he said in condemna-
tion of Walter's candidacy. "It is the Roosevelt nonsense." But characteristically instead of fighting Walters
in the open he "praised him away" to a neighbor university in the centre of the state where he could do
no harm playing Roosevelt politics. Likewise, although
he had always disliked "the Harvard gang" in the
faculty, "the culture crowd", and let them have few of the
niggardly plums he dispensed, yet he was outwardly cour-
teous to them, even to Beckwith, after "that dangerous
firebrand" had joined the executive council of the feeble
labor party in Eureka. Irritated by Clavercin's ill-
fated play and the attendant notoriety, nevertheless
he had refused to entertain the suggestion made by some
of the more scandalized trustees that the professor of
dramatic literature be asked to resign. "That would
be poor policy," he had counselled, "for all the noisy
radical element in the country would seize hold of it
as an excuse for attacking the university. Let him
sink into obscurity, which will soon come!" Patience
and prudence had been Dolittle's watchwords from
youth. He had observed that "noisy people" either

found it best to conform and shut their mouths or came to trouble in this world where what Dolittle called common sense usually got the last word.

In short, he was of the Hanna-McKinley breed, ardent about nothing, industrious, methodical, believing in a smug, orderly world run by people like himself, who were neither brilliant nor "erratic", but kept their accounts in order and never offended those in power. The trustees took great comfort in Dolittle after the uncertainties of Dr. Harris. He did not present them with unsuspected deficits, did not shame them into great exertions to keep the university afloat. If those among them who traveled away from Eureka discovered that the president of their university was generally considered an insignificant nobody, who made trite and boresome speeches, they shrugged their shoulders contentedly. Dolittle did well enough for Eureka, at present. "Nothing at all showy about Dolittle," they said, "but he is safe." To the students he was just "Prexy", a conventional, mouselike figure whom they rarely saw. To the faculty he was either negligible or the source of petty irritations. They reckoned up his increasing years and calculated the time that must elapse before the Board would retire him on a pension. . . .

Clavercin sitting opposite the president, whose watery green eyes regarded his visitor malevolently as from a great distance, became at once conscious of the insurmountable wall of prejudice that lay between them and talked badly, stammering, hesitating. Dolittle, brought up on an Indiana farm, disliked in general the Harvard product as snobbish and superior, and in particular there might very well still rankle in his memory a *mot* that Clavercin had made about his wife in those green years when he first met the lady. "Abel's Mistake, his One Great Mistake," he had called the tall raw-boned, nasal-voiced wife of the Senior Dean. The good lady was plain, small-town American and nothing worse. Her

efforts to preside socially over Eureka were gently humorous. She nudged distinguished guests with her elbow,
exclaiming,—"Now, you don't say!" or hid a coquettish
merriment behind a large hand, gurgling, "Oh, come
Mr. Blank" and a few innocent ways like that. . .

He knew that Dolittle had pronounced WHY? "dis-
gusting" and "degenerate" and had never looked with
favor on the growing popularity of the course in drama.
It was on behalf of this work that he had obtained after
long delay the present appointment with the president.
He must have something better than a graduate student
for assistant in a course that involved the examination of
so many student plays, also a better stage than the
crumbling wing of the old "temporary" gymnasium-
library. The dream of having a theatre where his
students might experiment in staging and acting their
own productions had gone glimmering with the death of
the sympathetic Harris. Latterly, however, there had
been a report that Caxton's Modern Language Hall had
been assured by the gift of a rich and learned Jewess of
the city, and Clavercin hoped the proposed auditorium
in the building might in some way be adapted for his
pet project. . . .

"We shall not build the Modern Language Hall at
present," Dolittle replied to Clavercin's appeal. "Labor
has made the cost of building in Eureka prohibitive," he
explained. This remark, Clavercin knew, was aimed at
his supposed sympathy with the new Labor Party. . . .
"And furthermore the Board would not favor devoting
so much space in the building to a theatre, which is not
properly a university undertaking."

"Why not?" Clavercin demanded sharply. "Don't you
consider the study and practise of an important branch
of literature suitable for the modern university—as much
as journalism or business administration?"

"I did not refer to the study of literature, properly
conducted, although in my opinion too much attention is

already given to literary courses at the expense of more important subjects. I had reference to the writing and staging of plays—to drama." (he pronounced it *drayma*) "which I understand is your chief interest."

Clavercin knew well enough how useless it would be to argue with this limited, prejudiced old man on behalf of creative effort in a university, but he could not refrain from asking ironically,

"Do you think methods of cost accounting more educational than the effort to express ideas in the form of plays?"

"It is more useful at least," Dolittle snapped, as he toyed with his eye-glasses in a manner he had assumed since becoming president, indicating that so far as he was concerned the interview had ended. Clavercin rose from his chair, feeling that the only suitable thing to do was to hand in his resignation then and there, but conscious that such a hasty act would simply please the old man he restrained the impulse. He would leave the university at his own convenience.

In the outer office fidgeted a number of his colleagues, waiting to see the president. Dexter was concerned with the fate of his famous "mouse-house", where under the care of an ancient dusty female innumerable generations of mice had been born, lived and died, for the cause of science. The next year's budget, now being prepared, had cut off the appropriation to maintain the "mouse-house", Dolittle for some reason not considering it necessary. Dexter was anxiously waiting his opportunity to convince the stubborn old man that without the mice his present work would be made impossible, knowing in his heart that this was precisely the end Dolittle had in view. Beyond him sat Paul Rymer, who had remained an assistant-professor for twelve years and was hoping against hope that the President would recommend him for the long awaited advance to associate professor. He knew that there were at least twenty more members of

the faculty in the same situation, and that not many of
them could receive the promotion. Who was to decide?
There was no seniority rule as in the army or the navy,
no responsible committee to examine his record and
determine on his claim against that of the nineteen
others. All depended upon the judgment, whim or
prejudice rather, of that one old man who stood between
the faculty with its clamorous desires for promotion and
equipment and enlargement of work and the Board of
Trustees, who had control of the resources of the university. As a matter of form these decisions were
referred to a select committee of the Board, but they
rarely if ever acted contrary to the president's recommendation. "Make him responsible—he ought to know,"
was their reaction.

In all the years during which he had been connected
with the university Clavercin had never had such a clear
insight into the system of the institution as this Saturday
morning in the president's office. Here in epitome was
the drama of American university life, in the figures of
these mature, intelligent—in some cases, like Dexter, distinguished men,—sitting in a row in the black office
chairs, like clerks waiting for their chance to defend
themselves and their life effort before the autocrat of
their destinies.

It was amazing, it was preposterous, he thought as he
gathered up his coat and hat and satchel of books, that
an old man of mediocre natural ability should have such
complete control over the fate of several hundred members of a faculty, many of whom were his superior in
character and ability. Nowhere else in the entire modern
world it seemed to Clavercin was there such an example
of pure autocracy as in the American university. Not
even in the great business corporations where the president was responsible not merely to a board of directors
but to a large number of stockholders, and was tested
day by day by the results he obtained. In a university,

outside of the faculty, nobody knew anything about the results the president was getting, and the faculty was powerless, except to gossip and grumble. He tried to think why it had come to this point of one man control, for it had not always been like this, and he concluded that it was because the trustees self-chosen to care for the university funds were busy and ignorant men, depending on their agent to inform them and to administer their great trust.

Outside the administration building students were strolling over the campus on their way to "classes" or "lab", or lolling about the benches discussing their own affairs. Around the entrance to Founder's Hall was the usual eddy of instructors and students, in which Clavercin encountered Caxton and Beckwith on their way to a meeting of the curriculum committee, which after a number of years of abeyance was functioning again. With his quick sense of the dramatic Clavercin recounted to these two old friends his interview with the president and the scene in the outer office of waiting supplicants.

"It's incredible!" he exclaimed at the end. "Think of the power that palsied old Donothing wields, over the destinies of several thousand human beings, counting both students and faculty, apportioning the income of twenty or thirty or forty millions of dollars. No prelate or feudal lord ever had a more complete sway. . . What we need is a revolution, right here and now!"

He looked across at the peaceable groups of students. "And if we all realized the absurdity of it that is what we should try for, first to throw out Donothing and then to inaugurate some sort of faculty rule."

"It's been tried before," Caxton said, "and has never succeeded. They fight among themselves for the spoils."

"At least there ought to be some appeal from the decisions of a president to the Board."

"No strong president will permit that," Caxton smiled wanly. "Just wait—Dolittle is near the end of his tether. I am told the younger trustees are getting tired of him and mean to retire him as soon as they can find a successor."

"And what is he to be like?" Clavercin asked. "Are we to be consulted in his choice?"

Beckwith laughed with gusto.

"Of course he's to be Lord Sanderson if not the Little President! . . . Better come into my labor college. No autocracy there!"

"And no salaries," Caxton gibed, with the weariness of the scholar who has already spent over half his vital years in patient waiting for an opportunity to do his own work.

"Yes, we are going to pay something," Beckwith assured them. "Not much of course, at first. But as labor wakes up and the union leaders realize what we are doing for their men the money will come fast enough. . . . At any rate the work is alive. They want it. No pounding your stuff into the closed minds of a lot of lazy undergraduates or feeding desiccated graduates material for their theses!"

This was Beckwith's way of keeping his spirit alive, his absorption in the new labor college for which he recruited teachers among the younger men in the university. He dreamed of its becoming a new and vital form of education, supplanting more and more the older universities, leaving them to sink into the desuetude of institutional routine, retreats for the children of privilege. . . . But that goal, Clavercin felt was a long way off in a dubious future, and he had no special enthusiasm for educating labor youth into a position of vantage. Education, the university, should lie outside that controversy.

"Come on into the meeting," Beckwith urged, seizing Clavercin by the arm, "and help us lick the science and business crowd. They've got a rotten scheme for . . . ."

For they were at it again, the revision of the curriculum, what Beckwith called "the second phase of the Thirty Years' War between Science and Culture." Old Tom Bayberry, now quite frail and looking forward to his retirement, sat through the long wrangles in the committee with a queer expression on his wizened face, now and then taking off his spectacles to rub his tired eyes and hide a smile. Although he was supposed to represent the classics in this eternal battle, taking the place of that stout campaigner Langdon, recently retired, Bayberry said little except to remark occasionally in a gently ironic voice,—"Gentlemen, they were saying just the same thing twenty years ago!" The younger men, especially the science group, who under the leadership of the chemist Pillbury led the present attack, listened respectfully to Bayberry's irony, then repeated their futilities.

This time it was "the group system" that the scientists advocated as against "the lax elective system" that had been in vogue since the founding of the university. The elective system, it was asserted, did not favor "concentration". Thirty years ago the elective system had been the novel, the advanced idea in education, by means of which the young mind was to be presented with such a dazzling array of intellectual dishes as to tempt him to eat something even against his will. The feast was prodigally extended before him in the thick pages of the university catalogue. But an increasing dissatisfaction with the results of this freedom of choice had grown among parents, faculty, the students themselves, as the numbers of idle students with their motor cars parked about the campus and their noisy fraternity houses increased year after year.

The Harris idea had been to extend the elective system democratically downwards by university extension courses so that as Clavercin once remarked,—"Any stenographer reading a novel on her way to the office might in the course of time pick up enough university credits to apply for a degree." All that sort of popularizing of education was falling into disrepute: the word now was quality, and the rounded graduate. So for the past year a carefully selected committee of the faculty had been working over a plan for regrouping all courses of instruction in an intricate scheme, each group presenting supposably a possible perfect education for some type of student mind. It was simple enough to make these groups in the rough. But as each group was supposed to include some general or "cultural" subjects to balance the "major" subject in the harmonious ideal of a complete education, all sorts of animosities and personal spites broke out between the representatives of the different groups. Was one course in psychology equivalent to a survey course in literature? The earnest professor of ethics almost tearfully besought the Committee not to neglect the study of philosophy, not to permit youth to leave the university without knowing what the greatest minds of all times had thought. After listening this warm afternoon to several hours of this display of the mediæval mind, Beckwith delivered himself caustically. First he sketched graphically the ancient and the mediæval conception of education, and the liberation of the human mind at the Renaissance, "which has proceeded steadily until the present day."

"What we are trying to do here," he concluded, "is to revert to the mediæval notion of the perfect education. We are trying again to square the circle, discover the impossible, an ideal education for every kind of human mind that comes into the university net. Our old way was safer because it permitted minds to discover for themselves their own salvation. We dislike the results because many of them remain as they were born, empty. So we are trying once more to play the part of Providence for the young. We set up a series of complete educations, like so many 'club' breakfasts on a bill of fare and say to the student, 'Choose! Each one of these menus has the requisite number of calories, the same amount of vitamins.' We have assembled here a deal of statistical information as to what our students have elected over the recent years, and we have had much expert opinion from the deans as to the results and from educational authorities as to what effect each sort of diet will have on the human mind. As grown men in a real world we should be ashamed of ourselves for wasting time over such a futile, such an unreal task. The day of the quadrium and trivium is definitely past. Nobody knows what is a perfect, a complete, an ideal education for another human being. No body of men can set up a standard of what educates and what doesn't. The human mind has long since broken from the theories of life which permitted any such formulation of the claims of knowledge. . . . It makes little difference what we decide here, how many slices of this or that subject Eureka will require for a degree. We shall be doing it all over a few years hence on an entirely new and equally erroneous basis—"

"What may I ask Professor Beckwith would he prescribe for the degree?" the dapper Little President interposed.

"Nothing!" Beckwith snapped back. "I would abandon the meaningless custom of giving degrees, which are nothing but certificates of residence, of value only to those who seek jobs."

"Gentlemen," said President Dolittle, who had been slumbering in the chair, it being one of the occasions when he presided in person, "do you wish to continue this pointless discussion or are you ready to vote?"

Beckwith turning his back on the president spoke directly to the members of the faculty.

"Yes, we shall vote the report and try the new system. But we all know that it will have no influence

on the future of education, as I have so often heard
it magnoeloquently asserted here. There is no known
method of discovering the ideal human education.
The most efficient education to-day is not being given
in our universities. It is being dug out of public
libraries, night lectures, technical journals, laboratories,
wherever a hungry mind can discover for itself—"

"Gentlemen," Dolittle's voice broke in irritably.

"One moment more, Mr. Dolittle," Beckwith remarked scornfully over his shoulder. "I do not often
waste the valuable time of this faculty. The gist of
what I have to say is this: under the disguise of a new
curriculum on the group plan certain departments in
the university are trying to boost their own wares.
Why not put the question plainly so that we may all
know what we are voting for? Do we want to turn
Eureka University into a trade school, for the study of
business administration, journalism, pedagogy, and so
forth? Why not be honest, if we do, and tell the world
that we are engaged here solely in showing the student
how to get a job?"

"Question! Question!" came angrily from different
corners of the room. Beckwith sat down, an amused
smile on his red face.

The committee voted overwhelmingly for the report.
Sanderson encountering Beckwith in the hall greeted
him affably, "Great speech, old man! It gave us our
majority!"

A smile twitched the ends of his little blonde mustache.

"That's precisely what I meant to do," Beckwith
rejoined, drawing out his watch to see if he could make
the next express to the city so that he could attend a
meeting of the council of the Labor Party, which seemed
to him so much more real than the vote of the Curriculum Committee.

Before the new group system of studies could be put into effect, which was to fashion at last the perfectly educated and efficient American gentleman, hustler and leader, prophet and sage and man of action,—before in fact the general faculty had finished its wrangle over the committee's report,—something had happened in the world which made the chatter about the proper ration between cultural and professional studies seem futile even to the faculty of Eureka.

CHAPTER FOUR

When Clavercin received Jessica's curt invitation to
accompany her to the Colorado mountains where she
had taken a cabin at a boarding-house ranch, he had
a sensation of surprise and quick response. There was
little, however, in the dry note to arouse elation. "If
you want to escape this dead town," she wrote in her
firm, small hand, "why not come out to the mountains
with me next week? Bring some work along as I shall
be busy with proof." It was like Jessica to propose
such a jaunt, dropping her suggestion casually without
concern for conventional implications, and it was also
like Jessica to guard cautiously her own independence.
It was what she called a promising "combination",
which had entered her mind when Constance Fenton
announced that she was going to an island on Lake
Huron with Louise Clavercin and the children in August
while Beaman stayed in the city completing a book.
Jessica thought that Clavercin would like the mountain
life and might prove companionable. She got a sense
of adventure from such impromptu "combinations". . .
"I am taking the afternoon train on Thursday. Bring
riding clothes," she concluded.

Probably she did not give the matter another thought
during the intervening week, but Clavercin while making
his preparations for the outing speculated vaguely about the
trip. At last, he felt, he might penetrate the mystery of
this enigmatic personality that had intrigued him all
these years. . . . When he passed through the Pull-
mans looking for Jessica and not finding her anywhere,
he had a nervous disappointment—she might have

missed the train or changed her mind and neglected
to let him know! As he returned to his seat he discovered her in a compartment behind a little table
covered with strips of proof. "I'll be through in a
moment," she said to him with a little nod of recognition, making a correction on the sheet in her hand.
Clavercin waited, smiling in amusement at the picture
she made. Surrounded by papers, open books, and proof
that she had pulled hastily out of a travelling case,
she looked like any serious lawyer employing his leisure
time on the train by going over his case. Her glasses
had slipped towards the end of her small nose and
her hair had escaped from the tight hat she was wearing over her ears. Yet in spite of her masculine industry and the disorder of her person she was indubit-
ably dainty and attractive, unmistakably feminine.
It was this subtle combination of male and female elements in her that made Jessica so interesting, so unusual,
Clavercin decided.

"There!" Jessica sighed, her eye running down the
long slip of proof. "Have you a cigarette?" She
pushed aside the mass of books and papers on the opposite seat to make room for Clavercin, and smiled at
him sunnily.

"I thought you weren't on the train," he remarked.

"I never miss trains. . . . I take a compartment so
that I can work and smoke when I want to," she
explained. "I don't like joggling about platforms or
sitting in the stuffy woman's room when I want a cigarette. Sometimes I go into the smoker, but that seems
to disturb the American man in his privacy. . . . This
is very pleasant!" she sighed, looking at the fields of
tall corn through which the train was clamorously rushing. "I always like a train, especially when it is headed
west, and tomorrow morning we'll be in the mountains.
You've never been there?"

Clavercin shook his head.

"Always go the other way when I get the chance," he explained.

"That's a mistake," Jessica pronounced thoughtfully, removing the cigarette from its holder with care. "Nothing freshens one like the mountains—and not too many people about! . . . What are you doing, your book?"

Clavercin explained somewhat wearily the collection of plays that he was editing for a publisher in response to the demand from colleges for texts of modern plays.

"There are so many things to consider, it's difficult to select the plays that will be understood and not shock our American prejudices," he said.

Jessica reflected a little while, then remarked,—

"But that's just what I should do, if I were doing such a book,—shock their prejudices!"

"And the publishers?"

Jessica shrugged her shoulders indifferently.

"Anyhow I want to do my own plays," Clavercin went on. "This is merely a pot-boiler, an academic pot-boiler," he iterated disgustedly.

"It's all pot-boiling," Jessica commented robustly, "except scholarship—and there isn't much of that. . . . Perhaps you'll write a play at the ranch!"

She smoked another cigarette reflectively. That was one of Jessica's peculiarities that she apparently thought seriously about what was said to her, and thinking made her silent, unresponsive for the moment. Clavercin watching her in this reflective pause felt that they had changed rôles in some fashion: she was the academic person, the man, while he was the receptive and creative person, the woman. Jessica he realised was somehow less concerned with him as a person than with the general social situation of the writer, the producer, trying to place the problem of his activity and existence in one of the categories of her well ordered mind.

"You've got a subject?" she asked.

"For a play? . . They are everywhere—you are one!" Clavercin laughed.

Jessica frowned inquiringly.

"I see you sitting here with your books and proof as the most significant sort of a subject," he continued gayly, improvising.

"All right," she replied, "I'll let you have myself for subject," and she gave a puzzled laugh. "And now I must get back to my proof!"

With a little gesture of dismissal she put her glasses back on her nose and took up another long slip from the pile beside her. "Shut the door, please," she admonished him as he departed.

Instead of taking out his own manuscript Clavercin went into the smoking car and over his pipe thought about his companion. Eureka might regard their journey together as an elopement, but it was not to be the kind of elopement that the EUREKA THUNDERER served up every morning with such relish. Later they had dinner and then smoked and talked in the compartment until Jessica again resumed her proof correction, with the excuse,— "I can't really play until I get this thing off!"

But after the proof there were notes to be collated, an article for the "Journal" written, and incidentally a lot of belated reading to be accomplished. Clavercin found that his companion was a very persistent worker, saving womanwise of the many idle moments which men usually waste in dawdling. The four weeks spent at the mountain ranch were only incidentally recreational. Clavercin felt obliged to work while Jessica was shut up in her cabin and thus not only got through the pot-boiling job he had on hand, but also blocked in his play, which fancifully he called THE SCHOLAR. "A new sort of scholar," he explained to Jessica, "not the usual stage product— one who turns scholarship into living.". . .

Late in the afternoon as the sun was slowly sinking in a cloudless sky above the mountain ridge Jessica emerged from her cabin in riding breeches ready for an excursion, and they set forth on one of the trails. The long hours of work behind her, Jessica was prepared for enjoyment and gave to it the same singleness of purpose that she put into her writing or laboratory investigation. She wanted to be amused or entertained and let her companion perceive that he was expected to satisfy her fastidious requirements. If she did not care for what he had to offer, she touched her horse and closed the topic by a long canter.

"You shut the door in one's face," Clavercin protested.

"When you are too prying," she replied with a little smile.

"But I want to know so many things!"

"That isn't the way to know—watch!"

They talked of his play, which was to be a comedy, and of the university, which was its background with the different personalities they both were familiar with.

"Just let 'em act out their ideas, behavioristically, and you won't get into trouble," Jessica counselled sagely. "Nobody knows when he's giving himself away in his conduct, but if you let 'em talk their ideas you will repeat the clichés and each one will tag himself."

The scholar woman, the chief character in the play, was to interpret the creed of absolute individualism in conflict with conventions.

"You must make her wise as well as clever," Jessica insisted. "Don't let her just exploit her antagonisms like the suffrage crowd: make her accomplish!"

And from that they wandered off into a discussion of the theory of living, which left them both thoughtful.

"You've left no place for feeling," Clavercin commented.

Jessica shrugged her small shoulders.

"There's been too much of that, in women's lives."

"Or too little!"

"Women are forever exploiting their emotions, and

those of others. . . . Besides I don't admit that if they
learn to use their minds, objectively, they will lose the
power to feel. But their feelings won't mess up their
lives and leave them flabby in middle age as so often
happens to them."

She smiled ironically at Clavercin's puzzled face.
Pointing to the distant view she remarked with sincere joy,—"That's great—the endless space! . . . That's
what I like most here, the long, long reaches of mesa
and mountain."

Thus she indicated another field of emotion than the
one which romantically filled his mind. They rode home
silently side by side. Clavercin thought much more
about his companion than she did about him. Her
mind as usual had departed on a solitary path which
she followed persistently to its end. He was thinking,
"Is her dislike for the personal, the subjective in life
merely a wholesome fear of sentimentality, the loose
emotionalism that has characterised women's intercourse with men—or is it a fundamental lack of the
emotional impulse in her?" . . .

"Why do you suppose those people at the ranch, the
college bred ones as well as the ones without college
degrees, all have the same flavor, like the soup?" she
remarked after a time. "Mr. Hopp, the lawyer with a
degree from Michigan, is just as uncouth as Parkers,
the flour mill man. Why doesn't the university do
something to their minds?"

"Because," Clavercin retorted quickly, linking the
observation with his own meditations, "the distinction
isn't a purely mental one. It's of the spirit, and the
spirit of the modern American university is precisely
the same as that of the market place. We haven't
anything special to give our graduates to distinguish
them from those without what we pompously call
'the advantages of a college education'. So they taste
all alike."

"Perhaps," Jessica replied dubiously. "But I think it is because the university fails to train their minds."

She was suspicious of the word "spirit". Too commonly it was used to cover vague and loose thought.

In spite of Jessica's impersonal habit of mind and the rigid devotion to work which she imposed, with the passing weeks came an increased sense of intimacy between the two. Clavercin disliking Jessica's purely mental attitude admitted that she was an excellent companion and playfellow, and that in their desultory conversations they had covered much of the ground of human relations without becoming self-involved.

As the time drew near for their parting, Jessica relaxed somewhat her impersonal discipline. "You are very understanding," she said with a flickering smile as they returned to her cabin after an evening walk, and with a slight caress she left him, startled, uncertain. It was as if another being within her, long repressed, held down by her uncompromising mind had suddenly escaped its bonds, a shy, childlike being awkward in expression. Thereafter Clavercin watched for the emergence of this hidden being, which had again been thrust back into obscurity.

"Why do you kill your emotions?" he demanded impatiently. "You've been doing it all your life I believe, deliberately killing them."

"I don't feel natural when I express them your way," she admitted, "in words."

But she was willing to listen to the creed of the romanticist as Clavercin poured it forth in reckless intensity,—the search for whatever might "extend life".

"You," he said accusingly, "think you are sufficient in yourself, your mind is all! . . . You have never given yourself to anything or any person."

"No," she said with a note of pride.

"You've experimented with love, no doubt," he threw

out at random, thinking darkly of the rumors about Rudolf Sheimer.

"Yes!" she admitted tranquilly. "It doesn't last."

"And you suggested this vacation as another experiment!"

She laughed almost gayly, at his reproach.

"I thought it might be a successful combination— and it has been, hasn't it?"

"Afterwards we go back to where we were?"

"Perhaps . . . Romance can't last long."

"So like a man you take a holiday now and then from your serious preoccupations, experiment a little with emotions, and then—forget it?"

"Something like that," she agreed readily.

"Do they satisfy, your diversions?"

"Not for long, but nothing emotional does really satisfy one for long."

And they were silent with their own thoughts. She would have him believe that hers was the perfected, civilised type of woman, untrammeled by prejudices, obligations, sentimentalities, with a disciplined mind that stripped every illusion from the human complex. . . . And yet there was the flickering smile, the shy caress of the little hand that denied her theory, her boast.

"Jessica," he said sombrely, "ours must be no philandering expedition. Nothing or all!"

She bent her head as if in acquiescence, then smiled mischievously.

"I suspect," he continued, "that all your life you have been searching for something lost, inside, something that would release you and let you live. . . . Most of us are engaged on that quest. Only you have tried to achieve with your mind—and have failed."

She nodded.

"We'll try something different, shall we?"

She was submissive, like a curious child, almost humble and very gentle.

"Jessica!" he cried tenderly.

The next morning Jessica met him at the breakfast table with her accustomed impassive expression. She opened a telegram, read it, considered a few moments, then remarked,—

"The children are coming out—they get here tomorrow night. . . . I'd like to have you see them. The boy is all right, going along in his school well enough. . . . But the girl! . . . I can't make anything of her—she's like every other girl."

Clavercin smiled.

He was sitting before the ranch house that evening when the two children arrived by the stage. The boy was fair-haired, slim, dark-eyed, like his father, with his father's quick response to his surroundings. The girl was slight for her fourteen years and very pale. She ran across the lawn and put her arms demonstratively around her mother. Jessica half turned her face so that the girl's kiss slid off the corner of her mouth to her cheek. To make up for the rebuff she patted her daughter's head. Clavercin divined Jessica's distaste for her daughter's effusiveness, also the girl's quick withdrawal at the emotional check. Mentally he compared this greeting with Louise's effusiveness over her young, which often made him uncomfortable because of its superficiality. . . .

The arrival of the young Mallorys made little change in Jessica's habits and pursuits. She questioned the boy closely about his term at the eastern school, saw that he got a safe horse and a guide and left him to make his own plans with his sister and the other young people at the ranch. Occasionally she joined Clavercin at tennis with the boy and girl.

"I put them on their own," Jessica explained succinctly to Clavercin, "as much as I can. I arranged to have them meet me here instead of waiting for them in Eureka so that they would have the experience of making the journey all the way from the east on their own responsibility."

Jessica, of course, had a carefully thought out theory of the whole matter, and acted up to it conscientiously. Nevertheless Clavercin after a few days of the family atmosphere, while admitting the excellent ideals felt an aridity, a lack of spontaneity created by Jessica's efforts to "keep the children from getting soft," as she put it. Reacting strongly from the "lazy mindedness" of the day she sought in every way to sharpen the intelligence of her young, letting their feelings take care of themselves. "There is a good geologist here, a man from the state university with whom I have arranged to take Ned on his hikes," she announced triumphantly at breakfast one morning.

There was German conversation before breakfast for May. So it went through the brief vacation in the mountains which the children were to spend with their mother. Clavercin in his talks with the children gathered that they liked their schools, felt more at home in them than in the Eureka house, and he did not wonder at it. There must have been something chilly in the impersonal atmosphere created by Jessica's rigid discipline. Yet both of the children were obviously proud of their mother, not only of her youthfulness but of her professional accomplishment.

"You know mother is terribly important," little May confided to Clavercin, "but we have a better time when we take trips with Father—he doesn't keep us always in school."

That was the phrase. Jessica would like to keep not only herself but the whole world at school all the time.

"Don't you ever let up?" Clavercin demanded laughingly one glorious afternoon when Jessica rose as usual to return to her cabin for work, the few minutes she gave to idleness and a cigarette after meals being finished.

Jessica did not understand what he meant at first.

"But I like my work most!" she protested.

"And the rest of us must take what we can get?"

Jessica did not reply. That, she had found, was a
convenient method of avoiding futile discussions about
"the imponderables", which quite literally did not count
for her. . . .

And so, returning alone to Eureka from the mountains,
Clavercin smiled as he recalled the romantic aspirations
that had lurked in the background of his consciousness
when he had set forth on this journey five weeks before.
If it had been a lovers' journey it was the strangest one
he could imagine and would be difficult to make intelli-
gible to another. His vacation had been profitable: the
pot-boiling text was finished and the bulky sheets of
THE SCHOLAR were also in his bag. He had an odd
sense of intimacy with the two children, especially with
little May, that he had not reached with their mother.
May, he suspected was acquiring data about her mother
which later she would employ in making her own account
with life, and not at all in accord with Jessica's theories.
Little May had her own charm, not so different from
Jessica's, but she would put it to quite other uses. That,
Clavercin reflected, was the curious method of nature
between the generations by action and reaction: the un-
intellectual background of the thread business had
brought out Jessica's intellectualism, and her own professional distinction would no doubt create in little May
a most domestic and sensitive woman, craving the very
qualities her mother's austerity had denied her youth.

Austerity! That was the note of Jessica Mallory. She
was the puritan reincarnated without religious faith.
She was austere with herself, with her family, with
Mallory of course, with all the world (so far as she
recognised an outside world). She would be austere
with a lover! Clavercin was uncertain whether he might
be put in the latter category, so austere had Jessica's
dealings with him been thus far. He had no doubt of

her liking for him, as a companion, "flexible" and "understanding" as she put it, and no doubt at all of his love for her. Her very reticencies and withholdings had whetted his imagination, and he found her clear intelligence extraordinarily stimulating. He had more will to do as well as more to think about and more "leads" for his imagination than for years past. "Mountain air works marvels," he said with a laugh. . . . He could even contemplate returning to the university without that sickening droop which the end of a vacation usually brought. Something had crystallised within him, a purpose, out of this fresh engagement with life. He had spoken to Jessica of taking a leave of absence in the spring and going to a little Alpine village he remembered to do over this new play. And Jessica had said something about an international congress of psychologists to be held in London the coming spring. Life for the moment seemed full of openings, less a matter of routine than it had six weeks before. Yet when he asked himself definitely what had happened in the Colorado mountains, there was little tangible that he could recall. Emotionally Jessica was as elusive as she was mentally definite. She had committed herself to nothing, except a pleasant "combination", and in less buoyant mood Clavercin asked himself if she ever could or would want to commit herself emotionally to any passion. That might be the price she had paid for her extraordinary control of herself, the price the intellectual was always paying for his clearer perceptions. Something habitually starved by his habit of life finally faded away. That was why university households had the meagre, forlorn air that too often they assumed, not because of lack of means to enjoy living, but because of the feeble sap that flowed dully through the veins of men and women professionally dedicated to the intellectual life. Few of his colleagues had a hearty, robust physique, the sense of physical enjoyment: they did not need the tissue. And still fewer had any passion about living, of any sort. It was not good form in polite academic circles to be passionate. Was this lack of passion, of physical and emotional virility, the reason why the vulgar public suspected university men, did not take the profession wholly seriously? Very likely. The professor was not frequently a whole man, and the unthinking, the instinctive person recognised his essential lack.

Yet scholarship to be enduring must be creative, must be based on all human faculties, emotional as well as mental, and the few great scholars whom Clavercin had known proved it. Learning to become productive must have within it the vital stir, compact of perception and imagination: must be creative. The mere accumulation of fact, the ingenuous composition of theory— "grains of sand"—Jessica had called her laboratory activity, was not enough. . . . "If I had the moulding of a university," Clavercin mused, "I would look for hearty men, good livers and lovers, passionate men, who thought with their whole being, not merely with their minds. . . . I'd get rid of the ascetic idea.". . .

Jessica certainly was not ascetic. In her own opinion she was a good Epicurean, daintily and discriminatingly selecting the viands of life. She was fond of the theatre, in a less degree of music and poetry. She liked to have Clavercin accompany her to plays and concerts. "I think more about plays with you," she said appreciatively. And they became closer, more like lovers under the stimulus of ideas that when on rare occasions they spent an evening alone in talk. Jessica, Clavercin divined, needed another temperament through which to enjoy. By herself she was unfertile. Scoffing often at her lover's "romanticism", nevertheless she needed the very element she scorned to wake in her a latent capacity to enjoy.

"Mother thinks too much," little May once said.

"She kills the fun of things." Such the drastic verdict of youth, even if only half true! . . .

As they came from the opera one night, the last resounding chords of "Siegfried" still reverberating, Clavercin pressed the thin arm beneath his murmuring,—

"You do need *me*."

"Indeed I never doubted it," Jessica admitted honestly.

CHAPTER FIVE

Jessica liked giving herself and her circle surprises: she would disappear from her workshop and from the university, turning up after a time in some unexpected quarter of the world where inclination or an opportunity for study had tempted her. Such furtive "getaways" satisfied her theories of personal independence as well as a latent craving for adventure. Nothing gave her a more immediate sense of triumph, of outwitting the world, circumventing tyranny, than to find herself in a Pullman compartment or on a steamer or in some large hotel remote from all claims, all supervision. Then she felt the same elation that a college youth has in his first spree: she shook her tiny hand at the proprieties. Now that she had given up long since any active participation in social life, in the usual avenues of activity, confining herself more and more intensively to her laboratory and her work, she was free to indulge this habit, for the children were ordinarily safely disposed in their schools, and Edgar was absorbed in his efficient activities, which had grown more numerous with the years. Just now he spent most of his time in Washington over the Larson Foundation. Jessica disliked Washington and saw no good reason why she should immure herself there in the home of all faded conventions. For that matter Edgar was seemingly content to live in an agreeable club. Thus her immediate family disposed of, each member busily occupied with his own affairs and independent of the rest, Jessica was free to roam much as she pleased.

She carried her work always with her, in a worn bag stuffed with books and papers. It was never long out

of her mind. Thus she maintained a continuity of
mental background which the idle traveler loses, and
received no agitating shocks from the frequent disloca-
tions of her environment. She could lose herself as
wholly in a bare hotel bedroom in the intricacy of some
problem as in her laboratory, perhaps more so. And
her "work"—sacred symbol—furnished the necessary
moral stability for a spirit essentially puritanical that
otherwise might have disintegrated in the release of all
obligation. Jessica not only loved her work more than
anything in life: she clung to it as a solvent faith, after
rejecting one by one all the more ordinary faiths of her
fellows. Like all faiths it was based on temperamental
inclination and in the last analysis was unrational.
Rudolph Sheimer, whose great influence on her mind
Jessica always recognised, had done much to formulate
this religion of work, to invest it with the sanctity of
science.

Early in their intimacy Jessica let Clavercin understand that nothing, certainly no love relation, might interfere with her work.

"My work," she said a little defiantly, as if she were
defending something sacred from a suspected inter-
ference, "is more important in my life than anything
else can be."

"Say than I am!" he laughed dryly.

"No, than anything," she iterated. "I'd never let
anything interfere with it. . . . It is more important to
me than any person, any relation could be."

After a long pause Clavercin remarked,—

"I don't see that there need be any clash."

"There need not be," she admitted, "but there often
is. Usually it is the woman whose egotism demands
sacrifices from the man, but the man too likes to believe
that his lovemaking is a woman's chief occupation! . . .
What would you think of a man who would put his
love interest before his work?"

"There ought not to be any conflict," Clavercin repeated weakly, feeling that there was a profound chasm somewhere between their natures on this essential matter.

The discussion closed with Clavercin's yielding the point and accompanying Jessica to London where a scientific meeting in which she was interested was to be held instead of "cutting all that out and going directly to the Continent," as he had rashly proposed. . . . Once away from Eureka, however, Jessica was more ready to enjoy than ever before. After the daily sessions of the congress the two went sightseeing and spent the evenings at theatres and concerts. They had a few idyllic hours at Bath, and then Jessica packed Clavercin off to Switzerland, promising to join him after she had exhausted certain opportunities at Cambridge which she desired to explore alone. He went ruefully, somewhat rebelliously, yet with a secret amusement over the situation, and dutifully scouted about until he found what he thought might charm Jessica in a little villa outside of Lausanne. He described its advantages so glowingly that Jessica arrived the next week. She brought with her a typist and announced that a young Englishman she had run across in Cambridge who was making some brilliant experiments in animal psychology might turn up any day for a visit. Thus they settled down to an industrious existence beside the Swiss lake. . . .

"I don't pretend to know how you put it over," Clavercin said with a touch of ironic amusement in his voice, as they sat on the terrace of the little villa in the lingering twilight. "But you do extraordinarily! Get your own way without any rumpus, make us all follow your tune."

Jessica smoked ruminatively as if she were giving this light observation as much attention as any new theory.

"Perhaps because I let the other fellow do as he pleases, too," she remarked amiably.

It was true: Jessica never made claims, never expected subjection. She wanted her own way, always, but if another's way conflicted with hers all she wanted was quietly to be allowed to take her own path!

"Don't you admit the possibility of a common way?" he asked.

"What's this?"

He looked over the neatly gravelled path that separated the small *pension* where he had his quarters from the villa garden and smiled. Their relation of comradely independence completely embodied Jessica's theory of sex relations.

"This is very pleasant," she sighed, rising from her seat and strolling across the little garden towards the lake.

They were passengers so to speak in the same boat, a comfortable one. There was nothing cramping, nothing permanent, nothing inhibiting in their responsibilities— and from Clavercin's point of view nothing creative in their relationship. It was like an agreeable dinner party *à deux*, or an excursion to a picturesque scene, or an hour at an opera. It was not life. For Jessica life went on in her head, in her "work", and she expected that her companion would carry on his own satisfying existence as she did hers. . . .

In the weeks that followed the outlines of their situation deepened but did not change, and they continued a friendly struggle, a running debate upon the matter.

"What you really want," she said scoffingly, "is just old-fashioned marriage. Run right home to Eureka!"

"Call it whatever you like," he grumbled, "there is more than this—if you want it!"

But he must admit that what they were having was stimulating and enticing if not all that his romantic imagination could conceive of a complete union of heart and mind. Jessica, although a bit of a prig and an indubitable intellectual, had sufficient personal interest to make the best of her delicate beauty. She offered a constantly charming picture and her very withdrawals of herself whetted curiosity. After a year of increasing intimacy there was nothing wholly known in her, nothing commonplace from repetition.

His play went rapidly. He read the scenes aloud as he finished them and although Jessica did not often agree with his thesis and never gave facile praise, her careful consideration of every line became the subtlest flattery. . . . Occasionally they made excursions to the celebrated shrines within reach. One of Clavercin's offices was to prepare fastidiously the program for these holidays and a success in avoiding fatigue or boredom gave him a curious sense of triumph. Jessica elicited all her companion's abilities to entertain her. And only rarely did he ask himself the stark question what might be her return for the constant thought he gave to her comfort and pleasure. Like the lady of old whose "exploiting habits" she condemned, Jessica would have replied coolly, "Am I not enough?" Or, "If it doesn't amuse you to please me, why take the pains to do it?" Her ultimate card so obviously held in reserve was indifference, the willingness to withdraw completely into her own sufficiency.

"Do you think you *can* love?" Clavercin once asked her abruptly.

To which after due consideration, she replied sincerely,—

"Yes, but not perhaps what you would call love, a kind of mystic absorption in another. . . . No, not that—ever!"

One lovely day on their return from an afternoon on the lake Clavercin reading out items from the Lausanne paper came upon an account of the assassination of the Austrian Archduke. "I wonder what that means," he commented, but Jessica evincing little interest as usual in political happenings he passed on to other matters.

Living much alone as they did, occupied by their work, Clavercin absorbed in his companion, and in the growing drama between them, they passed through the intervening weeks almost to August without being aware of the sultry European atmosphere. When Clavercin remarked at breakfast one morning, "It looks as if they were really going to war," Jessica replied,—"They are mad, just mad." Clavercin was sufficiently disturbed to go to Lausanne; he returned full of astounding news, which he related breathlessly.

"If there is to be a war," Jessica remarked casually, "we'd better be getting out of this place as soon as possible."

"Where to?"

"America I suppose," Jessica replied in an annoyed tone. She disliked to have her plans disarranged even by a war.

"Eureka!" Clavercin murmured. A picture of the white concrete walks between the familiar buildings, the dingy class rooms, the mustiness of stale food in the faculty club where over mussed tables his colleagues were no doubt debating the news of the European war, flashed suddenly across Clavercin's vision. He had given the university hardly a thought since he had left it four months before. If it had not been for this amazing event he would not have thought of it for another two months, at least. Slowly he posed the question,—

"But why go back—at all?"

Jessica gave him a long dark look. Through her mind there passed the memory of another occasion when a similar suggestion had been made to her. This time she did not hesitate, saying with a slight shrug of her shoulders;

"Of course I must go back. . . . And I could not carry on my work here, if they really get to fighting."

Thus pointedly she shifted the discussion from the plane of sentiment or passion to a reasonable practicality. Clavercin flushed, and remained silent. This was all it meant to her! He should have known it. . . .

"I suppose I ought to send a cable," she said at last. Clavercin went out to cable for her, and when he came back he found Jessica sitting beside the reading lamp, revising some recent notes.

"Any more news?" she asked casually.

"Lots," he said curtly, reading to himself the brief items of telegraphic news in the local paper. German troops had entered Belgium—it was real, then. And Jessica tranquilly revised her notes on certain animal reactions! . . .

They fought their way slowly into Italy through mobs of hysterical holiday makers trying to flee from Europe as from the plague. They were nearly three days on the train to Genoa. Jessica stood the fatigue remarkably because she was alertly interested in the spectacle of mob behavior. The war, Clavercin realised, meant almost nothing to her, just an incomprehensible outbreak of fury. But as a psychologist endeavoring to penetrate with a scientific method the dark places of human conduct, she was vividly alive to the abundant "material" offered to her in this dolorous journey. She got Clavercin to buy her a fresh notebook which she rapidly filled with her small script. She listened vacantly to his report of the news, his talk about the war, his denunciation of Germany. That meant nothing to her, apparently.

When at last they reached Genoa they had to wait a week in a hotel swarming with terrified Americans until passage could be secured in a ship sailing for the United States. Clavercin obtained a single berth by bribing a steamship agent. When he told Jessica she asked,—

"And what will you do?"

"I am not going back," he said abruptly, "at least not yet."

"But you will not be able to write over here in all this confusion!"

"I suppose not," he said looking at his companion with a slight smile. "Does it ever occur to you, Jessica, that there might be something else in life besides writing plays or making psychological investigations?"

Jessica Mallory did not reply to this direct question. She tranquilly finished her cigarette, then went to her room to pack her bag.

Clavercin bought some blankets and pillows to make the hole that Jessica must occupy for the voyage more comfortable, also a huge basket of fruit and wine. Although she seemed remote from him as a human being, ever since the news of the war had reached them, nevertheless he could not quickly get over the habit of looking after her comfort, of tending her. Whether his attentions, his constant care for her, meant anything to Jessica he did not know, any better than he knew what was the nature of her interest in him. As he stood on the stone quay watching the steamer slowly back into the harbor, his eyes riveted to the tall slender figure with a bright scarf wound about her head on the upper deck, he decided almost with indifference that he had been merely a convenience to Jessica, a sort of animated automaton, an improved "courier-maid". . . . Had any man ever been anything more to Jessica?

As he made his way slowly back to Geneva against the tide of fugitives, he thought occasionally of his companion sailing back to "home", to Eureka and Edgar Mallory, to her laboratory and wondered at the strange metamorphosis that a few brief days had wrought in his emotional life, and in his understanding of Jessica. Not that he flattered himself that he understood her even now! But he saw her, at least in relation with himself, without that veil of romance which he had tried so persistently for a year and a half to throw around her. The war might well dwarf all such personal pre-occupations so that they faded from the foreground of consciousness, submerged in the greater importance of the impersonal. For weeks thereafter he hardly thought of this woman, who for so many months had filled his imagination.

In the same manner the war had thrust out of sight almost at once the university and the intellectual life. Probably his profession had never engrossed his whole being as it ought, and now it had become wholly unreal. At Genoa under the influence of this tragic fact of war he had made that decision over which he had hesitated half a lifetime with an indifference and a certainty that surprised himself. He could not go back to *that* while half the world was burning up. Yet Romain Rolland's appeal to the European intellectuals to rise above the reign of unreason left him cold. He realised that the intellectual life in itself did not train men to understand themselves and their world. That was Jessica's mistake to believe that you could solve every dark place by thought. Without sympathy, or imagination, or faith. That was why she was content to heap up her little piles of sand industriously, tabulating the phenomena of the human soul.

PART FOUR

CHAPTER ONE

That the assassination of an Austrian archduke should keep an old man in the presidency of an American university was one of the minor ironies of the great war. Abel Dolittle was nearing his seventieth year when the war broke out, and even the more conservative trustees, those who had praised him for his "safety and sanity" after the death of the eruptive Harris, had begun to think that Eureka might benefit by a more progressive regime and to listen to the contemptuous murmurs of the faculty about their President. It was rumored that Doolittle would retire in the fall, and all the "possibilities" in the faculty were erecting timid hopes. Then came the war, and at first everybody forgot about Dolittle in the presence of more bewildering preoccupations. Later Dolittle was enough of a politician to turn the situation to his advantage.

The war got rapidly into full swing, verbally, in the United States. The correspondents, American and British, provided the American breakfast table with graphic descriptions of its horrors, and there were long editorial disquisitions on its origins and probable outcome. The universities buzzed with a real excitement, their faculties awakening from the somnambulistic dream of curricula and credits, of the conflicting merits of "science" and "culture". The "intellectuals" of Eureka, as all their brethren, swiftly became partisans in the controversy, and of course the great majority were partisans of "right against might". A few, a very few tried to use their minds and keep calm, but this attitude was so lonely, so unpopular that they soon were

235

forced to join one camp or the other. Poor old Eric
Schmidt stirred by a latent loyalty to his ancestors and
the more vivid memory of student days in Bonn splut-
tered himself into a momentary notoriety by defending
German "culture" in his class room. For which he was
sternly rebuked by Dolittle and warned henceforth—if
he hoped to receive his pension—to observe that strict
neutrality in word and thought recommended by President Wilson. Dolittle himself by this time was very
far from feeling neutral about the war. He confided
to Pliny Lucus (Canadian) in the sanctuary of the
Eureka Club that for his part he could not see how
any right thinking man, with red blood in his veins,
could remain neutral before a crime. Almost to a man,
he asserted, the Eureka faculty felt the same way, and
those who didn't would have the sense to keep quiet.

But not all kept quiet: Walter Snow had the temerity
to give an address in which he outlined with careful
impartiality the diplomatic snarls that had preceded the
present conflict and reminded his auditors that the
nations now arrayed against each other had been engaged before in many bloody wars. "And all of them
we must remember," he concluded, his sense of humor
bubbling up in his eyes, "righteous wars which national
honor compelled them to undertake. These wars don't
appear in the perspective of time so righteous or so
inevitable as they did at the moment. Interests were
at stake, often selfish interests, that were ready then as
now to gamble with human lives in the holy names of
justice and right!"

This being reported at the Faculty Club it was
recalled that Snow's wife had a German grandmother,
and the Snows were immediately put into the "Pro-
German" camp. On the next occasion when Beckwith
had luncheon at the club he was made to feel in the
many small ways by which civilized men indicate their

animosities that both he and Snow were no longer
welcome at the big centre table where they usually sat.
Characteristically Beckwith took the snubs with gusto.

"I suppose Snow and I are about the only neutral
members of this faculty," he remarked suavely, "because
we happen to know enough history to realise how
crooked both sides are in a war, and how misinformed
outsiders must always be. . . . England is doing her
best, naturally, to sell us the war. I hope we don't
bite! . . . Yes, Alsace and Lorraine . . . what of it?
They were not always French provinces, and as for
Belgium" . . . but what he had to say about Belgium
was drowned in a babble of indignant protest. After
an hour of this unprofitable argument Beckwith pulled
out his watch and jumped hurriedly to his feet.

"I'm due at a meeting of the arbitration board of the
Ladies' Garment Workers Union," he laughed, "a much
more important matter than what you and I happen
to think about the rights of the European mess."
Briskly, jauntily he hurried from the room, thinking,
"I shan't come here again until the war is over—sheep
minds!" while the men left about the centre table were
saying,—"Old Becky gone off his nut as usual. Just
to be contrary!" . . .

In October after the opening of the fall term Beckwith
had received a letter from Clavercin who was working
in a hospital in Paris. "At the close of the brief note
describing what he was doing, he remarked," I've
written Caxton I shan't be back until the war ends, if
ever. Dolittle can give me a leave of absence or the
other thing."

Happening to meet Jessica Mallory on the suburban
express for the city, Beckwith who had heard that she
was in Europe at the outbreak of the war, asked her if
she had seen Clavercin while she was there. Jessica
considering cautiously how much of the truth it was wise

to admit replied,—"Yes, I saw him in London last April."

"You know that he is staying on in Paris, doing war work?"

"Is he?" Jessica remarked indifferently and proceeded to relate some of the striking incidents of her journey to Genoa. Beckwith came back to his friend,—

"Clavey is taking the war quite hard . . . puts some sort of symbolic meaning into it!"

"I suppose he is romanticising it as so many are—over here!"

Beckwith gave an impatient shrug to his broad shoulders.

"I don't see how they can make this into a holy war!"

"They just want to fight!" Jessica affirmed. "It is terrible to see how the war fever is spreading . . . the stupid lies people will believe. Even Edgar feels about Belgium as if his own backyard had been invaded."

Jessica, who had long since abandoned "causes" and all belief in social amelioration, displayed an emotion about the war that Beckwith had never suspected in her. The war had roused the latent militancy of her Puritan nature as well as all her intellectual irony. Professionally it was affording her a wealth of illustration for her new book, "War Psychology", into which she was pouring herself with a dry malice. The war was a supreme illustration of the traditional tyranny of superstition, a kind of ritual of delusion invested with absurd authority by those who profited from its indulgence. To expose the methods of self-deception, the sinister means by which the fever was propagated and spread gave her a peculiar pleasure. All that Jessica disliked in human society and in human beings she could freely expose in her scrupulously impersonal discussion. . . . The two who had never been congenial suddenly found themselves drawn together by a common dislike of the war psychosis.

"You will be interested in what is happening in the Labor Council," Beckwith said. "Both sides of course are trying to get hold of labor,—the Germans to make trouble and keep the country from taking sides with the Allies, and the English especially to get us in. The Council is trying to steer a middle course and work for peace. It's a question which element will win."

Jessica listened to his sketch of the troubled labor situation, which reflected the mental uncertainty throughout the country. Beckwith described the secret plotting of the two forces. "If they'd only keep their dirty work for their own peoples!" he exclaimed. "They want to rush America into the war. We must do what we can to keep out."

He told of a proposed mass meeting to be addressed by prominent labor leaders and others on behalf of peace.

"The trouble is to find anybody with a national reputation who is willing to stand up and be counted in favor of peace. Every one is afraid these days and suspects his neighbor. That's war! . . . Well I must hustle over to my meeting."

"Do you want help—money?" Jessica asked hesitantly.

"Of course we always need money!" he laughed. "The war-makers have plenty of it."

The next morning when he found in his mail a cheque for a thousand dollars signed by Jessica Mallory, Beckwith smiled, thinking, "She means it! . . . I wonder what Edgar would say! . . . and Clavercin."

That morning he had read in the THUNDERER an impassioned article signed by Beaman Clavercin urging Americans to give their money to "help the great cause of human freedom," if they still felt "too proud to fight". Dolittle, Clavercin, Pliny Lucus, Edgar Mallory and many other earnest people took this haughty, disdainful attitude of injured national honor, while Jessica, Walter Snow and himself, who considered themselves equally high-minded and right thinking, were doing what they could to keep the country out of the war. . . . On his way to his office he had run across Constance Fenton going to some committee for helping the fatherless children of France.

"And how about the fatherless children of Germany, whom the Allies are trying to starve?" he had asked her.

Constance's soft lips tightened cruelly,—

"I'd like to see 'em all dead, every one of them!"

And the United States was not yet officially at war! . . . Beckwith stripping the envelopes from his letters, looking sharply for contributions or favorable replies to his appeals for help in organising his mass meeting smiled quizzically to himself, thinking, "Such is human nature. . . . But old Beaman—what got hold of him?"

He did not suspect the large part that Jessica Mallory had had to do with Clavercin's passionate advocacy of the war.

The beginning of the next term President Dolittle introduced in the faculty a motion requesting the government to provide instructors for military training in the university. In spite of indignant protests from a small minority, the motion was promptly carried by a viva voce vote. Presently two tough ex-army sergeants could be seen behind the new Modern Language Hall barking commands to a couple of hundred students, who ran hither and thither in breathless bewilderment.

"Almost all the members of our faculty," President Dolittle announced to the reporters in his office, "I am glad to say are patriots."

"If it hadn't been for you and me and a few others, Snowball," Beckwith scoffed, "he could have said, *All* our members!"

(Pliny Lucus an unofficial head of the local branch of the American Protective League had warned President

Dolittle of the sinister activities of Professor Beckwith working through the Labor Council, an old antagonist of the traction magnate, "We have our eye on him!" "So have we," the university president rejoined.)

"They ought to make old Donothing a major general," Beckwith remarked, "for distinguished gallantry in the rear."

CHAPTER TWO

When Jessica Mallory looked out from the platform of the immense auditorium into the sea of white faces that filled every corner of the big building and heard the clamor of those outside trying to force their way into the "pacifist" meeting, she had a flutter of emotion long unfamiliar. It had been some years since she had addressed any large meeting, and then only decorous academic gatherings whose reach of emotion covered boredom and intellectual interest. Never such a seething mass of men and women! She reflected with a characteristic detached irony that here before her eyes as in a vast laboratory was the raw matter of her recent studies in war psychology; also that the simple truths which she intended to present to them as a result of those studies would be like snow scattered on a hurricane sea. As she told Beckwith when he had urged her not merely to assist this anti-war protest with her money and her name but also to appear on the platform, "stand up and be counted with the other yellow dogs, pro-German and pacifist," he put it, she felt that the project of a big meeting was an empty gesture.

"You will convince nobody," she said, "and you will give more powder to the war people." Yet she had agreed, after Senator Ryder had prudently refused to speak and other well known people had withdrawn from the unpopular movement, to mount the platform with the little band of pacifists and radicals that Beckwith had collected and "be counted." Something grim within her Puritan stock responded to the challenge,—a substitute as she said to Beckwith for the militarism now so rife in

the world. She too could fight in her way, in a losing
cause, the perpetual fight of reason against unreason!
As she composed herself in her chair in the front row
she glanced at the little band on the platform and smiled
at the inequality between them and the hungry mob
beneath and up above in the great auditorium. So few
against so many

"Kind of noisy, ain't they?" the man next her remarked. His bony, livid face leered out disdainfully at
the crowd. He was a radical, a "labor" lawyer, of un-
savory repute among the conservative citizens of Eureka.
Jessica divined that his presence on the platform was
due as much to a thirst for notoriety as to ardor for the
cause of peace. The war had been championed by the
"respectables", his usual foes. Beyond the lawyer sat
Beckwith, looking worn and troubled. Jessica knew that
the publicity caused by his activity in the present affair
was intensely distasteful to him. "I accepted the chair-
manship," he told her, "because if I didn't the thing
would get into sinister hands, and I could keep it to its
legitimate end,—a protest against our being rushed into
the war by a hired press." Beckwith, of course, knew
what would be said of him at the university, that he was
"pro-German" (already a hateful epithet) and guilty of
involving the university in an almost unpatriotic cause.
To which he answered, "We are not at war,—quite yet!"

Beckwith's ardor for lost causes, for struggling weak-
ness, for unpopular people and movements was almost
as inexplicable to Jessica, keen psychologist that she was,
as was Edgar Mallory's easy conformity. To one, whatever "leading people" did or thought must be right,
while to the other it must be wrong! That peculiar
spring of tenderness for the oppressed, for the under dog,
which was Beckwith's moving force, was entirely unin-
telligible to her. She could be roused by injustice, once,
many years ago before she realised that injustice so
called was but one of the component factors of life, and

she could fight as now for reason against unreason, but not like Beckwith for the little, the weak, the downtrodden. The submerged did not appeal to her. Beyond Beckwith sat Marion Eave, the head of the university settlement, who had won a national position from her wise, unsentimental championship of social causes, which she was now bravely risking in behalf of pacifism. "Lady" Eave as she was called by her feminine admirers, sat with closed eyes, gray-haired, bent, tired. How many abortive efforts to lift humanity had she not spent herself upon! She had said to Jessica Mallory,—"One is compelled to be an opportunist, to lend a hand to this or that movement as human interest gives the chance." So she had lent her reputation to this forlorn effort to keep the country out of the war. What a faith—in something!

Behind the speakers sat a small group from the Labor Council, a few of Beckwith's students who had come in anticipation of a scrap, Walter Snow, smiling and cheerful as usual and some stray persons who liked to sit on platforms even in unpopular gatherings.

The great organ (which was always out of tune) was rumbling forth patriotic airs, and a resolute group of men and women immediately beneath the stage were trying desperately to labor through, "My coun-try, 'tis of The-e-e," while the tramp of newcomers in the aisles kept up. The clamor about the doors became so bad that Beckwith rose and went outside. After a time he returned and whispered to Morarty, a well known labor leader, who picked up his hat and coat and disappeared into the wings. Beckwith leaning across Mrs. Eave whispered,—"Must have some one to keep them quiet outside—overflow meeting in the park." There was a gleam in his tired blue eyes. He had expected that their protest would fizz out in a half filled hall, and instead the meeting promised to be huge, unwieldy. Jessica smiled, realizing that even with lost causes numbers were heartening. Presently Beckwith stepped to the front of the stage and raised his arm for quiet.

It was obvious that not all in the hall had come in the sacred cause of peace. There were cat calls, whistles and jeers from the outset.

"The Kaiser's secret agent," some one shouted from the balcony. Another, "Put him out " and so for a few deafening minutes the sea of people agitated itself until after a row in the balcony stopped by a policeman a voice sang out,—"Let the professor speak!"

Beckwith seized his opening.

"Thank you! I did not know that I should have to take refuge in my cloth," he said pleasantly, and plunged into a statement of the purpose of the anti-war meeting. The United States had not yet been dragged into the gulf of war—"because of rats like you—" Beckwith nodded and went on. Both sides were exerting every energy to get the country into the war, openly and secretly. There were sinister influences at work throughout the nation, and it was time before it was too late for sober reasonable folk, if there were any left, to demand a hearing and ask why and how their country should be led into the war. "What are our war aims?" Beckwith demanded. "Let the president put before the country the facts—"

"Every one knows them!" a red-faced close-cropped man interposed insolently from below the platform.

"I do not know them!" Beckwith retorted. "Suppose Mr. Penniman that you come up here on the platform and tell this audience why your newspaper has suddenly changed its tune and begun to urge America into the war."

Penniman, one of the owners of the EUREKA THUNDERER, a young man who had recently become a trustee of the university, rose and stepped into the aisle.

"I don't have to get on any platform to tell the

professor that," he shouted. "I am an American, I believe in my country, I—"

The storm broke from every quarter. Cries of "Pro-German—coward—traitor, put 'em out, Wobblies," filled the air. At its height it seemed as if a riot would end the meeting, as if the waves of faces would overflow to the platform and sweep the speakers into the wings. Beckwith remarked hoarsely,—"Penniman has packed the place with his Vigilants!" (An organisation for running down "German plots" that had already begun to terrorize the city.) The police either made feeble efforts to quiet the disorder or looked on apathetically. It was not until the settlement worker, Marion Eave, had risen and stood patiently waiting to be heard that the sea began to subside into something like calm. For the moment the passions of the audience had been assuaged; many there recognized the worn face of the settlement worker for whom they had a latent respect and were willing to hear what she had to say.

She spoke quite simply, quietly, of the conditions in Europe from which she had just returned, the misery, the infinite misery of the little people in all the belligerent countries, the horror of a modern war behind the front. "You don't get that, even in the most vivid despatches. You have to go into the people's homes, see the lines of black clothed women applying for help, the huddle of fatherless children in the refuges. I've seen all that, and that is why I am asking myself, 'Is it necessary to add to this mountain of human woe?' If it is necessary no honest man or woman would avoid the issue, but many of us cannot persuade ourselves that it is necessary for our great country to add its weight on either side to this load of misery. We do not believe that anything can be accomplished by more fighting."

There was comparative silence when the next speaker rose, the radical lawyer Simon Draught, but the calm produced by the settlement worker's dispassionate speech did not continue long. Draught was keen, ironical, contemptuous. He spoke of the money made in the United States out of the war, the debts contracted by European governments. "Those same fellers want to make more money as well as get back what they have loaned to England and France—that's natural enough—I would myself if I were in their boat. But I don't want our sons to fight for their money," and so on,—words that were received enthusiastically by the majority in the hall. When he got to an exposition of the way in which public opinion in favor of the war was being created, the opposition led by Penniman became noisy again.

"Why," Draught said slipping a wet tongue over his dry lips, his hands thrust deep into his trousers' pockets, "our friend Penniman here who is trying to make things lively tonight with his Vigilants could tell you no doubt just how England is selling us this war! Talk about the Kaiser—"

He got no farther. The meeting was again in wild uproar, the majority trying to throw out the members of the Vigilants, who seemed to have the support of the police. Beckwith leaned over to Jessica Mallory.

"Stand up," he said. "Just stand!"

She rose obediently, a sense of the ridiculousness of the whole situation steadying her nerves. She stood there singularly girlish, slight, between the small group on the stage and the glare and blare of the audience. She had intended to speak on the psychology of war, using some of the familiar data of her new book. While she stood in the midst of tumult calmly, placidly as in a lecture hall an idea came to her. Seizing a moment when the noise fell perceptibly she spoke. Her voice came out with surprising clearness, each word distinctly enunciated.

"Children," she said and waited. In the next pause she shot out in a lower more conversational tone,—"For you know you act more like bad children than anything else! Like noisy, quarrelsome children. You should be

be put on bread and water." She waited pleasantly
smiling until the audience startled into silence was ready
to give attention. "Observing your conduct in the mass
here this evening while the speakers were trying to reach
your minds I realized better than I ever had before just
why the peoples of the world still fight. It's that child
mind which you show most when you get together. It's
that child mind which skilful people are playing on to
get all of us into this bloody nonsense going on in
Europe. Try for a few minutes to-night to lay aside
your childishness and figure out just what it will mean to
a hundred and ten millions of us if we go on the loose
and add our force to the unreason of the world."

She talked on easily, slowly, of the psychological laws
involved, of suggestion, imitation,—of war psychology,
finding illustrations in the cries and actions of the meeting. Soon she heard a laugh, a detached unconscious
laugh.

"Ah," she remarked, "the first note of reason.
Thanks!"

She sat down abruptly when she had finished and
received some scattering applause. Beckwith taking
advantage of the calm read the prepared resolutions
calling upon the government to declare the aims of war.
"They all know over there what they are fighting for—
they have the booty divided already in their secret
treaties. Let us understand what we are fighting for—
let us go into this thing like men, not children, with
our minds clear about what we are doing!"

Bedlam broke loose once more, fights occurring in the
aisles until Beckwith declared the "resolutions" carried
and the little group on the stage scattered hurriedly into
the wings. Jessica, much amused by the belligerent
temper of this pacifist meeting, floated out along with
Beckwith into the street, which was one black surging
mass. If the emotion inside the hall had seemed childish, futile, outside the churning mass of humanity was

more like moving matter than something with conscious will.

"Come on," Beckwith shouted into her ear, "Draught is speaking in the Park!" At the end of the side street, the strip of park was black with massed thousands, struggling to get nearer the raised pedestal of a civil war general that decorated one end of the Park. There Draught holding his soft hat in one hand and waving it back and forth to emphasize his words was haranguing all within sound of his shrill voice. The thin lips in his livid face were distorted with the effort to make the surging mass hear.

"Friends," he yelled, "they call us traitors, pacifists, cowards. I'd rather be a pacifist than any," and there followed a stream of obscene profanity which was greeted uproariously by those in the mob near enough to hear. Jessica absorbed in the spectacle of Draught's passion,—a bitter, vindictive hate although voiced in behalf of peace,—became separated from Beckwith, who presently took the lawyer's place beneath the bronze figure of the civil war general and began to speak. He had lost his hat in the crush, his loose silk tie was torn from its place, and waved in the air. Head very erect, shoulders braced, he too looked like a warrior, not unlike the stern-faced man in bronze above him.

"They tell us that this war is a crusade for the right, but the statesmen on both sides keep on trading lands and peoples yet to be conquered. The only crusade I will fight in is one for peace. They tell us that this country wants to go to war with Germany. Look around you! If every citizen in this country could—" the rest was drowned in a roar as a platoon of mounted police sent to dispel the crowd came slowly down the avenue. The last words heard by Jessica far away as from a fading scene were, "They have to call out the police to keep us quiet!"

The stream of hurrying people fleeing before the mounted police swept Jessica Mallory towards the railroad station where she arrived with flushed cheeks and beating heart. "I wonder if I too am getting the disease," she said to herself. "It's contagious, a real germ, the germ of hate, I believe. Beckwith has it too, working in him—only he hates hatred and injustice and war. And I hate unreason!" Then she dozed off in the suburban car filled with peaceable lethargic men and women, reading the last war extra with its broad band of display type, "Defeat of the Italians—Débacle," etc. She woke automatically at her station and descended with others into the quiet side street. "I wonder if it could get them as it has the others," she mused. "Of course! They are just the same sort of people who were howling at that meeting." Then her mind turned to Edgar who had cabled that he was on his way home, having been abroad on a Red Cross mission to Bulgaria. It was lucky that his arrival had been delayed. Although she had given the reporters her professional name, Dr. Jessica Stowe Mallory, no doubt Penniman had recognized her on the platform and would see that she got all the publicity possible from her connection with the pacifist meeting. Hitherto she had avoided anything that might give her husband annoyance through publicity of her views, but tonight she felt indifferent.

"He'll have to stand it," she said wearily, as she turned up the path to her home. "We can't think alike about so many things!"

The coming summer she would insist on taking the children out to the cabin in the Colorado mountains, to keep them away from the mounting war fever, especially strong in the East where the children were at school. Young Edgar, barely fifteen, talked wistfully of

the boys in St. Stevens who had left school already to
enter the ambulance corps and "see the war." Jessica
realized with a pang that in this first great public crisis
her children felt much more with their father than with
her. "Mother is queer," they said among themselves,
sensitive as the young always are to any divergence
from the norm of action or belief.

CHAPTER THREE

Mallory on his way to Eureka read the lurid account in the "THUNDERER" of the pacifist meeting, which had ended in street riots and the dispersal of the mob by the police. "The leader of this pacifist and pro-German group," so the account ran, "was Norman Beckwith, the well known socialist professor at the University, and among the speakers was Dr. Mallory, wife of the former Dean," and then in true newspaper irrelevancy followed a personal account of the Stowe family and her marriage, ending, "Dean Mallory is at present in Europe on a Red Cross mission to Bulgaria, under the auspices of the Larson Foundation."

When husband and wife met at the breakfast table they greeted each other amiably, calmly, as was their wont, as if they had not been separated for six months.

"How was the crossing?" Jessica asked.

"Comfortable enough—after we got out of the submarine zone. The Sheimers were on board, coming out here."

"So he wrote me," Jessica replied equably.

"I believe he is a German agent!" Mallory exclaimed.

"Oh, don't get that mania!" Jessica said wearily. "You know his wife's people live here. Very likely she wants to see them and get away from the war for awhile. I should think she might!" After a moment she added, "I cabled them to visit me."

Mallory gave his wife a long, searching look.

"That is going pretty far, Jessica," he said in a low voice. "We shall be in the war if what I hear from

Washington is true before the month is out, and you have asked a German spy—"

"See here, Edgar! We are not in the war yet, and you don't know that Rudolph is a German agent."

"He has all the marks of it," Mallory fumed.

"Of course," Jessica continued equably, "and if I had known you were coming back so soon I should not have asked them here. Anyway they may not find it convenient."

She rose to leave the room for her morning hours of work as was her custom.

"Jessica!"

Something unaccustomed in her husband's tone arrested her, a note of appeal, almost of pathos, in his usual matter of fact voice.

"What?"

"Can't we get together on this?" he said, stressing slightly the "this", indicating how momentous to him the present crisis appeared. He made the unwonted demonstration of putting his hands on her shoulders and drawing her slightly to him.

"Why on this more than on other things?" she asked crisply. Nevertheless, she made no effort to withdraw from his tentative embrace and smiled slightly into his sober eager face.

"Because it is so—fundamental!"

"To you, not to me, Edgar. I don't see War as fundamental to anything, merely a demonstration of perverse unreason. I let you take the war your way and don't interfere, and you must let me take it my way—and not interfere. With the children, either," she added more seriously. "They are not to be inoculated with the disease if I can help it."

"You can't!" Mallory said firmly.

"Perhaps not, but I shall do what I can to keep its suggestions out of their lives."

"There are some things, Jessica, beyond reason, deeper than reason. That you have never discovered."

"Fighting isn't one of them," and with that retort, the two parted. It was the first and the last open discussion of the war which they had. As Jessica sat down to the proof of "War Psychology" she reflected on the breakfast table conversation, trying as was her wont after any experience or human contact to relegate its meaning to some category of her own thought. "Edgar believes in the state, in patriotism, in war and all that," she mused. "I don't. Furthermore he wants his own tribe to believe with him, to act with him, to feel with him. That is the solidarity of the family he talks about so much. And I suppose that his egoism receives a blow when he discovers that he hasn't imposed on the tribe, on his immediate dependents, his own beliefs and convictions—just as in religion. Because we married and shared our lives to a certain extent, have the children, he feels that we should share our beliefs and ideas. I wonder how much of it is mere pride on his part in not having the world know we don't agree about such things " and with that query unanswered Jessica turned to her proof.

That evening Beckwith came in with Walter Snow to talk over the pacifist meeting and settle some accounts. Mallory's presence caused a restraint that amused Jessica, who let the others talk. Snow gave a hilarious, burlesque account of the turbulent meeting.

"They all wanted to fight," he roared, "the pacifists worse than the others, and they weren't happy until they got out into the street and had a free for all with the police to finish it off! . . . Oh, you ought to have been there, Edgar!"

"Hum!" Mallory commented glumly, and to Beckwith he said abruptly,—"What possible good could it do, Norman?"

"Not much perhaps—but it was worth doing!"

Beckwith's face still bore traces of the strain of the

previous night. There had been a disturbance in his
lecture hall that afternoon caused by outsiders who had
come there to make trouble. He had received threaten-
ing letters and knew that he was followed by men,
probably agents of the Vigilants, spying on his movements.

"I can't see that," Mallory observed coldly, "and you
ought not to involve the university in such a controversy."

"Why not?" Beckwith snapped. "You and Dolittle
and a lot more are involving the university in the war as
fast as you can, aren't you?"

"See here," Jessica interposed, "if you men are going
to wrangle over the war you can go somewhere else. . . .
Out there!"—and she pointed to the campus where an
unusual crowd had gathered around a big bonfire.

"I wonder what they are celebrating to-night," Mallory
said. Let's go over and see."

"It's an anti-pacifist demonstration," Snow laughed.
"I heard they were going to hang you, Beckie!"

"I must see that!" Beckwith roared.

While Jessica hunted for wraps the men stood watching the fire and the crowd across the street. Jessica
coming back into the room perceived that the old
friends who had seemed so antagonistic a few moments
ago had forgotten their differences and were joking with
each other over the scene below. "Children," she
thought, sardonically. "There's war for you!". . . .

The vacant oval in the centre of the Eureka campus,
reserved according to the building plan for a Gothic
chapel, was the scene of student celebrations organized
in haste after a football victory or other athletic event.
To-night a huge pyre had been built of packing cases
and broken chairs, and around this was gathered a
rapidly swelling circle of students and many who were
not students. Strung upon an electric light pole on the
edge of the oval was a scarecrow figure clad in cap and

CHAPTER FOUR

Clavercin's articles in the Sunday THUNDERER had been a great inspiration to those with allied sympathies all through the early months of the war. They had largely retrieved the disfavor caused by his play— WHY? which had long since been forgotten. Caught in the backwash of the Marne tidal wave he had witnessed many harrowing scenes among the refugees and the gangrened wounded slowly brought into the improvised hospitals by crawling trains and had ardently embraced the cause of the invaded. The war presented itself to him with a dramatic simplicity and intensity, which he translated into those early articles, incorporated afterwards in a book, "The Great Cause", much read especially in the East by those who were mortified by their country's hesitation in taking sides in the war.

"Clavey's got it bad," was Norman Beckwith's comment when he read these fervid denunciations of the devastating Hun.

"He's too near to see it," was Snow's apologetic explanation.

During the second year of the war, almost imperceptibly the tone of these weekly articles changed and rumors came back to the campus brought by stray workers in the American hospitals that Beaman Clavercin had become a "defeatist", something almost worse than German at that time.

"He's beginning to see," was Beckwith's comment. "Poor Clavey! By the time his eyes are wholly opened this country will be mad for the war!"

On the entrance of the United States into the conflict Clavercin's articles disappeared from the editorial
page of the THUNDERER.

"His stuff is too academic," Penniman explained when
questioned. "Now that we are in the scrap, we need
more close-ups, not arguments and sermons. Anyway
he is too literary. What people want to read is eye-
witness stuff!" and the great Penniman, who with his
close cropped hair looked more than ever like an ex-thug
went to "the front" in person, and sent back lurid if
illiterate accounts of what he saw there.

Meanwhile Clavercin's friends learned that he was ill
in Switzerland, and then late in the spring of 1917 he
came home and appeared once more on the university
campus. He came back like a silent ghost to a strange,
empty home,—for already the university had "got into
the war" with a zeal that threatened to leave the
abandoned class rooms and laboratories to the care of
janitors. As he walked slowly up the side street towards
the campus it seemed to him that he was returning
after death to the spot where he had begun his life. He
remembered that other morning so many years ago when
he had approached the new university from the same
direction, his heart filled with such tremulous expectations. At the corner where he had hesitated before
crossing the river of mud, in place of the "temporary
library and gym" soared the lofty Campanile, from
which at this mid-morning hour the chimes were sounding gayly, cheerily, "Onward Christian Soldiers, March-
ing as to War",—in these days the one selection ren-
dered. He paused beneath the Campanile to listen to
the bells, recalling Edith Crandall, Harris, old Harden,
other ghosts of the campus, the hopes and fears and
struggles of all those years while the university was in
the making. What would they say to the khaki clad
young men of the R. O. T. C. now performing with
considerable alacrity their evolutions in the centre oval

of the campus around a few pieces of light artillery that
the government had sent from its storehouse for local
color? "Right fours! Halt!" and a stream of professional profanity from the tough ex-army sergeant in
command. The youth of the university, so indifferent
as Clavercin remembered them were now "all in it",
with the same zest they had formerly shown about their
athletic games. Many had already "gone over" in one
formation or another.

The faculty also had been "mobilized", and every
member who could obtain a place in the war machine
had fled to Washington or was preparing to depart.
Already many of them had donned khaki, which had an
odd, humorous aspect on their thin legs, on the aging
narrow shoulders of the "scholar-soldiers". Clavercin
dropped into Dexter's laboratory and found the biologist engaged in carefully measuring out his precious
anti-pneumonia serum to be forwarded to an army
encampment.

"It came through right, just in time for the emer-
gency," he told Clavercin gravely. "We are getting the
best results from its use. I had a chance to join one of
the ambulance units and go over, but I feel this is more
necessary. . . . Of course you'll be going back?"

"No, I shan't go back," Clavercin replied shortly.

"Washington?"

"No, I am going to teach if they want me—and
there's anybody to teach." Dexter looked at him with
curiosity.

"What's the matter? . . . Malaria? Flu? . . . Oh,
they'll want you. It is almost impossible to keep any
professors here."

From Dexter's laboratory he sought Caxton, who was
cleaning out his desk preparatory to leaving for Washington. Caxton was in uniform with a captain's stripes
on his tunic.

"Military intelligence service," he explained to Clavercin, "in Washington . . . training applicants, you know. I've quite a staff. Want to come?"

Clavercin shook his head with a wry little smile.

"I've seen all the military intelligence I can stand!"

Caxton, who was too much preoccupied with his own affairs to ask questions, continued to talk as he emptied drawers and shoved piles of student papers into the waste basket.

"You won't find many left in the department. Flynn is in charge. Poynter has gone with Red Cross; Organ is teaching meteorology over in France; and Lambert is helping Mallory on the intelligence tests in Washington. . . . They are drawing heavily on the universities in every line. Sanderson is running a bureau in the Loan Department," and he ran on enumerating the members of the faculty who were serving in one branch or another. . . . "The war will last a long time, I think, another five years. I hardly expect to be back before that—who knows?"

It was apparent that the war had touched the stagnant pools of the university to life. Caxton with a lifelong experience of thwarted power had found in it a responsible and active post. The inferiority of the academic life, so coarsely voiced by Aleck Harding at the last Wind Bag, was about to be disproved. The country in its crisis needed trained minds, the special knowledge of the university. Clavercin mused over the irony of the situation that he should now be returning to the university as to an asylum, while his fellows who had functioned in it so much more contentedly were fleeing its seclusion into the din of war. It was as if all the long years of abstractions, of repressed ambitions, of class room routine and unreality were now revenging themselves in the glorious release of energies that the war offered.

"Beckwith is here," Caxton remarked, with a slight reserve in his voice,—and Snow."

"Yes, I am lunching with them. Won't you join us?"

"No," Caxton refused briskly, "I am lunching with General Bord and some of his staff at the Eureka Club."

There was a touch of superiority in the scholar's voice, quite pardonable, a little amusing, indicating his sense of importance. His was one of the best minds in America, Clavercin reflected, as he left Caxton's office, not merely in his own narrow line of scholarship but as a mental machine, and it took the bloody insanity of a world war, a chaos of misery, to awaken its possessor to a sense of importance and dignity! A Caxton to be proud of lunching with a few stupid army officers, to be inflated by the task of educating young men how to collect information from spies and prisoners . . .

It was the close of a class hour, and about the entrance to Founder's Hall, which already was assuming the dinginess of age, together with a thin coating of ivy, students were congregating as usual, smoking cigarettes, chatting with each other between classes. There were noticeably more women among them than men, and some of the younger girls were also in khaki, with insignia pinned to their coats. The great game of war had penetrated to Eureka, with its thrills and excitements and pretenses. Eureka was actually more warlike in appearance than Paris, Clavercin reflected. A few thin, white-faced youths walked briskly off in the direction of the library, graduate students no doubt, to whom the din of war meant nothing except that it had removed from the class rooms those teachers whose courses they desired to take in order to complete their work for the higher degrees. They were pacifists by temperament and occupation.

Clavercin met old Tom Bayberry on the path to the Administration Building and stopped to chat with him. The archeologist's legs looked unsteady and his bony face was more twisted than ever. He was puzzling over a letter written in childish script in French. "One of my orphans," he explained to Clavercin, "I've adopted three. This one lives near Nancy. She writes very nicely to her American *grandpére*. I suppose the village schoolmistress corrects her letters   Here is her picture," and he fished from an inner pocket a small photograph showing the indeterminate features of a little girl. "Classes? I've got four students in one and two in the other."

Thus even Bayberry participated in the war through his "orphans". That had become a practise especially among bachelors, too old for any form of service, to "adopt" French children, sending them gifts, exchanging letters. "I've taken on another," one would say to a friend. "How many have you?". . .

The pleasant spring sunlight filled the open places of the campus, falling full on the oval where the R.O.T.C. were still performing evolutions directed by the barks of the old sergeant. Clavercin realized in one swift perception how much of Dr. Harris's grandiose program had been filled in, how large the "plant" of the university had become—all now turned into an army camp to "help win the war."

The President's office was quieter, more retired than ever. The smiling young woman who reigned in the outer office beamed happily on Clavercin.

"Yes, the President is expecting you!" and she disappeared.

Portraits of General Foch, of Marshal Joffre, of General Pershing had been hung on the walls, also a few garish war posters. Clavercin recalled that the university had given recently an honorary degree to Joffre, a great ceremony by which the university acclaimed the war. How Dr. Harris would have enjoyed that occasion!

Clavercin did not have long to wait in the empty outer office, and his reception by Dolittle was in happy contrast with his last interview with the university president.

"So glad to see you back, Clavercin!" Dolittle

suggested by the evolutions of the R.O.T.C. on the campus oval. "Every department almost is able to contribute something of value to the common effort! It is a great demonstration to the community of the usefulness of our higher institutions of learning!"

And he believed it, Clavercin reflected, as Dolittle ducked his silk hat into the waiting limousine and with a little nod to him wheeled away in that peculiarly nervous rush that war was cultivating in every activity. The war had surprisingly rejuvenated Dolittle. He was once more feeling his own importance, which was the psychological basis of youth. So it was with the scholar Richard Caxton, with the scientist Dexter and his pneumonia serum, the physicist who was teaching young men how to adapt artillery fire to the weather, to Maxwell who was engaged in calculating the cubic contents of ships and how to pack away in each boat the maximum load, to Mallory who was putting into practise those theories of testing human adaptabilities hitherto worked out in laboratories with the aid of questionnaires. To all these and many more the war had given a sense of reality to their work, to their lives. Odd! In him the war had developed a sense of human futility the longer he had stayed in Europe, the nearer he had come to its myriad manifestations. Long since, the fables about the issues of the war circulated by statesmen and writers had ceased to stir him; it was with a sense of ironic humor that he discovered their renewed potency in his own country. . . . So he was returning to the university as to an asylum, just as his fellows were escaping from it into what seemed to them reality!

In the months that followed while the country "got into the war" deeper and deeper, Clavercin felt the healing of his academic task. He entered his rather empty classroom with a new sense of repose, of enjoyment, as to a temple in which enduring verities might be considered instead of fretful temporalities. Outside the student band might blare out "It's a Long Way," and other martial ditties, while the thinning ranks of the undergraduates showed more and more khaki, within his lecture hall with its long shadows at twilight he could forget for a time the din of unreason in the world and attach his mind to the fundamental truths of the spirit. For the first time he thoroughly enjoyed his teaching although the material in his classes was unusually mixed, graduate students, women auditors, undergraduates. In the dearth of courses students took what they could get. For the first time his task had a dignity, a meaning to it. Because of the absence of so many instructors he gave the general survey course of literature, usually designed for first year students, and was making it over into a brief history of the human spirit with its currents of fundamental impulses and aspirations. He felt that he was not teaching literature, something stored away in books on library shelves, pawed over by dull minds, annotated and explained, but life itself. All the emotions, all the experiences of his own life, especially of the recent years, went into his interpretation of the human spirit, as expressed in the written words of the old texts. As he came down the centuries into modern times, drew near the contemporary maelstrom of the world, the currents merged into a roaring cataract. Often he wished that he had the special knowledge of the biologist, of the psychologist, of the historian, so that he might trace more surely the multiform weave of the human spirit. To teach literature properly one should be equipped with all the sciences and all the philosophies!

At the end of his lecture he came away from the class room exhausted, but at peace, assuaged, having given all that was within him for his hearers to take or leave, to assimilate or reject as they might. He came out into the cool twilight of the autumn or winter day while the

CHAPTER FOUR

Meanwhile Beckwith's militancy had turned into new fields. The conscientious objectors, of whom there were a few among the students, appealed to Beckwith for advice and protection. One rather talky, white faced young man with literary aspirations made himself their leader and hung about Beckwith's apartment for weeks undecided whether to attempt flight or to go through with the rôle of martyrdom recommended by his mentor. Finally he surrendered to the authorities and was shipped off to Leavenworth. He was succeeded by a furtive little cockney whom Snow had discovered and bailed out of prison on the charge of sedition for his editorial utterances in a little labor sheet. Then came stray Hindus, who had escaped from India and were being pursued by the British secret service. Clavercin after listening to these representatives of revolt protested to Beckwith,—

"They aren't worth it, Norman, the risk and trouble you take for them. That Duncan lad is a plain shirker. He's the kind that would wobble through life anyhow, and it is only his ingrowing egoism that has landed him in Leavenworth."

"You are hard on the boy!"

"And as for the cockney, according to his own story he has welched on every job he ever had. . . . Dass I don't wholly understand, but he is using the war I suspect, as an opportunity for revolt."

"Of course! Why not? Others are using it—the big capitalists especially—as an opportunity for exploitation. They are buying organized labor by high wages and exemptions, and combining against unorganized labor. . . .

Besides the individual doesn't matter, how inferior he may be. It is the idea we have to fight, the idea of tyranny which the war is fastening on us all."

It was this growing intolerance, this tyranny of the majority over the individual, over the minority, that especially aroused Beckwith's flaming protest. In his resistance to the brutal will of the majority, he lost sight of personal qualities. To Clavercin on the other hand, it was the quality of the individual that counted most. Sincerity, honesty, steadfastness appealed to him. The tricky players of the game, the self-interested and the trivial, aroused his contempt. Nevertheless Beckwith had reacted unerringly to the gangrene of the war spirit—its intolerance—and almost alone here in the temple of the university he fought every manifestation of the hateful spirit which was spreading its poison throughout the world.

"You must do this and that, you must think as we do," the triumphant majority shouted in chorus. "Why?" Beckwith demanded imperturbably. "In all times of crisis like the present the majority has been found to be wrong in the end. I deny its authority!"

So he organized committees, drubbed up meagre sums from sympathetic persons to maintain his protegés in their revolt.

"I don't like what your friend Beckwith is doing," Louise Clavercin said to her husband censoriously. "Maida Grant was talking about him at luncheon to-day and said if the university authorities didn't shut him up the army intelligence office would. He's on their lists you know."

"So am I," Clavercin replied amiably, "because of my favorable review of Barbusse's book last spring. So are a lot of our leading citizens for one absurdity or another. That doesn't mean anything!"

"It was a horrid book," reflected Louise, who since she had joined Maida Grant's bond-selling organization had grown oppressively patriotic. "It isn't the time to air such views when everybody is doing his bit to win the war."

Clavercin visualizing the large impressive Maida addressing gatherings of applauding citizens in her bond-selling campaign remarked, "What a lot of fun you women are having with the war! Even Constance Fenton has shut down her crèche and is running about speaking on food conservation. What will you do after the war?"

"Go into business!" Louise retorted, "and make some money."

Drawing on her driving gloves she departed in the gray-painted Ford that stood outside the front door when it was not careering wildly hither and thither on some war errand. Clavercin mounting to his disorderly study collected books and papers for the afternoon lecture. He realized that to Louise, to Maida, even to dear old Constance his assiduity in teaching classes in literature at the university "while we are all doing our best to win the war" seemed quite unmanly, betraying a native impotence of character. The emancipation of women had come through the opportunity the war had offered for their public services. So they scurried over the country selling bonds, talking at luncheons, encouraging humbler housewives to save food. They had compelled the orchestral association to discharge old Gluck because he had neglected to obtain his citizen's papers thirty years ago when he came to America. "Besides he's horrid, you know, with girls." "But you never found that out before the war," Clavercin had protested.

"Oh, well"—

When they gathered after their exhausting labors at some pleasant dinner party where the food regulations were ingeniously evaded, they talked gravely of the reconstruction of society after the war. "One will have to do real things to get social position, not merely be rich and give nice parties," they said. Then drifted into the usual gossip about jobs. Oh, yes, the war was doing much for women, and they were mostly for it heart and soul.

CHAPTER FIVE

I.

After the Armistice they came back, slowly, reluctantly, when their different war "services" terminated, from camps, from Washington, from "the other side," came back to the university. Not all. Some of the younger men having enjoyed the tonic atmosphere of the competitive life, the freedom and delight of male companionship outside the campus, found other promising avenues into that new world every one talked about those days. Day, a promising instructor in Clavercin's department, stayed on in France, organizing instruction for the troops left there, Bard in chemistry was employed by some crafty men who had bought up German patents cheaply; one of Sanderson's best men was hired by a New York bank. But the older men returned to the academic nest, discarding regretfully the uniform, their honorable khaki and spurs, feeling somehow that the great vacation of all their lives had ended, with the freedom of being "under orders"! Now they must enter the treadmill once more and give orders to themselves. They must resume the dull tasks of study and classroom, get out of the desk drawer the old lecture notes, which looked more dingy and lifeless than after the usual vacation. Caxton, who refused to consider the Armistice as final, stayed on in Washington until the following spring. He had made an astonishingly good intelligence officer mitigating regulations with a little common sense, and after his experience with some thousands of undergraduates had acquired a shrewd judgment of young men. To go back to his

274

dusty office in Founder's Hall every morning and worry over the text of Chaucer had not the same reality it had had before 1914.

So gradually they got back to the common level of the old daily task, in a world not so new and "reconstructed" as they had fondly dreamed it would be, thanks to their exertions in beating the Hun. For a time some of the glamor of the war hung about their minds: they swopped experiences over luncheon in the faculty club, held reunions, revived old animosities and disputes, criticised the roster of club members who had done war work. And once more they revived the pleasurable emotion of an unrestrained hatred of the Reds, the terrible Bolsheviks and their unpatriotic sympathizers at home. But this aftermath of the dear, delightful war spirit also wore off in time under the steady grind of the old mill, and the grudging reminder of the scholar's conscience to remain skeptic and try to see the other side. The talky ones, the propagandists and speech makers, kept up a chatter over the peace treaties; for Eureka had its representatives in that grotesque assemblage of academic "experts" at Versailles. Chittering the head of the history department, boasted for a time, "I made the Polish corridor!" and Dolittle had something remotely to do with the Turkish treaty. For a couple of years after the Armistice they carried on their verbal warfare, defending the treaties, and felt that they had had a hand in molding destiny, at several hundred removes from the centre.

For once the university had been in touch with actualities. To be academic, with a professor or doctor before one's name, had not been a cause of tolerant contempt, on the part of the "men who do things". To be academic had not been a reproach; often a recommendation. Faculty members felt, "They had to come to us with some of their problems,—they did not know—and on the whole we did our part well, certainly as well or better as those cheeky men of affairs who bungled ships and aeroplanes and grafted scandalously". The university, they felt, had acquitted itself handsomely in the national crisis, had proved its worth, its importance, and they meant that never again should the university slump back into insignificance. In this new world, which they had helped to make, their place should be both more honorable, with enhanced prestige and more comfortable, with higher salaries. Just how they did not know.

And first of all they were overwhelmed with students, their classes crowded beyond endurance. For the youth of the country had flocked into the universities in astonishing numbers after the war. "We showed them we had something here they would need," the professors thought complacently. Also, it was true, that there was less for them to do, now that its youth having been made into good fighters the world suddenly decided to settle back into peace. "You might as well go back to school for a few years," parents said, "and prepare yourselves," —for what? For that new world. Besides parents had the money, much easy, cheap war money, and the boys, girls too, deserved a vacation, a little petting and loafing and bragging. So back in floods they had come to the pleasant walks of academe, to the halls of learning and the sound of chimes, the rah, rah of football and jazz and bootleg liquor and all the rest,—to the university.

Now what should they do with all this promising, clamorous youth,—what should they teach them? They were a bit tarnished, some of them, by their war experience, disillusioned, frustrated, with a nonchalant "show-us" air they had never had before. It was the old question, but more urgent with this mob of disillusioned youth.

At the first full faculty meeting many of the old faces reappeared, singularly freshened and fattened by the war. Mallory who had come back from Washington, with a medal, some said to take over the presidency, others said to leave Eureka for a much more important post, was there, sitting beside old Bayberry, gaunter and homelier than ever and a trifle unsteady on his thin legs. Also Clavercin, whiter, grimmer, burning to speak out at last in behalf of a new university. Beckwith was there, in worse repute than ever since his connections with the imprisoned pacifists, the communists, and all the other "down and outers" as Mallory mockingly called his proteges, and beside him Walter Snow with a fresh repertoire of the foolish doings of his colleagues with the map of Europe. And of course Sanderson came, more self-assured and provocative than ever, his mustache thicker, in the centre, shaved back at the sides like the youth of the day, full of the "splendid record of my department"—every man in it having "served in some useful capacity the duration of the war." In this new academic world as in the new outside world there would be ready for him a suitable place, a very responsible place, nothing less than the presidency of Eureka, at last.

For old Donothing in spite of his talent for publicity, for pronouncing authoritatively the current commonplace, had reached the end of his long academic tether, and was about to retire, "as soon as a suitable successor could be found."

Past seventy, in this new, newest of old worlds there was obviously nothing more for him but a harmless old age spent in writing his memoirs. His good friends in the British propaganda service had invited him to join one of those eminent junketing parties popular after the war to look into the Chinese situation, which would occupy him, thanks to the leisurely and luxurious manner of such excursions with its official entertainments, at least a full year. So this might well be the last full university function at which he would preside. (He had already officiated in the giving of honorary degrees to French, Italian, English, dignitaries, civil and military. . . . As he sat on the platform dais at the end of the bare faculty room surrounded by his minions, deans and secretaries, his little yellow eyes blinking out on the faces below him, some of whom he could remember for over a generation, listening to the lisping secretary of the curriculum committee read the long delayed report on the reorganization of courses, he might well conclude that the "safe policy" had succeeded. Eureka was "sound," ready to leap ahead to those new "opportunities for service," which luncheon club orators were so fond of celebrating. In the report furbished up by the glib secretary there were paragraphs about the "quickened sense of service," the position the university should take in "our reconstructed world." Those two honorable words, "service" and "reconstruction" were so much overworked that Beckwith suddenly leaning forward remarked to Mallory, "We are in short to remake the universe and serve everybody from charwoman to God— we are *it* " . . . Finally the secretary's lisp died away, and Dolittle coming back from a long reverie of China and boards and banquets mumbled,

"Gentlemen, you have heard the report of the curriculum committee, which has been delayed due to the interruption of the war. What is your pleasure?"

"I move," Beckwith said in flutelike tones, "that the committee be discharged and that the report be laid on the table until we know more about that New World the report seems so familiar with."

A dozen members of the faculty rose nervously from their seats, and there was the usual mess of motions, counter-motions, amendments, withdrawals, points of order, characteristic of Anglo-Saxon procedure applied to faculty meetings. Dolittle sat in puzzlement, while the wrangle proceeded with acrimonious exchanges that displayed temperaments rather than convictions about the curriculum. At last after an hour's waste of time, as the sun was disappearing behind the Campanile, the faculty got at the report itself and the debate began

acidly, tempers having been strained by the preceding
futilities. Heads of departments had their say. Sanderson, recognized leader of the committee, made a
brutal attack on the "futilities" of "culture," to which
Caxton retorted sneeringly against "business colleges."
Bayberry rose waveringly from the rear of the room.
The president who had been dozing as if from his seat
of vantage had already passed beyond all this academic patter into the larger life of international conferences, recognized the professor of Greek with relief,
shutting off the eager youngsters who were panting to
speak. Bayberry so rarely spoke in faculty meeting, although he was punctilious in attendance, that he was always
listened to respectfully. The room settled into quiet,
curious to hear what one so remote from life in subject
and thought might have to say on the burning question
of the great future.

Although he represented, Bayberry said, one of the
least practical branches of learning, one that attracted
least the modern mind, nevertheless it was traditionally
the oldest culture on the globe; so something might be
said for the Greek point of view even in a world of
tanks and aeroplanes and publicity bureaus. "We
know that these ancient sages were concerned with the
same puzzling question,—what is education? . . . Nobody knows—that is the simple truth. It is like asking
what is nourishment or clothing One thing for one
man in one time and circumstance, another in a different time and circumstance. There is something both
ironic and pathetic in this recurrent strife among us
doctors of learning, each working for his own subject,
his own craft, trying to make out of the scraps of knowledge we have an ideal balanced ration of education like,
an ideal suit of clothes, standardized for all youth. It
can't be done, gentlemen! You will take another unit
away from English or Modern Languages and give its
place to some form of science or business administration.

That will not make education for education is within!
. . . You talk of the new world, of reconstruction and
all that. I venture to say that to our successors here
it will be found to be much the same old world we have
known, essentially, with the same problems, the same
enigmas, because it will be a world of men and women.
. . . . I shall vote, therefore, as I voted when the
question of curriculum first came up before this faculty
in President Harris's time, as I voted ten years later
when the existing arrangement was introduced—I shall
vote 'no!', not because I am opposed to change, to experiment, but because I do not believe that we or any
similar academic body of men can establish arbitrarily
an ideal of education, of life for the coming generation
by taking a pinch of this and a dash of that and combining them with something else in so many units and
thus make a suitable intellectual ration for all spirits.
Let us leave the eternal problem to the generation now
entering the university. Let them choose from the feast
we offer whatever they happen to want!"

He sat down as abruptly as he had risen, and there
was a squirming in the room, whispered conferences
among the leaders, interrupted by the tired, droning
voice of Dolittle, "Are you ready to vote, gentlemen?
Let the secretary read the amended proposal as it now
stands," and the Little President lisped for a few minutes; then the faculty proceeded to vote without much
confidence in what they were doing, and the President
announced more briskly than he had spoken hitherto,—
"The measure is carried. A motion to adjourn is in
order."

Thus the new world was ushered into Eureka.

CHAPTER SIX

Efficiency was the watchword of this new world, with "reconstruction" and "service" hanging vaguely in the background. Everybody realized that a brand new curriculum recognizing "functional subjects" did not make a new educational world. That was the screen behind which the "new forces" must operate. What men talked about among themselves was a new president and "the Drive." The two went together! The new world demanded an immensely increased endowment and to procure this it was necessary to secure a "magnetic" personality for president. Mallory was persuaded to lay aside his other ambitions for a time and accept the leadership of the "Fifty Million Dollar Endowment Drive," which was to recreate Eureka, give it the equipment and the "plant" to meet its obligations in the new world.

"Why fifty millions?" Clavercin inquired plaintively.

"Because it is a big round number. You must think in large terms, Clavey, these days. . . . Pretty soon they will be asking you to declare your needs for prosecuting your studies and you must be prepared to ask for five millions—for that theatre, you were always talking about, a library of dramatic literature, at least five new instructors, and a perpendicular rise in salaries, say twelve thousand for you, Clavey."

"I don't want it," Clavercin replied sombrely, unable to respond at once to Beckwith's facetious acceptance of the new world. "I think we are paid pretty nearly enough for what we do as it is. What we need—"

"For heaven's sake, man, don't talk that way in

281

public: they will think you crazy," Beckwith warned.
"Dick Caxton is head of the publication committee to
get out our literature of needs. He and Mallory will
show you what you want!"

Indeed, a new wave of enthusiasm began to run
through Eureka, for "the bigger, better, best of universities," and members of the faculty who had waited
anxiously for a five hundred dollar increase in salaries
now talked in millions. Every one was doing it. The
"drive" had become one of the most popular features
of university life. Under Mallory's inspiring leadership
with his genius for organization, a new method of getting money for the drive was introduced. Instead of
dropping into some rich man's office or lunching with him
privately and tickling his vanity until he consented to
become a donor, there was an army organization of
drive leaders, whose business it was to cover every possible contribution to the fund. "We are not going after
the philanthropist class," Mallory announced. "The
day of individual benefactions, of a rich man's buying
himself into respectability and social consideration has
gone. Of course," he added hastily with a humorous
grin, "we'll not refuse any tainted money, but there
isn't enough of it! To accomplish what we are after
we must make the smaller people contribute. We
must make the comfortable middle classes feel that this
is their university, not only our own graduates but all
earnest men and women who believe in better things.
We must make it a religion to give to the university,
not a social gesture!"

And that was the note of the new world: everybody
who counts must support the things that count.

"You are selling the university to the public this
time," Beckwith carped, "instead of a war! It will do
less harm."

"Precisely!" Mallory agreed readily. "And you,
Norman are one of our best assets, if you did but know

it. Your radical friends are so disturbing to all decent-minded, prudent citizens that they want something done to prevent the curse of communism and chaos. So they are sympathetic to the claims of religion and education, as they never were before; they see that we are the cement of society, and if they wish to leave their money to their children in peace, or even enjoy an orderly death, they must contribute to the cement fund, must patch the crumbling walls of society. . . . So instead of discouraging you in your efforts to get the wobblies out of jail, to stir up insurrection in India, to recognize Russia, and all the rest of the radical pro-gram, I tell you to go right ahead and get all the pub-licity you can for your activities. Every column you receive works for us, and means thousands of dollars to the drive fund."

The two old friends laughed amiably. Probably Mallory had a better understanding of Beckwith than any one of Eureka, and for his part Beckwith respected Mallory more than he did any other conservative mind. In essential character they had much in common; it would be difficult to account for their divergence in action and belief.

"I see your point, Edgar, but I can't help you rake in the endowment. Would you like my resignation?"

"Never!" Mallory laughed tolerantly. "Of course you are a reproach to the university in some quarters, not so important as they once were. But you are an invaluable asset to us in other ways than I have just mentioned. When we are told that you are dangerous and subversive to the social order we reply that we do not agree with your views, of course, and deplore your present activities and associations. But a university should be tolerant to heretics. You are our foremost heretic! So we point to you and say to any critic, 'Eureka tolerates Beckwith because we know he is sincere and able and stimulating to students. Our students are too mature, too sane to be carried away by his social vagaries!' "

"Thanks, Edgar, for your frankness," Beckwith grinned. "Now that I realize my usefulness to the institution as a horrible example I can prosecute my radical activities with an easy conscience. And you might help me with Heune's case. Some of our witch burners want to deport him. It is outrageous!"

He related forthwith at length the history of the Russian student, who had been peaceably working his way towards a degree when he fell into the net of federal and state authorities spread to catch the seditious.

"He was working in a bank up town. Somebody in Washington discovered his name in the rolls of the communist party and had him clapped in jail. That was a year ago. Snow and I bailed him out, and he found another job, with the federal reserve branch here. Thinking he was safe from further persecution he sent for his old father, who is now on the way over. An order has come through from Washington ordering him deported in the next boatload of aliens that this land of the free is shipping back to Europe. . . . A word from you to the proper authorities in Washington might very likely get him a reprieve until his case has been thoroughly looked into. He is no more a communist than you or I, Edgar. Why, he is a government employee! What do you say?"

Mallory's smiling face sobered.

"I'd rather it were a contribution to one of your down-and-out funds Norman," he said at last. "I'd gladly give you a cheque. But in my position, with all the liability to misrepresentation—"

"I see! You don't want to be compromised."

"It isn't so much myself as the university," Mallory said hastily. "I have no right to involve the institution in such a controversy."

"One might think that the business of a university is

to champion the victims of intolerance," Beckwith suggested with gentle irony.

"You can't antagonize the community. We depend on the community for our support, our influence," Mallory protested.

"And for the success of the Drive" Beckwith added. "So instead of getting loose from the prejudices of big donors by going to the public for support, the university places itself under stricter bonds than ever not to offend the ideals of its supporters. The philanthropists of the last generation to whom Harris appealed were often liberal-minded men, willing to keep their hands off the university, but henceforth we are to be bullied by the opinions of the middle class, the conservative, well-to-do citizen! God help the university if that is to be its destiny."

"Oh, you take too gloomy a view of the well-to-do citizen," Mallory protested. "He isn't such a bad fellow. We molded him at any rate. He graduated from some college, for the most part, and it is his recognition of the good he got from it which is making him loyal to us now," and he ran on in the style of the drive literature, being turned out to the tune of busy typewriters in a nearby office.

"I know the song," Beckwith interposed. "Even old Dick Caxton has turned his hand to *Scholarship and Citizenship*. Flynn did *Eureka, the City, and Eureka the University,—Shall They Advance?* I suspect you, Edgar, of being the author of the *Dialogue with a Dean!*"

"No, no," Mallory laughed. "That was the Little President; didn't you recognise his style in the up-to-date man of the world Dean?"

"Well, then, you turned off *The Quest of Truth*, celebrating all the services to humanity that the university has accomplished."

"That was a composite. Dexter helped!" the new president admitted, laughingly.

"And *A New Epoch at Eureka*, Beckwith continued pitilessly, enumerating the titles of the drive "literature," "with a ten million laboratory for business science."

"We had to give Sanderson that, he's so infernally successful in bringing in money!" Mallory explained ruefully. "But we are going to build Caxton a special library and—"

"And a new faculty club house, I hope? And raise salaries all around so that every professor can own a Ford sedan and keep a smart young lady secretary with a typewriter? . . . Oh, the New Epoch at Eureka will be another crop of buildings and 'facilities'! Hope you'll get a better architect than Harris had, by the way! Well, your drive is running to plant and equipment, true to form. Good luck to you! I hear you have forty of the fifty millions in sight."

"Not quite that," Mallory corrected cautiously. "But we hope by the end of the year to make some interesting announcements on the drive."

"The women are in it too," Beckwith went on, "it isn't safe to go down town in the train unless you have pinned to your coat 'I have done my bit and more' for Eureka! Quite right, Edgar," he continued his banter as he groped for his hat. "Customer ownership, every student a stockholder,—that's the slogan! The community's university, for upholding the community's ideal of service with profit. Well, I must be off. I am lunching with Jessica, trying to interest her in my kind of a university, my labor college. We can't rival your plant, but we have a large field,—ten to fifteen millions of labor families."

Mallory's face assumed a curious expression at this last sally.

"Perhaps you will be more successful with Jessica than with me," he remarked dully as Beckwith disappeared from the president's office.

The outer office was no longer the cold, somnolent

place it had been under Dolittle. Mallory had insisted
when he assumed the responsibilities of Eureka that if he
were to conduct a successful drive for fifty millions he
must delegate the various functions of the president. To
the Little President had been assigned routine administration, with a corps of young deans under him. Caxton
had been given charge of the literature of the drive,
Sanderson the social activity of the drive, and so on.
Office room for all these had been found in convenient
proximity to the president, so that this wing of the big
Administration Building resembled closely an army headquarters in full blast, with a noisy chorus all day and
far into the night of typewriters. Chairmen and chair-
women of the many committees to which the active field
work of the drive had been entrusted, now sat around in
the outer office waiting for a few words with the drive
leaders. Beckwith, as he passed among them, observed
that the personnel of the drive was much the same as
that of Penniman's Vigilants. Just as the most active
propagandists for ward had been drawn from the ranks
of "our social leaders", so now the most active workers
for a new epoch at Eureka were from the same aspiring
class. "After all," he reflected, ducking his head to
Louise Clavercin, who was chatting with big Mrs. Grant
and Constance Fenton, "it is *their* world. The war
hasn't altered that fact!"

The women were all in it! They had got the habit of
"doing big things" during the hectic war months and
were loath to slip back into obscurity and dinner parties.
The women were behind all the university drives in the
country and Eureka women, who had been prominent in
selling war bonds and running war charities fell upon the
big drive as a heaven sent opportunity. Louise Clavercin had discovered a pleasant individual niche for herself
at last. She had become liaison officer between the city
and the university, which involved a great deal of dining
out and lunching and interminable conferences. She had

become very intimate with Maida Grant, who had promised Mallory to "get Eureka society behind the drive." Louise was her adjutant and obeyed orders, collecting the more presentable members of the faculty to be infiltrated into dinners or to offer parlor lectures at the homes of important people. Often she had an informal sort of committee meeting at her house so that Clavercin formed the habit of lunching always at the club. "Poor Beaman is so delicate," she would say in explanation of her single appearance at a dinner. "You know I think he has never recovered from his war work, poor dear!" The tradition grew that Beaman Clavercin was a victim of melancholia and extremely trying to his charming wife, who was an angel, "and so clever." In this affair of the drive which brought her into close relation with the president of the university Louise Clavercin at last achieved the role originally designed for her by Jessica Mallory as Edgar's official wife. They telephoned each other a dozen times a day, avoiding so far as possible personal interviews. When a meeting was imperative, it took place either in the city or by chance at tea at Constance Fenton's, rarely at the Clavercins'. Jessica humorously noting this effort to avoid gossip suggested as she departed on a winter trip to South America, "Do ask Louise to come in here while I am away. . . It would save you both so much time."

Mallory put this down to his wife's peculiar sense of humor and did not reply. Jessica, who was now enjoying full control of her father's estate, had insisted on contributing generously to the drive before her departure.

"I gave Beckwith the same amount for his labor college," she explained. "I don't believe in either, you see, and it is only fair to do for you what I did for him, to be impartial. When I come back maybe I'll give you some more. The money seems to pile up and up at the bank. I'll see which educational enterprise shows the best promise!"

No wonder Jessica Mallory had finally achieved the reputation not only among the college wives, but in the city of being "queer." "If she would only find some one on the way to South America," Louise daringly suggested to Constance, "and never come back!"

"Oh, they say she has found 'some one' before, several times," Constance retorted with an amiable laugh, "but she always comes back. That's her kind," she mused, with a certain girlish cynicism which she had never lost over the vagaries of human loves. She had never married and still lived in a wing of the big brick house, the main part being occupied by the university creche and kindergarten. Some said it had been Clavercin who kept her from marrying, others Mallory, from the necessity of having a romantic explanation.

She herself explained frankly,—"I just don't care for men, having to look after them I mean. I like babies, and nowadays one doesn't have to marry to have all the babies one wants! I've thirty in there every day, besides my own specials."

Her specials were the four orphans, all girls, whom she had adopted from time to time, as occasion came and the helpless child appealed. Clavercin remembered the night when he was dining with Constance Fenton in the big house with a merry company—she was only twenty then and loved gaiety. A servant whispered in her ear—"Long distance." She had excused herself, and when she returned a little flushed she announced, "You'll have to play by yourselves to-night. I'm off for Michigan. Beaman do look up the trains for me. . . . Yes, it's a baby—parents just killed to-day in a crossing accident, and some friend has telephoned me about their child." That was the first one, Maude, who was now in the university. Clavercin who had kept warm his affection for Constance through all the vicissitudes of his career now received over a cup of tea after his late class the latest gossip about the women's end of the university drive,

"Maida Grant is clever," Constance gurgled confidentially. "She's worked off that Women's Hospital she used to organise balls for, you know. She got bored with it—it was always in need of money—and so she has handed it over to the university. She's very able, Maida, an important person in the City. They can't put over any big thing from a reform mayor to a university drive without her help. I wonder how her husband likes it Or Edgar Mallory for that matter," she added with a chuckle.

"Marriage is no longer woman's destiny," Clavercin observed tritely.

"Oh, it never was—merely an arrangement for having children," Constance volunteered hardily. "How much better off we'll all be when we don't make that natural desire so painful socially "

"You talk like Jessica Mallory."

"You know I like that woman!" Constance observed triumphantly. "I didn't used to—thought she was a prig and fearfully selfish."

"She *is* something of a prig," Clavercin sighed.

"But she is a wise woman all the same. She never fools herself long."

"I wonder if that is the highest praise a human being may aspire to?" Clavercin remarked sentimentally.

"Oh, yes, for a woman it is!" Constance rejoined positively, bending a smiling face over the tea tray. "Of course men must be able to fool themselves with one thing or another—and we women have to help them in their make-believes! That's our lubrication function as Jimmie Flynn says. And we perform best when we aren't fooling ourselves . . . . There's dear old Uncle Tom coming across from his house to get his tea," she remarked, pulling down a shade in the front window of the big room, which made it seem more livable. "I always give him a signal when I am to be home, by leaving up this shade "

Presently the Flynns dropped in on the way from the city, each with a small child by the hand. Clavercin realized that pretty Mrs. Flynn had lost much of her good looks. "Getting old like all of us," he commented, "all but Constance and Jessica Mallory! They will never grow old, Constance because she was born radiant with the simplicity of a child, and Jessica because somehow she has achieved peace with her mind. One is purely instinctive, the other purely mental, and both have rounded out themselves somehow as no men I know have done. They have filled out their characters and got into adjustment with life—one by plunging into it breathlessly, the other by withdrawing from it discreetly !"

They were talking about the drive. Jimmie Flynn had been addressing a gathering of women in a house on the other side of the city.

"We have too many rivals in the field. Vassar has just combed the city, and Elmwood is beginning. However, we have the biggest body of graduates, and ought to beat 'em to it! Besides Eureka is the home institution. Let the East look after its own colleges, I told 'em."

"Patronize your *naborhood* druggist," drawled Bayberry with a chuckle.

"Sure . . . We are as good as any of 'em!" Flynn rejoined with the imperturbable complacency of Eureka. "The missus and I want to get that trip to Europe when the drive is over. Mallory has promised it !"

"The drive will never be over," Clavercin sighed.

"Oh, sure," Flynn rejoined. "We've twenty in sight already, and Mallory expects to wind it up by Christmas in a whirl of last hour pledges. I think he has some special gifts in reserve, to announce when the proper moment arrives."

Flynn was enjoying Constance's good bread and butter and tea, hungry after his exertions in the city. He took the drive optimistically, naturally, as he had taken the war, the university, Eureka, life. There seemed to him nothing derogatory or unseemly in a university drive for money. That was the way one worked these things. The technique of arousing the community had been immensely improved by the experience of the war, and Eureka was employing the last wrinkles of salesmanship learned in the Liberty bond selling drives. They were receiving pledges on the instalment plan,—so much a week or month,—also writing endowment insurance, on a scheme that Sanderson had worked out. "You give the university so many thousands and we guarantee you a fixed income for life. Our tables are much more favorable than those of the best insurance companies, etc." Another plan was "the favorite professor endowment." A prospective donor or a group of donors could select one of the popular professors and contribute a fund for his endowment, also for his retirement allowance. That scheme was "taking like mad."

"Adopted orphans!" Bayberry chuckled, wrinkling his thin face ruefully.

"It gives the individual touch. Lots of folks want to see the object of their benevolence. If they can't afford to give a building that they can look at, they can take pleasure in their own professor!" Flynn chatted on amiably. "Our most dangerous competitor is the church movement: endowment for poor ministers. That is just getting started. It's a pity we can't come to some sort of arrangement with them, division of the territory or a percentage basis. There's a danger in overworking the community. They may go on a gift strike if they are teased too often."

"Not while they are in fear of the Reds!" Clavercin suggested as he rose to leave. "They are your best

friends, as they were to the bitter enders in the war.
Anything to keep out the Bolshies—that's your winning
slogan!"

"Oh, we are working that! We tell them no educated
person will stand for communism. The church and the
university are the two great bulwarks of society as it is,"
Flynn purred, quoting from the drive leaflets.

The Flynns, were in the thick of the drive, in the
ranks, trying to secure hundred dollar subscriptions from
young graduates and ambitious households that expected
to send their children to the university some day. They
left "the big graft", as Flynn would put it, to Maida
Grant, Louise, Mallory and the other drive leaders.
They belonged to the democracy of the university and
functioned there happily.

On either side of Constance Fenton's kindergarten
home were fraternity houses; also across the street all
the houses once known as "professors' row" were now
occupied by these colonies of the new rich youth that
flocked to Eureka. They had driven out the faculty,
who had retired either into more economical flats or
block houses on quieter side streets. On a warm spring
evening like this a clamor of youth came from the open
windows, the noise of musical instruments badly played,
shouts, and songs. Up and down the street on either
side motor cars were parked close, expensive cars in
which boys and girls packed tightly rushed back and
forth on aimless business. When a fraternity gave a
dance the noise kept up far into the night until occasionally the good natured police on the beat intervened
on behalf of the private citizens who still lived in the
neighborhood. At last Eureka had become not only
popular but even fashionable. Moneyed people from
the surrounding states sent their children here rather
than to eastern colleges. The community had become
rich in the war, and this was its flowering.

Clavercin asked himself if they were the same sort of

youth he had known first at Eureka, with merely another veneer? These boys and girls whom he encountered on his twilight walks in parked cars 'with curtains drawn, on lonely drives in the parks. While their elders were bickering over the right sort of education for a reconstructed world, they went gayly to jazz, bootleg gin and whiskey, sexual freedom, with a new note of scorn or frank indifference for the old commandments. "Get the dough", "Put it over", "You have but one life to live", were the profound truths they seemed to have brought back from Armageddon. It was to provide this youth with more commodious quarters and to pay their instructors more highly that the great drive for the fifty million fund had been organized.

That was unfair, the sour prejudice of age, Clavercin knew well enough, for behind this noisy façade of the fraternity houses was the great mass of the student body, hungry and eager, poor rather than rich, seeking life.

CHAPTER SEVEN

Jessica did not like women. She thought she understood them better than they understood themselves—that was her profession, and it was true that she had a keen perception of their pettier sides. Women did not like Jessica as a rule, and while admitting that they could not understand her explained her conduct unpleasantly. Jessica got on much better with men than with women, but as matrimonial superstitions still largely persisted even after the war her opportunities socially were limited. As the years passed even men bored Jessica, and her interest in all human beings was more quickly exhausted, so that her life became solitary, at times lonesomely so. Ned and little May had been so well trained to take care of themselves, to become complete individualists that even before they had finished college they had both settled their own lives without much reference to either parent. May had become involved with what Jessica called a "dancing partner"; Ned was following the vagaries of a woman older than himself, who had had several pasts. She was quite capable of giving the boy some of the emotional warmth that he had failed to get from his mother. Jessica returned one day from South America to find the young people thus thoroughly "on their own". Edgar in his way was trying to make the best of the situation especially for the girl and had the "dancing partner" at the house. After the first family meal the two parents looked at each other, baffled.

"What on earth can she see in him?" groaned Edgar.

"Sex," Jessica answered with professional brutality.

Edgar who had never got used to the scientific approach fussed with the fire, suggesting over his shoulder,—"She might have got that—and something else!"

Jessica, ignoring her suspicion that little May may have sought the most extreme opposite to her own mother, remarked placidly,—

"She'll divorce him within three years—pity!"

"Pity! I should say it was," Edgar responded vivaciously.

"I mean it's a pity she should feel she must marry him at all."

"Of course—and why should she?"

"Because all you 'good' people make her think it necessary. . . She might so much better have the experience and once over it—forget it!" Jessica continued placidly.

"May is not that kind, fortunately," Edgar protested.

"No, unfortunately!" Jessica agreed,

Mallory gave his wife a long searching look and then asked in a troubled tone,—

"Jessica, doesn't this,—this personal situation with May,—give you doubts about some of your theories?"

"Why should it?" Jessica replied briskly, and to avoid further discussion took up a book she was reading on the mental habits of monkeys. More and more Jessica had become engrossed in purely mental occupations. She felt lost without a piece of work or an absorbing problem into which to duck when anything threatened her serenity. She could "dope" herself with her intelligence as other human beings did with emotions or drugs, dulling any uncomfortable sensitiveness to environment or circumstance as now.

"If I should continue the discussion, we should merely get angry," she thought to herself. "I could not make him understand. . . And I can do nothing to prevent

May from getting what is coming to her, and so I had
better not think about it at all. . . . ."

Presently Edgar left the room. Jessica could hear him
in his study talking in low tones with May, who was
spending this evening at home because of her mother's
return. They were doubtless "talking the matter over",
a futile proceeding that made Jessica shrug her shoulders,
but one that always seemed singularly comforting to
Edgar and May. . . .

The one woman in the university whom Jessica ex-
cepted from her dislike of women was Beatrice Snow,
Walter Snow's young wife. Beatrice was a sculptress of
local repute, and she had not allowed matrimony to
interfere with the slow, methodical prosecution of her
profession. They had no children—Beatrice held that
professors and artists should not encumber themselves
with offspring. It was said also that young Mrs. Snow
had induced Walter to refuse an advantageous offer from
a neighboring university because she did not want to
leave the stimulating atmosphere of Eureka just as she
was becoming well known. The Snows were apparently
happy and self-absorbed, all the more since the German
terror of the war time which had caused Snow to withdraw from association with his colleagues. He admired
his youthful wife greatly and believed devoutly in her
gift. In fact the couple had come to live almost entirely
in Beatrice's "gift", her present and future fame.

Snow in his bachelor days had acquired a shack beside
the Lake at some distance from Eureka, a fisherman's
two room cottage to which he had taken his friends on
holidays. After his marriage he had added a roomy
studio perched on the extremity of the high bluff over
the lake where Beatrice did much of her work while
Walter played housekeeper and cook or walked alone
up and down the lake shore. Jessica shortly after her
return accepted Beatrice's invitation to the shack for the
week end, largely to escape what she called the "crisis

atmosphere of the home", created by Edgar and May.
Ned had gone to California with his lady and had not
thought it necessary to return to welcome his mother, a
neglect that Jessica would never have remarked upon to
anybody but which stung a little. As she made the slow
journey to the shack along the lake shore in a train that
stopped at one ugly village after another, Jessica's meditations that spring afternoon were not pleasant, and yet
her usual mental medicine did not work. A dozen times
she took out from her bag a book or a bit of ms. or a
copy of the Review which contained an important article,
but she could not concentrate her interest, become im-
mersed in a train of thought as usual. Her glance
wandered out over the light grey and blue surface of the
lake, the one lovely object in a sordid landscape of
factories and sluttish towns, but across the spring
shimmer over the water came a vivid picture of May's
small, unformed face, distorted by conflicting emotions.
"She would not stick to her college work, although I
warned her," Jessica thought, "and now she has nothing
but her emotions to meet life with. Such a pity!"
Something remotely like misery settled into her own
mood. "Come!" she braced herself and once more set
her mind on her work. . . .

The Snows always made much of Jessica. She had
created a scarcity value for herself among the few people
she saw anything of, and took considerable pains to
maintain their regard for herself. Today as she sat after
tea on the studio veranda looking out over the placid
lake into the sheen on the west, she was almost content
once more. Walter was boisterously recounting for her
benefit university history for the past six months while
Jessica had been absent.

"The Drive has been everything! It took the place of
the war, of the Bolshies. A new form of patriotism . . .
Beatrice and I lived out here to escape the Drive. Beckwith? Of course he's put himself in wrong, by con-

ducting his own special drive for funds for his labor college. Haven't you heard about the labor college?"

Jessica vaguely remembering a cheque she had given Beckwith before leaving for South America nodded and inquired,—"How is it getting on?"

"It's great!" Beatrice chimed in enthusiastically. "We are all going to resign from the university and teach in the labor college. Summer courses,—out here on the Lake, in history and politics and art and cooking and swimming—"

"The new education will be more eclectic than Harris ever dreamed, in his most Barnum days!" Walter Snow interjected.

"Norman promised to come out tonight. He will tell you all about it and make you a trustee and head of a department, too," Beatrice chuckled.

"Extraordinary, that man's energy!" Snow mused. "After sustaining conscientious objectors during the late insanity and protecting the victims of the witch-burner since, he has been encouraging the Hindus to throw off the hated English raj and last winter was in deep in the coal strike. . . Came near being arrested with Hoffman at a communist meeting. . . Every time he's licked before he starts, but doesn't seem to know it. And now it's this labor college which is to educate the new generation of workers so as to enable their leaders to compete with the bosses more on a level. . . Extraordinary man!"

"Norman surely has one good time living if ever a professor did," Beatrice laughed gleefully.

Later Beckwith arrived, red and perspiring from a long walk around the lake shore, with Clavercin trailing limply behind him, also a short thick-set young man who was introduced to Jessica as "Palli, one of the teachers in the labor college." Beckwith at fifty was physically hard and sound, a trifle balder and heavier than in his youth, but with the same gusto about living, the same ironic passion for ideas. Nothing had fretted

her. She looked his way and seemed to be expecting him to speak.

"There's the moon!" he exclaimed pointing to the thin silver blade just emerging from the undulating surface of the lake.

Jessica looked in the direction he pointed and nodded. Was she remembering that night in Colorado when they had watched the moonlight on the little mountain lake? They had been close then and that afternoon on the lake at Lausanne, just before the war. . . Probably she was not remembering: Jessica did not believe in recalling such moments once passed. She regarded that as being "soft"—besides it made her uncomfortable, and she did not believe in making herself uncomfortable. . .

"What are you doing now? I saw you had a play on this autumn—was it successful?" Jessica inquired.

"It ran four weeks . . . No, I can't say it was successful. But I liked doing it."

"What was it about?"

"Oh!" Clavercin paused, then said briefly, "The usual theme,—what's it all about—living. . . It would not interest you, Jessica!" he concluded laughing, as he saw a familiar frown gather about the high white brow. "It was about the eternal secret, and mysteries, and all that," he went on using terms that he knew Jessica disliked as "meaningless".

"Still romantic?" Jessica questioned .

"Incurable."

"Still expecting the solution in the depths of another's emotion?"

"No!"

Jessica poked a stick into the sand while she thought.

"But I am glad I have lived in the faith of *some* solution somewhere, not merely accumulating experience," Clavercin insisted. "After all, failures are as illuminating as triumphs."

"That's true," Jessica admitted, and they were silent

before the hopelessness of their minds ever completely understanding each other. Silence was more sympathetic than words. . . .

" . . We are back in the university just where Harris started us," Walter Snow was saying to Palli with a burst of hearty laughter, "more buildings, bigger salaries, more plant. And the world is back pretty much where it was before the war, trying to feed too many people and scrambling for the fat things."

"There's always a struggle for the place in the sun," Beckwith admitted. "But it's the other fellow's turn now."

Palli nodded his black head.

"You bet—and he's going to get it too!"

With a cry, half yelp and half crow, he plunged into the dark lake. Jessica rose leisurely and moved after him.

CHAPTER EIGHT

Again an academic procession wound across the Eureka campus following the old trail of the cement walk first laid out in the Harris days. It kept on past Founder's Hall, out through the gap between the burly Administration Building and the Modern Language Hall, crossed the Boulevard, in considerable disarray due to the speeding traffic. The black mortar boards and flowing gowns, a few silk, many of less luxurious material, with the doctors' colored hoods, bobbed into the sunken roadway, and reappeared on the other side before the excavation for the new College of Business Science. There a small gathering of people in the neighborhood attracted by the students' band and the gowns and hoods watched with momentary curiosity the ceremony of laying a corner stone. There were three addresses. Mallory quite imposing in his gown, tall, square-shouldered, pale, smooth-shaven, alert, spoke briefly of the recent effort of the university to "enlarge its facilities and provide for the needs of the new world." "In dedicating this great building to the service of business," he said, "the university recognizes the significance in modern life of the economic factor."

Pliny Lucus, who had given the building, next spoke panegyrically on the civilizing influence of trade from the time of the ancient Phoenicians to the present day, and somewhat floridly sketched the dawning future of mankind when "under an improved and extended system of commerce all peoples shall be as one," and the will to fight (bloodily) would be forgotten. Sanderson who concluded the speech-making emphasized the peculiar contribution of ideas and ideals which the university had to offer business life. "We are all in business!" he concluded.

Tom Bayberry's thin lips moved in an ironic quaver as he murmured,—

"Yes, the business of life!"

There was some confusion over the affair of cementing in the box of prepared documents (which contained among other things a copy of the Versailles Treaty and a complete set of the Drive pamphlets, together with the day's THUNDERER and the World's Almanac). The audience tittered with relief over Sanderson's somewhat plethoric handling of the trowel and applauded mildly Pliny Lucus's deft way of splashing in the mortar, not realizing that his introduction to the business life had been as a mason's assistant. This ceremony over, the caps and gowns wandered back in little groups to the campus, passing on the way the site for the new medical buildings to be erected about a large hospital. That corner stone was being saved for another occasion, thriftily.

At the luncheon which followed in the university commons there were a number of "snappy speeches" in the "lighter vein", for which Mallory still retained his taste. The theme of these was of course the success of the great Drive. The big gilt hand of the Drive clock on the face of the Campanile had been pushed to the thirty million mark that morning, which was considered the present goal, although as Mallory warned the trustees facetiously, "This is but the end of the first half! . . ." From the Drive the speakers moved naturally to "Superpower," a word then just coming into common use. Pliny Lucus described enthusiastically the effort being made to link up all the little scattered units of industrial power throughout the nation into one great system of superpower, and likened it to the movement in the church and the university to enlarge the scope of their influence by drives and amalgamations, "so as to canalize efficiently the mighty stream of idealistic purpose."

Beckwith, who had come in with some others after the luncheon and was leaning against the rear wall of the commons, shouted "bravo" so loudly that the audience craned their heads to discover who was making a disturbance. Pliny Lucus subsided abruptly into his seat next the president, and Mallory tactfully started the band playing Alma Mater. Then Maida Grant, who with Louise Clavercin was seated at the speakers' table, rose massively to speak on behalf of "Women in the Drive and in the World," and paid some pretty compliments to the ability of Eureka's president, and the generous response of big business represented by Mr. Pliny Lucus. She took occasion in referring modestly to her own efforts to shy a rock at Beckwith and "that malcontent minority; we used to call them traitors during the war,—and they are traitors to society still!" She said that she was proud to be a woman helping to create a man-and-woman world; one thing women could never be converted to and that was communism in any form. Some flighty persons had been flirting with communism even within the walls of the university, theorists merely, but *dangerous* theorists. The best answer to them was this magnificent college of business science. It was considered the speech of the afternoon. Once again the band played Alma Mater, and the audience joined in singing, a bit uncertainly, the academic hymn and then broke up. As they trooped through the cloisters to the street the chimes from the great Campanile rang out, "Oh, be joyful!" The repertoire of the chimes had improved during the present administration, but this touch was not unpremeditated. The lively carol rang gayly into the winter twilight and many heads craned upward to the belfry, beneath which extended the gigantic hands of the drive clock, pointing to the illuminated figure thirty.

Students lined the street about the base of the Campanile and cheered as the distinguished guests and faculty appeared. It was felt everywhere that this was a great day for Eureka, a more imposing, more dignified triumph than the university had witnessed since Harris had bestowed the doctorate on the lumberman Larson or the football team had beaten Yale ten to nothing in the home stadium. All the distinguished guests were smiling and joking, as they pushed through the crowd of students and motors on their way homewards. Jimmie Flynn was confiding to Constance Fenton and Tom Bayberry the itinerary of that long anticipated excursion to Europe. Caxton in a fresh silk gown with a brilliant purple hand was sketching to Lucus a magnificent scheme for coöperation between European and American universities in the exchange of faculties. Maida Grant sipping a restoring cocktail at the Clavercins' sighed, —"That's over! Now the next will be—"

"What?" Louise Clavercin demanded hungrily.

"A new president for Eureka."

"You think Edgar will leave us?"

"I know it," Maida said, closing her eyes impressively. "He told me as much at the luncheon."

Louise Clavercin had already received from his own lips this information, but she discreetly permitted Maida to think that she was hearing it for the first time.

"It will be a fearful loss to Eureka!"

"We couldn't expect to keep him long, he's so splendid! . . . What will Jessica do!"

"Oh, Jessica is beyond such trifles. She will write a new book or organize another expedition to Asia or Africa!"

Shortly after the triumphant climax of the drive the news spread over the university campus that the efficient Mallory having fulfilled his promise to the Trustees was about to be translated to some mysterious post of responsibility in the East under the auspices of the Larson

Trust. Some said it was philanthropy, others education, —a new kind of educational survey of the world,—at all events a position highly paid and extremely important, which would necessitate a great deal of travel and public speaking. The trustees were already considering presidential material in the faculty and outside and had asked certain influential members of the faculty to coöperate in the selection of the new president, an innovation that created a very happy impression on the campus.

And yet when this informal committee representing the faculty canvassed the situation they could come to no agreement about a candidate. Of course Sanderson was in the thought of all, but as one member put it, "We have had about all of Sanderson we can stand,— we don't want to become just a College of Business Science." Poor Jorolman of Education was no longer even considered because of his marital griefs. Odd as it seemed the name most insistently mentioned on all sides was that of Norman Beckwith. No one denied his ability and his devotion to the university. The voices of the thousands of young men whose imaginations he had touched were coming back to the campus in no uncertain tone. "Beckwith is no Red, he's just alive. The world is moving; move on with it!"

A few years before Beckwith had been burned in effigy in the oval of the campus because of his pacifism. But many of those who were most vociferously for war in those days had become devout pacifists by now. Even the red of the Russians no longer seemed so gory or so dangerous as it had just after the Armistice. As remembered, many of Beckwith's most hated remarks became merely caustic common sense premature in utterance, perhaps. Whereas, as his partisans pointed out,—"The spirit of the man is more truly modern than any of us!" The movement for Beckwith at first taken as a joke rapidly gained ground, eliciting the support of all the so-called "progressive" and liberal spirits in the communities. His enemies—and he had not avoided making enemies where possible—under the leadership of old Dolittle, who had come back to Eureka to write out the memories of his wonderful experiences, became alarmed and laid their lines of battle "against radicalism in Eureka". The matter threatened to become acute, for it had been some years now since the pursuit of the Reds, and people's emotions were hungering for a rousing fight. The trustees were supposed to be about evenly divided between those who would rather resign than allow Beckwith to become president of Eureka, and those who admitted guardedly that they would vote for any candidate that had the support of the faculty. But the faculty thus appealed to was helplessly divided and uncertain. In the height of the campaign Beckwith characteristically went off to Europe for six weeks, saying, "I am not a politician looking for votes." This indifference whipped up the ardor of the young supporters of his candidacy, and when he returned the fat was still in the fire, sizzling.

"Do you really want it, Norman?" Mallory asked Beckwith when the two met by chance in New York.

Beckwith colored like a youngster.

"Some times I think I do," he admitted, "but not unless the better part of the faculty and the trustees want me unreservedly."

Mallory shook his head soberly.

"You know that could never happen. Not for years! It would be a long and a petty fight to maintain your leadership. The majority of faculty and trustees can't understand what you are after, and would suspect your every move."

"I suppose so!" Beckwith admitted, a little wistfully.

"Wait another ten years!" Mallory urged.

"Oh, hell, by that time our labor college will be running Eureka off the field!"

They laughed companionably.

"Not so soon as that, Norman! It's more likely Eureka will be affiliating your labor college."

"See here, Edgar," Beckwith said after a time, "Sanderson is not to get it?"

Mallory shook his head.

"Not a chance. Every one is fed up with business administration and business science."

"Who is your dark horse?"

"What would you say of Dexter? Now that his wife has died he has no encumbrances. He is in science, and it is along that line the university can advance most easily. He doesn't make enemies. He is not brilliant but everybody respects him—and his professional reputation is first rate," the president maker affirmed.

Beckwith nodded approvingly.

"Good man, old Dexter!"

"Neither radical nor conservative, just a hardworking, clear-headed, good-tempered scientist!" Mallory pronounced eulogistically.

"You ought to marry him to Louise Clavercin or Maida Grant, and he would be perfect!"

"Perhaps that can be arranged, too," Mallory concluded.

THE END